# A Thai Bride

## Toi's Story

Daniel McKenzie has spent the past 30 years working in the creative industries as a musician and song writer and although he has been writing for some time, this is his first publication.

## Acknowledgements

This work has only been made possible through the belief and love that others have shown to me throughout my life.

I would therefore like to thank my loving and nurturing parents, for teaching me to strive to do the best in everything that I undertake and who have been my lifelong inspiration.

Janet and Jeremy Davis, who have shown me the true meaning of kindness and are people I aspire to; you have my sincerest gratitude.

I would also like to thank Jenny, Suzanne and Denise, who apart from my mother, have been and still are the other significant women in my life and like my mother, try to keep me on the straight and narrow, with varying degrees of success.

I would also like to thank all those who found the time to proof the manuscript and helped with the editing of this work; your help has been invaluable.

I would like to also thank my publisher, who without, this book would not have life.

# PREFACE

As I sat down to start this book, well, to do the research, I only knew that I wanted to write something that worked for the betterment of the human spirit.

Having considered writing a "How to be successful in business," or some other laboured story from my life, I instead decided that I would produce something that would have a wider appeal. My aim to produce something meaningful; something that anyone can pick up, understand and relate.

I must say, that though I make several references to self-help, this is not a self-help book; more, a book that will hopefully make you take a moment out to think.  Well I suppose you can take anything out of these writings and if they help you, then that is a good thing, isn't it?

Anyway, it was at the start of this research period whilst on a shopping trip, that I met a woman, who at this point will remain nameless; who provided me with the inspiration for the production of this work.

I met the woman whilst waiting in a queue, waiting to be served and I got talking to the well-dressed and well-presented 55 year-old.

Our conversation started on how the length of the queue was too long and how much better things were in the old days. She asked me about myself, so I gave her a brief history, which she seemed to find interesting, as did other members of our queue.

I asked my questions and learned that from very humble beginnings she'd made a success of herself, which made our life stories similar.

In her youth she'd worked in catering, becoming the managing director of a small firm and then had invested wisely, making a lot of money in the process. She hastened to add that she'd successfully raised three children, something of which she was very proud.

So, it was clear that she was financially secure and during the course of our conversation said that she was truly happy, well, apart from waiting around in the queues at the local shops.

This prompted me to ask her why she did her own shopping, when she could quite easily afford to get someone to do it for her.

She indicated to me that getting out among the populous made her feel alive. She also said that she busied herself with doing charitable work, often manning soup kitchens, sometimes handing out blankets to the destitute and was often out visiting friends and family.

Her replies prompted me to ask if she was truly happy, as all of the running around and activity that she undertook had the look and feel of a person in search of something.

However, before she answered, our conversation was

ended abruptly as it was now her turn to be served, so we said our goodbyes and went on about our business.

Some weeks later as I scanned through the message boards of my local paper, I came across a message, which read; "I am trying to find a man who I spoke to as I queued in the Harrow Branch of Marks and Spencer in the St Anne's Centre, four weeks ago. I would really like for him to get in touch with me."

As I had been in the store at around that date, I immediately thought of the woman who I had spoken to some weeks before. Could this message be for me I thought. My suspicions were confirmed when the message went on to give a fairly good description of me.

What could this woman want from me? I thought.

With a mixture of suspicion, fear and I suppose, interest, I telephoned the number given in the message, which seemed to ring for an age before someone answered.

I immediately recognised the voice on the other end; it was her. So trembling as I spoke, as for some reason fearing what was to come, I proceeded to introduce myself and quickly gave her my full name in case we were somehow disconnected; she would then at least have my full name, as I thought she would then be in a position to look me up.

She recognised my voice and gave her name, then after a short exchange where we verified who we said we were; she went on to tell me that she'd spent the past three weeks trying to get hold of me. Indeed, this was the second week that she'd run her add in the local paper; this information only serving to intensify the anxiety that I now felt.

After apologising in advance for taking up my time and then in an apologetic tone, she began to tell me that she couldn't stop thinking about the conversation that we'd had in the shop, specifically, the parts about her happiness.

She conveyed in a now rather defensive manner, though she had always thought she was happy with what she'd achieved in her life, she thought that I had hit upon something relating to her "searching for something."

Over the past few years, she'd felt a high level of anxiety; it was as if there was something missing, something that she should have done, something that was preventing her from being truly happy. I noted that she had contradicted herself, as she didn't really know whether she was happy or not. She went on to tell me that she'd thought about the story that I told her about my life and believed that I sounded happy, or more precisely, content; and contentment was something that was missing from her life.

I thought it strange that a person with as much life experience as she had should want to confide in me, and as suspicious thoughts swirled around in my mind, I struggled to keep up with the conversation.

We talked for about 20 minutes before I thought our time would be better spent talking face to face, therefore suggested that we meet up to discuss things further and we agreed to meet at her house the following day.

* * *

The woman lived in a big house in leafy Hertfordshire; she had definitely done well for herself I thought as I drove up the quarter mile driveway to her house.

As I reached the house, I noticed that she was there waiting on her doorstep, smartly dressed and made up, as if about to meet friends at a posh restaurant, putting me to shame, as I only donned an old tee shirt, a pair of worn baggy jeans and my saving grace, a new pair of Nike trainers, but I felt comfortable.

We greeted each other like old friends when she invited me in, with me nonchalantly giving her a peck on each cheek. It was strange; I hardly knew this woman, but it felt as though we had known each other for years.

The inside of her home was as impressive as it had looked outside, which reaffirmed that this was a wealthy person.

As we retreated to her drawing room; her domestic help appeared, a woman who seemed to look at us disapprovingly. Well I suppose a strange man in his mid thirties and a 55 year old and our seeming familiarity could to some people have been construed as somewhat inappropriate. The woman asked for tea to be brought in, which the helper agreed to do.

We embarked on our discussion and quickly found that we wanted to explore what it was to be happy and from early on, contentment and satisfaction figured quite highly.

I took the chance to tell her a bit more about my life, as I wasn't really prepared to go right into my personal stuff as we stood in Marks & Spencer a few weeks earlier: Instead, giving her a happier view, or version of how my life had unfolded.

I now went into some gritty detail, telling her how I had been married with two children, owned a nice house, held down quite a good job five years earlier and how I had taken it all for granted: And, how by not paying attention to what was really important to me, had cost me the lot and nearly my life.

After being divorced, I somehow turned to alcohol to try to dull the way I felt about what I perceived had been done to me; you know, a couple of glasses of wine here, a couple of shorts there, all I hasten to add taking its toll, and how a couple of years later I ended up in intensive care facing multiple organ failure.

After pulling through and with months of recuperation, I found a way of not just coping with the pain, but beating it. I searched myself to find out how and why I went into self-destruct mode, finding that hate had figured quite highly.

I hated my ex-wife for divorcing me; I resented my children for seemingly taking her side, and hated my immediate family and friends for what I saw was the cause of my heart ache; their years of dependency on me.

It was only when I changed the way I thought and felt about people and situations, did I begin to live again.

I first began by stop blaming others for what had happened, took responsibility for what had gone before and prepared to accept responsibility for me and my future.

Over time I began to love again: Surprisingly I found that I loved my ex-wife; not in the way that I had done before, but this time as the mother of my children and a friend.

I also realised that my children had not taken sides, but had only reacted to my over compensating brought on from the guilt that I'd felt for no longer playing such a major role in their lives, and I suppose the feeling that I'd somehow let them down.

Only when the hate had gone did life really move on, and I truly felt contented, or truly happy.

The woman seemed to be impressed with my story and after answering a few of her questions I realised that I had talked enough about myself, as I sensed that she really wanted to talk about herself. So to make our discussion tangible and have some practical meaning, I quickly made her the subject of our discussions.

This suited me as I was in the middle of doing research for the production of a book, so it gave me the opportunity to put my experiences and theories to the test and to gather information.

So here you are, my story; though the names of the characters in A Thai Bride, are fictional, the story has its basis in fact.

In memory of those who perished in the "Great Flood"

Northampton 1998

# CHAPTER 1

Cold and raining heavily, a gale blew across the Nene: Toi awoke feeling comfortable, warm and totally at ease. Only moments earlier she was cold and in pain, feelings which had now dissipated. On opening her eyes she saw her parents, older sister and the faces of many more almost forgotten friends merged into a living collage; a collage that depicted a marvellous yet confusing tapestry, which represented her life experiences.

From her vantage, she saw Graham on his knees, hurriedly tying up what looked like a large bundle, his face red and awashed with tears; all the while mumbling to himself.

"I told you I'd find someone else, I told you, I told you."

Instinctively knowing that she couldn't communicate with him directly, in her mind she lovingly told him that everything would be all right and that he shouldn't cry, hoping that somehow his subconscious would pick up on her thoughts.

Using some makeshift weights which he fixed to the bundle with some barbed wire that lay in a tangled roll, he nervously looked around, peering out into the darkness, ensuring that he was alone, before pushing it into the water.

As the bundle slid over the edge, she caught sight of a distinctive yellow coat, her yellow coat, and in that moment she understood what Graham had done. In that moment she felt a peace that was never felt in life, in that moment she was free, she was happy.

\* \* \*

9 weeks earlier…

Sarah sat staring out of her front room window, watching the rain; it was mid-February and turning out to be one of the wettest winters in living memory, and the latest weather report forecast more rain.

She sat there silently thinking about work and what she would be doing that week.

She was the assistant manager of the kitchen at the International boys' boarding school and was also what she always said that she would never become; a dinner lady. It was a job that she hated, but owing to her financial situation, it was a job that she had to keep to make ends meet.

Having recently been promoted to kitchen assistant manager, she'd beaten off the other staff in the kitchen to the job, leaving the atmosphere not at its best. However, the way in which the school operated made her promotion and resulting salary increase well worth it.

The school catered for children of the rich and famous, the aristocracy, actors, musicians and business people alike. It was therefore open all year round, as the children were either, taken out, or as in many cases, left for the school to look after during more conventional holiday periods. This meant that she had to work all year round, rather than in standard term time, but did get the weekends off, as vending machines substituted dinner ladies, which gave her time to spend with her own children.

Her thoughts were broken by her son Carl, who couldn't find his football boots.

"Mum, where's my boots? I'm playing football today," He shouted from upstairs.

"They're where you left them, out the back somewhere, I think." She replied, the level of her voice tapering off to a whisper as she reached the end of her sentence, now thinking, *why don't you just come down and look for them.*

Now returning to her thoughts, she rehearsed a conversation that she knew she must have with her manager Karen, as even their relationship had come under some strain in recent weeks.

Karen was upset that Sarah got the assistant manager's position and made her feelings known at every opportunity, which was the main reason why the atmosphere in the kitchen had been quite bad in recent weeks. Sarah had been chosen to replace the last assistant manager by the company's regional director, who believed that she was destined for a job in area management. She was 'made from the 'right stuff,' he told Sarah and was eager to, 'fast track her.' This of course, rubbed some of the other staff up the wrong way, and led them to think that the motive for his continual interest in Sarah was more than just professional.

She continued rehearsing the conversation to ensure that she would get things right later, as most of the time, Karen displayed a tough woman image, which at times could be quite intimidating. This didn't help, as ever since childhood, Sarah had been quite timid; not surprising then that the people in her life had always used her in some way.

She'd always found it hard to say "No" and paid for this with a failed marriage and a year of depression. However, her doctor and therapist were surprised at how suddenly she'd come out of the depression given her history. She put her recovery down to a couple of books that she'd read and discovered why saying "Yes" to everything could be just as negative as saying "No."

* * *

As a fifteen year old she was influenced by an art teacher, a popular new age/hippy type; he told her class that to embrace life, one had to say 'Yes' to everything. In hindsight she thought that was a bit of a stupid thing to say to a class of impressionable fifteen year olds.

It was only 20 years later and with some enlightenment; information that she gathered from her books as well as her ex-husband, before she managed to create a balance and her life really began to move forward.

While married, her husband hid behind a positive persona,

which created a regime where words like 'no' and 'can't', were rarely used. In the end being 'positive' proved to be his tool of manipulation and at the same time his Achilles heel. But, the information she gleaned from him in relation to the positive use of 'creative visualisation' came in very handy and was about the only useful thing that he left her with; well, apart from her children and the house that they lived in. He was the person that got her into reading self-help books, teaching her about the importance of visualising one's goals and desirers.

Ironically he was the first victim of her visualisations or goal setting, as she started to imagine life without him and within a year had divorced him.

It was interesting how quickly his positive persona unravelled as they switched positions, with Sarah taking more control as she became more confident, learning to detach herself from situations, looking at them more objectively and had also learned to feel guiltless about hard decisions that had to be made.

This was another reason why she was able to divorce the man that she thought dragged her down, with no regrets: Also the reason why she'd applied for the assistant manager's position.

* * *

*There is no way he'll be playing football today,* she thought, referring to her son Carl and looking through the front bay windows, seeing the rain falling heavier now.

Feeling as miserable as the weather, she knew she had to snap out of it, and as she stood up picked up her half-finished rooibos from the coffee table and shouted.

"Come on you two!"

Before taking another mouthful, finishing the cup.

After placing the cup back onto the coffee table, she stood in the middle of her magnolia coloured living room, and fixed her shoulder length shiny blond hair into a ponytail, all the while staring at her pale reflection and into her grey blue eyes.

"Come on!"

She shouted once more, as she flicked her hair through a thick elastic band, now grinning at her reflection, trying to make herself feel better, only to spawn the thought after looking at her cheeks. *Oh! I've got to lose some weight, no wonder no one wants you.*

"Come on!" She shouted once more.

It was Monday morning, the start of a new week, time to get the children off to school and time to go to work.

\* \* \*

The barge 'The Duck' sat on the canal at Croxten and was in a sorry state. As well as needing a good clean and a lick of paint, there was junk everywhere. An old metal grey and rusted red watering can where flowers once grew, a heavy looking roll of rusting barbed wire, several empty flower pots, and a couple of crates of rain filled beer bottles among other things adorned its deck . Inside wasn't much better either: It had an old Victorian feel about it, but in a cheap 1970s reproduction way. It was dark, dank, with the odd cobweb and it was hard to see how anyone could have lived in it.

Inside Graham sat staring at the rain through the first starboard porthole, as if waiting to see someone come past along the canal path. The rain seemed to be never ending and it felt as though it had been falling for weeks.

He sat there, trying to contain his mood which wasn't at its best. He'd wanted to travel to Northampton on the barge over the weekend, to see his seventy-five year-old mother, but couldn't owing to the weather, that had been so bad that he'd decided not to go. He'd promised that he would make the journey up and now feared that she would complain that he was a bad son, and that he didn't love her.

He hated when she complained about him, but had put up with it all of his life; which had a profound effect on him. Married three times, he found that he couldn't hold down a relationship owing to, what his last 'Relate' counsellor diagnosed, "an anger management problem." Like most men, he hated women nagging, however, unlike most men this led him to hold women in low regard, and he acted chauvinistically towards them. Suffice to say, he didn't have many women friends, indeed, he didn't have many friends at all.

As his wife Toi nervously cleared up after breakfast, the rattle of the crockery on her tray broke his train of thought.

"Can't you do that quietly, I can't hear myself think?" He growled.

Already nervous, his voice startled her and she dropped the tray she carried, the crockery falling, smashing into pieces which scattered about the floor.

Leaving his seat, Graham rushed over to her and grabbed her right arm.

"Are you stupid or something? That tea set belongs to my mother." He roared.

Actually, his mother gave him the tea set because she didn't want it. She thought it looked ugly; a £4.99 present bought from Woollies by some obscure relative 10 years earlier to celebrate her 65th birthday.

Toi, a small Thai woman, slight in build, cowered, with her left hand above her head, waiting to defend an expected blow, all the while apologising for breaking the crockery.

After catching sight of a book that rested on the coffee table, Graham paused for a second as if in thought. He had caught sight of a self-help book that he'd bought in the hope that it would help control his anger and change his outlook on women. He was already half way through it, and though he thought there was a lot that he could take from it to improve his situation, his outlook on women had changed little.

Toi yelped as he threw her to the floor, the look on his face now filled with venom.

"Get out you stupid woman," he shouted. "One day I'll get rid of you and get myself someone else. Go on, get out; go to work."

He turned his back on her as she got back to her feet and struggling to keep the tears from welling up. She tried to apologise once more, her voice falling upon deaf ears, as he was back staring at the rain, thinking about what had to be done.

Now crying, she turned to look at him once more while putting on her coat, but knowing better than to make a fuss, she left the barge and hurried on to work with the rain still falling heavily.

## CHAPTER 2

The kitchen was cold and always took an hour or so to warm up after the weekend. On Monday mornings it had the look and feel of a morgue about it, tiled from floor to ceiling, terracotta floor, white walls, with stainless steel workbenches. The utensils, knives and serving spoons were stored on stainless steel trays, as if sterilised and ready for use. The green of the first aid box on the wall next to the store cupboard, and bright red of the extinguisher and fire blanket always stood out, catching the eye as one entered, as well as the smell; a mixture of stale chip fat and lemon smelling kitchen cleaner, a reminder that it was really a kitchen.

The hard faced Karen was already in and dressed for work when Sarah arrived, her freckled pale almost grey coloured skin, white coat and netted peak cap contrasting against her red hair; it was 8:30am and still early.

At home, Carl had found his football boots and with his sister Louise, had been rushed to their grandmother's house and dropped off earlier than usual, she would take them to school today.

As Sarah entered the kitchen, Karen mumbled something that resembled,

"Good morning"

"Morning, nice weekend? Did you get up to much?" Sarah replied brightly, asking an open question, putting Karen on the spot.

Not wanting to make conversation, Karen tried to find a way of replying as briefly as possible without really going into any detail.

"Yes, my weekend was good." She muttered sullenly, now frowning; wondering why Sarah had arrived to work earlier than usual.

*Here we go again*, thought Sarah, feeling Karen's questioning eyes and defiant body language. *But I'd better get on and do this.*

Knowing that Karen came in to work about half an hour early every morning, Sarah had made sure she'd arrived before 9am, before the other staff arrived and now alone approached Karen, her face wearing a nervous grin. Karen looked back suspiciously, her furrowed brow clearly seen beneath her netted cap.

Feeling a bit apprehensive, Sarah started.

"Look, Karen, the atmosphere in here seems to be getting worse."

She paused momentarily, waiting for Karen to respond and when nothing came back she continued.

"I've worked here for a while, I don't want your job, I just want to work and earn a living,"

Though she'd rehearsed what she wanted to say, she appeared frightened, and through a trembley voice, her words were coming out all wrong.  Karen still silent, arms now folded and head tilted to one side, knew exactly what Sarah tried to communicate but still said nothing; wanting Sarah to squirm and suffer, penance for having the favour of the regional director.

As they stood there, Karen couldn't help thinking that Sarah's wining sounded pathetic, and the little attention that she afforded Sarah were quickly taken up by her own thoughts.

* * *

As Karen's mind wondered, it took her back to Debbie's house; a friend, work colleague, and a pest at times, who she'd known since her school days and though they were not the best of friends, they'd always kept in touch.

Debbie on the other hand, had always put much more stock in their friendship, often leaning on Karen in her times of need.

A year earlier, the police had arrested Debbie's husband Michael, on a wife battery charge.

While Debbie sat on the floor, her facial blood vessels beginning to flush where they had come into contact with a fist and as she cried out to the police to.

"Leave him alone he didn't mean it."

The police hauled the violent Michael out of his home while Karen stood in the middle of the kitchen thinking how pathetic Debbie's wining sounded.

"What the hell are you doing?" Asked Karen, "He's just given you a hiding; the bastard needs locking up."

"But I love him," Debbie sobbed, clearly embarrassed, head down, eyes fixed on the grime stained red and white vinyl floor tiles.

Karen, repulsed by Debbie's statement, began to reply, but before she got a word out, the women noticed one of Debbie's children standing in the kitchen doorway after being woken up by the commotion.

"Go back to bed love." Debbie sobbed.

But, her child just stood there rubbing her eyes, a look of bewilderment on her face, before Karen stepped in.

"I'll take her," said Karen sternly. "You just get yourself cleaned up. The police are going to be back in a minute to take your statement."

As she took the frightened child back to bed, passing through a dark hallway, a police officer entered through the front door that had been left open, and as the two women passed, they acknowledged each other with a half smile, in sync knowing that the situation here with Debbie was completely wrong.

Karen tucked the child in, kissing her on the forehead, before telling her that everything would be all right; that, "mummy would be all right".

She purposely slowly and quietly descended back down

the steps, trying to hear what Debbie had to say to the officer.

As Karen reached the kitchen doorway, Debbie sat at a table holding an ice pack to her brow, trying to magic away the bruises, which were surely going to appear, with the officer taking notes.

In a corner by the toaster, on top of a work surface, stood six empty beer cans, next to them, two chardonnay bottles, one of which was empty and the other half full.

Debbie slurred as she spoke, giving away, that she'd been drinking, but Karen still wanting to see the best in her friend, in the end conceded that Debbie's judgement must have been compromised, well, in relation to the defence of the man that had just beaten her up.

Wanting to help, but given Debbie's state, Karen knew it would be hard to make her see that she needed help; that she needed to get away from him.

"He didn't mean it." Debbie slurred, defiantly as Karen entered the room. "He'd lost some money, he was just a bit angry, that's all."

With her eyebrows raised, the officer shrugged her shoulders in frustration.

"Look I don't want him prosecuted." Said Debbie now with her voice raised.

"Mrs Hersham," The officer replied, "as I said, we don't need a statement from you for us to press charges, but this has got to stop, and we would prefer it if you did give a statement."

Shaking her head, Debbie looked down at the vinyl tiles once more.

"Mrs Hersham, how much have you had to drink?" Asked the officer now showing some annoyance, "Are you in any fit state to be looking after children?"

As Debbie looked up, opening her mouth as if about to speak, Karen interrupted.

"I'll deal with this," she said, now feeling it was time for her to intervene.

* * *

Karen's focus was dragged back to the here and now, as Sarah began another sentence, but before she uttered a word, the kitchen door flew open; it was Toi who was soaked.

In her haste to leave the barge she'd forgotten to take her umbrella and was now soaked through to the skin, the rainwater dripping from her head into her face, however, did not mask her tears.

Eyes red, her nose running, shivering and now teeth chattering, she looked a sorry state. Seeing her distress, both Sarah and Karen for that moment forgot their differences and rushed to her aid.

"What's wrong?" Asked Karen.

Toi looked at Sarah's expression; head half tilted and eyes

beginning to water in sympathy, which was all Toi needed to see for her to burst into tears.

"Come on Toi, what's wrong?" Asked Sarah.

Toi's grasp of English wasn't the best, but she did the best that she could, and while taking in large gasps of air as she tried to hold back the tears that were now streaming down her face she responded.

"It's Graham," she sobbed.

Karen seeing that Toi had started to shiver interrupted.

"We'd better get you out of those clothes, before you catch your death."

Toi stood motionless for a second not knowing what to do, for some reason waiting for Sarah's approval. Sarah nodded in agreement, before all three left the kitchen and walked silently, apart from the occasional sniff from Toi, down a long dark corridor that led directly to the staff changing room.

The changing room was small, dimly lit and housed more grey coloured lockers than was needed for the number of staff employed in the kitchen on two of its four eggshell coloured walls. A doorway at the back led to a WC, which the staff seldom used, as they found it smelly. Four wooden benches adorned the two remaining walls, one of which Toi sat down on when she entered the room.

As she began to remove her wet clothes, Sarah and Karen tried to avoid looking at Toi's body, awkwardly staring at her face, only occasionally glancing downward, both admiring her tiny size zero frame. She stripped down to her uncoordinated pink bra and white knickers, which were also wet, before moments later being handed a towel, which Sarah had taken from her locker.

"Now," said Karen. "What's this about Graham?"

Toi had calmed down a little, though her eyes were still red and puffy where she'd cried so much.

"It's nothing." She replied.

"Come on Toi; you're one of my staff and if you're upset when you come into work, then it becomes my business," said Karen, her tone now less sympathetic.

With her head now lowered and rubbing her hair vigorously, Toi replied.

"Really it's nothing."

Karen now beginning to feel irate, was about to open her mouth when Sarah interrupted.

"Why don't you get Toi a nice hot cup of tea, to warm her up?"

Sarah winked and then gestured with her eyes and head, hoping that Karen would understand that with her out of the room, she might stand a better chance of finding out why Toi had come into work so upset. Karen glared at Sarah for a second, before Toi's head appeared from underneath the towel.

The three women looked at each other a moment, before Karen, now unable to hide her annoyance said,

"OK, do you want sugar?"

# CHAPTER 3

Now with Karen out of the room, Toi felt that she could talk. She trusted Sarah and felt in some way connected with her, as just like herself, Sarah for some reason had brought down the wrath of the other staff and was being treated badly.

Toi herself was employed as a dinner lady; Sarah's replacement and being the new person had been picked on. Only in the job four weeks, she was being subjected to the prejudices of her work colleagues; she was a Thai bride, good looking, slim, and came to the country married to one of their own. To the people that she worked with, Thailand was synonymous with lady-boys, under aged sex, and where perverts went to get their kicks. They likened her to a prostitute; however, they dared not tell her that to her face, through fear of being fired.

Nevertheless, they made much of her poor command of English and constantly ribbed her about not understanding them when they asked her to do things around the kitchen. She hated this, but it was the lesser of two evils as the job got her off the barge and away from Graham, if only for a few hours.

Toi opened up while she changed into her kitchen whites, talking about what had happened that morning. While she spoke, Sarah couldn't help thinking about her own situation and how she was treated by her ex husband; though no violence was involved, she understood the mental anguish that being in an abusive relationship could bring. She knew that only Toi could put a stop to it happening, that she would have to be strong, and that Toi had to take control of the situation if she was going to be successful.

Noticing what looked like bruising on Toi's back, she gently rubbed a hand over them.

"Is this what he's done to you?"

Toi nodded and then explained that she wanted to come to England to get away from the poverty of her Thailand home. She was raised in a shack in Bangkok and heard that there was a good life to be had here, in the UK. Some of her friends sold themselves as prostitutes to raise cash to leave, while others like her, found middle aged Englishmen who wanted wives to look after them back in England; so she went out and found Graham.

He told her that he lived in a big house in the centre of London and that they would want for nothing. He had made it sound like a fairy tale, and that coupled with her eagerness to get away, meant that she didn't take much more convincing; two weeks later, they were married and back in the UK; it was only then that she found out the real truth.

Though he'd lied about his situation, she learned to 'love', no 'appreciate' him, for giving her the opportunity to leave Thailand, but she was still deeply unhappy. It wasn't that he didn't have a big house, nor was it that they wouldn't want for anything; it was that he lived on a barge.

When Toi was seven, her sister was found, drowned in the Chao Phraya River.

After mysteriously going missing, (presumed kidnapped) for a year, her fourteen-year-old sister returned home, where it seemed not much was made of her disappearance as the family were just glad to have her back. However, she had changed; she looked and acted much older than she had done before. She now wore makeup and adult clothes, which to the annoyance of her parents, attracted the attention of older men. She also stayed out late and generally seemed to have more money than her parents, which fuelled rumours that she was now a prostitute. A few months after her return and while she was out, two men came looking for her, saying that she owed them money; it wasn't long after, that her body was found in the river where she'd drowned. The death of her sister left an indelible mark on Toi and now she was terrified of the sea, rivers and waterways.

* * *

Graham didn't work; he said that he "couldn't", because of his bad back. He instead spent his days drinking anything he could get his hands on; bought from her wages and government handouts.

Toi also went on to tell Sarah how he didn't like her going

out or talking to anyone, and that he had beaten her a couple of times after he'd caught her talking to their neighbours.

She began to cry as she told a story of how she'd met up with her Thai friend Abhasra, who had arrived here from Thailand a month before her. She'd married a man from Surrey and seemed to be living a good life.

"I had to lie to him," said Toi, referring to Graham. "If he'd known that I went to meet Abhasra, he would have beaten me. I told him that I'd got some extra work at the school and would be out all day."

Through the tears, she couldn't help but smile with genuine happiness for her friend's good fortune, as she described where Abhasra lived.

"She lives in a nice big house in a place called Cobham, in Surrey, with a very nice husband. She showed me some pictures"

It's near London you know." She said, forgetting that Sarah was native to the UK.

Sarah smiled. "I know."

"Abhasra cooks and cleans, but, I know that her husband loves her and she is really happy."

Sarah put her arm around Toi's shoulders,

"Things will work out for the best," she said, just as the changing room door flew open; Karen returning with a hot mug of tea, which she handed to Toi.

"Is everything alright?" she asked, directing her question at the pair of them.

"Yes," they replied in unison.

As Toi sipped the tea, Karen gestured to Sarah by way of moving her head towards the door. Obviously wanting to know what had happened to Toi, thought Sarah.

Standing up, Sarah turned to Toi.

"We've got to go and start."

Toi looked up from her seat and nodded.

"You take your time." Sarah continued, a sentiment mirrored by a nod from Karen who had begun to head towards the door.

Sarah turned towards the door, noting the frustrated expression on Karen's face.

Pursed lipped Karen held the door open, letting Sarah through, before leaving the changing room herself, releasing the door, letting it silently close on its hydraulic hinge, catching a long sniff from Toi as she tried to clear her nose.

The women walked slowly down the dimly lit corridor towards the kitchen.

"Well?" Said Karen impatiently.

The suspense was now killing her and Sarah knew it. Not fifteen minutes before, she had me in a similar position and was milking it, she thought.

But thinking that she was better than Karen, she quickly

filled her in on what had happened to Toi that morning, omitting to tell her the parts about how Toi came to be here in England, focusing instead on how badly she had and was being treated by Graham.

"Bastard!" Said Karen.

As she heard how he didn't like Toi going out or talking to the neighbours and fell silent when she learned that Toi had bruising to her back and arms.

"You mustn't tell anyone," whispered Sarah.

But her voice fell on deaf ears as Karen, still silent as they reached the kitchen entrance, with her eyes fixed firmly ahead, was, for that moment deep in thought; deep in a world of her own.

Realising that something she'd said had got to Karen, Sarah repeated a little louder

"You mustn't tell anyone, Toi told me in confidence."

But, Karen was still silent.

"Karen!" Said Sarah loudly.

Startled, as if just awakened, Karen was now back.

"Yes, yes. I heard you."

Suddenly, in front of them, the kitchen door flew open; Debbie, Jenny and Jane, the other dinner ladies came through the other way. They had arrived for work, and the sight of Sarah and Karen, together, and the look on Karen's face, obviously not a good one, broke their chatter.

After a momentary silence, they all had their usual Monday morning greeting and spent a minute chatting about the weekend.

"So how's the teacher's pet today," said Debbie, not missing the chance to have a dig at Sarah.

\* \* \*

After Debbie's last violent episode a year ago, Karen convinced her that she should give evidence against Michael, which she did reluctantly; and given his violent history; he landed a short stay at one of Her Majesty's hotels. It was inevitable then that this led to the break-up of Debbie's second violent marriage.

On his release, he demanded that she left the family home, and wanting to avoid a fight; or that is what she says, she reluctantly agreed and moved into the local women's shelter with her three young children, and desperately needed money.

Karen, feeling largely responsible for what had happened, promised Karen the vacant assistant manager's position when it came up, even though she knew that Debbie may not have been the best person for the job. The intervention of the regional director put pay to any designs Debbie may have had on the position and left her blaming Sarah for her current hardship.

\* \* \*

Karen quickly intervened, rebuffing Debbie's dig at Sarah.

"That's enough! There's work to do and you're all meant to be in the kitchen and ready for work at nine. So come on, chop, chop!"

The women stood motionless for a second almost in a state of shock, as for them Karen in a roundabout way had just defended Sarah, which was unexpected.

"Come on, what are you waiting for?" Karen continued.

Jenny and Jane turned, hurrying off towards the changing room while Debbie stood there for a moment staring at Karen in disbelief.

"You too!" Said Karen.

Debbie rolled her eyes and tutted as she turned and ran down the corridor to catch up with the others.

As she caught up with them, she whispered.

"I don't think she got any at the weekend." Before the three women burst into laughter.

"I heard that!" Karen shouted back down towards the women; not really hearing what Debbie had said, but knowing Debbie, what she'd said was probably rude.

Sarah and Karen went through the doorway, back into the kitchen.

"I don't dislike you," said Karen.

Sarah stood there silently, not really knowing what to say. The day seemed to be unfolding better than she'd expected, in terms of patching things up with the other women in the kitchen.

"It's just that head office shouldn't have employed anyone without my say so".

Sarah nodded.

"I know you're the best person for the assistant's job and, potentially my successor".

*If only you knew.* Thought Sarah

Karen held out her hand.

"Lets' start again shall we?"

Sarah nodded before they both shook hands.

Five minutes later, the four other women entered the kitchen; it was time to begin work.

# CHAPTER 4

Two weeks later, Sarah sat staring out of her front room window watching as the rain blustered around in the wind. It was 9am on a Saturday morning; the kids were up and behind closed doors in the other reception room, the sound of Nickelodeon filling the background.

She sat thinking about how much better things had been at work; how Karen now treated her with a bit more respect, which seemed to have rubbed of onto the other women, well, apart from Debbie who still seemed to be holding a grudge.

During the last week, Karen had said something to the women about Toi's situation; now in sympathy, they had in the main, stopped talking behind her back and had calmed down a little about her poor use of English.

They were now finally starting to get to know her and though still a bit suspicious, they also found her intriguing. Not only was she an attractive woman, she also possessed an inner beauty, which made the women take to her.

Maybe it was her Buddhist calm; the gentle way that she addressed them, or the way she bowed her head slightly when she greeted them; whatever it was, it worked.

But her newfound popularity did breed some jealousy and one day last week the women forgot themselves. Under the guise of Toi's poor use of English, they'd been a bit nasty towards her, which led Sarah to defend Toi, saying that she was having to learn a third language, as she already spoke Thai and Burmese. She then had a dig at the other women, by telling them that they struggled to speak their first language "English," properly, which did not go down too well.

The other women didn't speak to Sarah for the rest of the day, but she didn't mind as she had Toi to talk to. *They talk a lot of rubbish anyway,* thought Sarah.

That said, things were better than they had been. It seemed as though after what had happened to Toi, the women had been left thinking that they'd found some common ground, though Sarah struggled to see what real common ground had been found, well, apart from the obvious, 'a dislike of men.' It was evident that all of them, had at some time had major run-ins with men, which left them a bit jaded. But a dislike of men was a little too negative for Sarah who was now determined to change that collective feeling. Perhaps with a little more reading; something on positivity would help. Something that she could impart on the others. *A trip to Waterstones in the week,* she thought. *Yes, a little retail therapy and a good book would help.*

\* \* \*

Enviously Graham stared out of the first starboard porthole at the neighbouring barge as it slowly pulled away from the bank. 'The Raven' was in pristine condition; painted red, black and grey. The light pine coloured deck complementing the highly glossed outer of the wheel room, epitomising what most barge owners would want a barge to be; and Graham was no exception.

Though it blustered outside, the sight of 'The Raven' in those moments strangely brought a little warmth into his life.

He stood there, a half-drunken bottle of cider in one hand and a document in the other. He turned as a worried Toi broke his thoughts as she entered the room.

"Come on love, you need to sign this," he said being unusually nice.

"Sign what?" She replied.

Unable to contain himself he flipped and now with voice raised said.

"I told you, these papers! They're so you can stay in the country." His voice returning to calm as he remembered what he had to achieve.

Now cowering, "Oh yes, yes those papers," she replied apologetically.

After laying the documents on the table he pointed to where she should sign,

"Sign here," he said.

To his annoyance, she looked down at the document and slowly studied it, as if carefully reading it, and now clearly irritated, he tapped the document at the point where he wanted her to sign, knowing that she had no idea what she was looking at given her poor grasp of English.

"Sign here, and here," he growled.

Toi looked up, reached across the table and picked up a pen; she signed the document then looked up from the page.

"Do I have to go?" She asked.

He took a swig from his bottle and belched out loudly.

"Yes, you live on the water, so you have to learn, it's the law," he said, before belching once more.

"Please, I hate it, I'm frightened."

"You have to learn. Come on, just get your things ready."

"I have." She replied.

As he put the document into an A4 sized manila envelope, she stood there for a second looking at him and then around the ramshackle cabin, which was not too dissimilar to the one that she'd grown up in.

Taking herself back home, to the masses of rusting corrugated rooftops, underneath a stained black and grey Bangkok motorway flyover, she remembered the stench of the mustard coloured effluent flowing through an open sewer in the street, next to food being prepared for her consumption, mixed into the fumes from the roadway above. And as a child, trying to dodge sexual predators as she lived, begged, and slept on the sidewalk. She was just better off than the caged dogs that were destined to fill tourist stomachs. But it was her Thailand, where she'd grown up.

She remembered how he'd acted when they were there; he was so different; he was so nice, but that all seemed such a long time ago. Now she couldn't help thinking that she would have been better off at home in Thailand and had travelled halfway around the world to realise this. There, she lived in poverty, but she was happier than she was now.

Graham slurped another gulp of cider, trying to get the taste of the envelope gum out of his mouth and then belched loudly once more, breaking the silence.

Already knowing what the answer would be, she asked,

"Are you ready?"

She wanted a lift.

"Ahh," he replied shaking his head. "I've had a drink so you'll have to walk."

There was a momentary silence while they both listened to the rain beating down onto the deck and roof of the barge. Knowing she would be soaked if she went out there, even with an umbrella, she looked at him, trying to make her face as sad as possible, but he was not moved.

"I'm going to the loo, and I don't want to see you here when I come out, and post this." He said, handing her the envelope.

"But it's raining," she whined.

Graham thought for a split second and in that moment, she hoped he would change his mind.

"Just go!" He said, to her disappointment, before grabbing a newspaper that he'd bought a couple of days earlier and then trundling off to the toilet.

After waiting for a few moments to ensure that he'd actually gone, she rummaged around in her right hand coat pocket, before slowly pulling out a mobile phone. Holding it up in the direction of the toilet so she could keep an eye on the door, she quickly punched in a number.

Seconds later, she whispered into it.

"Hello, yes; he's drunk and won't take me."

After pausing for a second while the person on the other end replied.

She then replied. "Yes, I'll meet you by the bus stop, bye."

She hung up and the phone went hastily back into her pocket just as Graham startled her by shouting from behind the toilet door.

"Are you still here?"

After grabbing her bag, she tiptoed into the hallway, past the toilet door, making her way up the stairs to an entrance hatch, passing two bright yellow life jackets at the top. She put her umbrella up, before lifting the hatch, stepped out onto the deck and was almost blown off her feet as a gust of wind caught her umbrella. She quickly grabbed the rail at the top of the hatch as the wind again took hold of her umbrella once more. Now terrified, she worried that she might be blown off into the canal, and as she couldn't swim, that would be the end of her.

There was a momentary break in the wind and the opportunity that she wanted. Fumbling with the umbrella, she managed to put it down, then under her arm, before edging along the side of the barge until she was opposite the canal path. After taking a deep breath, she jumped on to the wet but solid ground, slipping forward as her feet hit the path, almost losing her footing and falling backwards into the fast moving water. But, she managed to stay upright and breathed a sigh of relief, glad to be off the barge and back on solid ground.

With the rain still lashing down, she put her umbrella up again and made her way to the safety of the road, taking small steps on the slippery canal path, trying to keep her balance.

Through the first port side porthole, Graham watched as another gust of wind caught her and as she struggled to keep her umbrella from blowing away.

* * *

She was soon at the bus stop where she waited under the shelter for a couple of minutes, before a red car pulled up and tooted. She ran over, the rain still lashing down and got in.

# CHAPTER 5

Half an hour later, Toi was looking somewhat uncomfortable as she stood by the side of a swimming pool, debating whether to get in. The chlorine fumes emanating from the pool were strong, and from time to time she squinted, causing her eyes to water lightly, giving some relief.

She wore a light brown two-piece bikini, something that you would see worn on a sunny beach in Spain, which looked a bit out of place given the weather.

A swimming instructor tried to reassure her that it was safe to get in the pool, as she would only be in 3 feet of water. The other people in her group were children; they were all in the pool having fun, their playful noise echoing around the pool area. Many of their parents offered encouragement through the glass that separated the swimming pool from the lounge viewing area.

"Mrs Morton, it's quite safe to get in, the water is warm," said the swimming instructor.

Toi said nothing and just stood there squinting.

The 19-year-old instructor eyed her attractive frame, causing her to feel more uncomfortable, which prompted her to fold her arms across her chest in an attempt to cover herself up, which immediately reminded the instructor that he was there to do a job and not to eye up his clients.

"Look, all the kids are in."

She frowned.

"I can see that!"

"OK, OK, take your time, no pressure." He replied, now seeing her annoyance.

His attention was suddenly taken up by a commotion over the other side of the pool; a girl was screaming as a boy in her group splashed her. Now with his eyes firmly fixed on the commotion, the instructor realised that he'd already spent too much time with Toi.

"Just let me know when you're ready to get in," he said, before hurrying across to the other side of the pool and then blowing his whistle, trying to catch the attention of his learners.

Toi put her arms back down by her sides, then nervously folded them across her chest once more, looking over to the lounge area where Sarah, the driver of the red car that had stopped to pick her up earlier peered through the glass.

Sarah tried to offer encouragement by nodding and smiling, hoping that Toi would conquer her fear, hoping that she would join in with the rest of the class.

She'd brought her swimming costume just in case she had to get in the pool, but really didn't want to as it was raining and cold outside and worst still, she would have to redo her hair. But as Toi had been standing by the side of the pool for ten minutes and now that the instructor had walked away, she thought that she ought to go in to show Toi that there was nothing to fear.

A few minutes later Sarah was in the pool holding Toi's hand; ten minutes after that and like one of the children, Toi splashed around the shallow end, not wanting to venture any further than waste height where she couldn't firmly put her feet on the bottom of the pool.

Minutes later the instructor reappeared, telling Toi that it would be hard to teach her to swim in such shallow water, but he would try. However, he disappeared for the rest of the session, choosing instead to spend his time coaching the children.

To help Toi, Sarah decided to tell her about creative visualisation and how using the technique could help her learn how to swim. After spending a minute or two sorting out the translation in to Thai then back into English, she asked Toi to close her eyes and imagine herself swimming freely in the sea. Even more.

"Imagine being a strong swimmer, swimming freely in the sea and enjoying it."

Toi did this for about ten seconds before first opening one eye and then the other. The women chuckled, before Sarah told her that she should try the technique every morning for ten minutes before getting out of bed and that this will help her to become a good swimmer.

Being sceptical, Toi's smile became a grin, before she burst in to laughter.

"What's so funny?" Asked Sarah.

"Well, how would doing this help me swim?" Toi chuckled.

"Not only will this help you swim, it will help you to become an expert swimmer."

Toi's laughter faded as she looked at Sarah in disbelief, the expression on Sarah's face showing that she was serious.

"Look, you told me that you wanted to come to this country and how you went out and found an Englishman, how did you do that?"

The expression on Toi's face was now one of puzzlement.

*How did that have anything to do with swimming?* She thought.

"You probably imagined meeting an Englishman in a bar and then him whisking you off to England?" Sarah continued, "Is that right?"

Toi now, more confused than she was before, just nodded.

Sarah seeing her confusion and now herself frustrated said.

"Oh, it doesn't matter; just imagine swimming in the sea every day, OK. It will help."

Toi smiled and nodded.

The women were in the pool for about half an hour before

Toi said that she should be getting home, as she had to get Graham's lunch ready.

After climbing out, Toi asked Sarah to wait for her while she spoke to the instructor, and while she wasn't eavesdropping, Sarah overheard Toi apologise to him for not getting into the pool sooner. She also asked about more lessons, the instructor directing her to reception where they would take her bookings and give her more information on the pool opening times.

This didn't come as a total surprise to Sarah, as Toi, in the end seemed to enjoy herself. What Sarah didn't know, was that Graham had paid for the swimming lessons, and lied to Toi, telling her that if she wanted to stay in England she must learn how to swim, as it was a legal requirement. He told her that the English were an island race and everyone from an early age had to learn how to swim. Toi, not native to these shores and having no reason to disbelieve him , agreed to learn.

In the changing room, as the women changed, Sarah noticed that Toi had fresh deep red and blue coloured bruises on her chest, which clearly came as an embarrassment to Toi, as she quickly tried to cover them up. However, Sarah said nothing, deciding instead to save any questioning for another day, as it had already been quite an uncomfortable day for Toi.

\* \* \*

It was still raining when the women got outside and they quickly ran to Sarah's red Yaris and got in. It was then that Toi caught a glimpse of the folded envelope in her bag, remembering that she had to post it.

"I've got to post this letter." She said, pulling the crumpled document from her bag and then carefully trying to straighten the creases.

"Can we stop at a post box before you drop me off?"

"Course we can," Sarah replied, noticing that the letter had no stamp on it.

"Oh, but it hasn't got a stamp on it," she remarked.

Toi looked at her puzzled.

Sarah pointed to the letter and mouthed

"It needs a stamp, the letter."

Toi now understood.

"Ahh a stamp. Oh no, he will be angry if I bring it back with me, can we get a stamp now?"

"Give it to me and I'll post it, I've got loads of stamps at home."

"Are you sure?" Toi replied, now unsure about what to do. "It's for me to stay here, in England."

"Don't worry," replied Sarah, seeing Toi's concern, "I will post it, I promise."

After a moment in thought, Toi agreed. *That should be alright.*

Sarah dropped Toi off by the side of the canal; they said their goodbyes and Sarah drove away.

It was only drizzling now, so Toi didn't bother opening her umbrella. She got back to the barge, let herself in, and found Graham who had been drinking all morning waiting for her. He was quite drunk and now wanted his lunch.

"How'd it go?" He slurred.

Toi smiled, "It was good."

"I told you you'd like it; did you book some more lessons?"

"Yes, at the reception, I can go on Tuesdays after work."

"Good." He replied nodding.

Well, what's for lunch?" He said now changing the subject.

"Oh, I'll just make something now."

As she turned to leave the room, he remembered the letter.

"And that letter, did you post it?"

She paused for a second, unsure if honesty would be the best policy and then with some apprehension told him what had happened; the fact that the letter had no stamp, and that Sarah said that she would post it. When Graham heard this he flew into a rage, talking about how he'd told her to post the letter and if that "bitch", referring to Sarah, didn't post it, Toi would be kicked out of the country. She found it hard to understand why he was so mad, what was going on, surely Sarah would post the letter.

Graham was even more annoyed to hear that she'd met

Sarah to go swimming. What was she doing meeting people behind his back? *I've got to teach her a lesson.* He thought.

* * *

Sarah got home a few minutes after dropping Toi off; she hurried inside, got a stamp from her utility draw, licked it, carefully fastened it to the top right hand corner of the envelope, and then rushed out again. She knew that the post was due to be collected any time soon, so had to make it to the post box before the post-man.

The post-man arrived as she got to the post box, so she handed him the letter, not before noticing that it was addressed to Sun Alliance, which was puzzling. Going by what Toi had said, it was more likely to be addressed to the immigration office, or some other government office and not what she understood to be an insurance company. *Maybe Toi had got it wrong* she thought.

After returning home Sarah began to get lunch ready and whilst on autopilot reviewed her morning. She'd helped her friend by using positivity and visualisation techniques and it seemed to be working. *If I'd been thinking this way years ago*, she thought, *my life could have been so different, so much better.*

*But, I've got my children and that is at least one good thing that has come out of my dysfunctional life.* She caught herself being negative and then told herself that she should have *'No Regrets. What's happened in the past has happened and I should be looking to the future. Things will be different now.*

## CHAPTER 6

Jenny walked to work most days and today was no exception. After dropping her children off at her sister in law's house, like clockwork she walked the mile and a half to work.

As the wind toyed with the tails of her cream and red Mac and brown skirt, she began to wish that she'd worn trousers. *'Bloody weather'* she thought.

Every day thoughts of her family and childhood filled her mind; she thought about how close she'd come to having a nervous breakdown nine months earlier, following the death of her father: And how she was still not on speaking terms with her mother.

She'd always been close to her brother and quite often talked about him to the other women in the kitchen, building him up, as if trying to pair one of them up with him, but always avoided talking about her childhood and her parents, as if therein laid a deep dark secret.

The fact is, as a child she was sexually abused by her father and now blamed her mother for letting it happen.

For some reason she still felt love for her father, as she'd developed a shared dependency for his attentions, in a "Stockholm Syndrome" sort of way. She didn't want to love him, or miss him, but found that she couldn't help herself and hated herself for it.

While married with two children, she was introverted and

the other women handled her with kid gloves as they saw her as being emotional, as she would burst into tears at the drop of a hat.

* * *

The kitchen was filled with excitement as Jenny entered; Sarah had told the women that she'd been swimming with Toi and what a good time they'd had.

"Swimming!" Said Debbie, "I haven't been swimming in years."

Then admitted that it was about time her children learned. Sarah had made it sound so good that all of the women seemed to want to go, including Karen.

"Any fit life guards there?" Asked Jane.

"Trust you. Always the one to be thinking about sex." Jenny replied, removing her coat.

By now Sarah was blushing, something which Karen noticed.

"Ahh!" "So there were some fit blokes there then? I can tell by your face," she said, before they all burst into laughter.

The excitement was broken by Toi's arrival; as she stepped through the doorway, there was a gasp and the women stood speechless, looking at her almost in a state of shock.

What had left them speechless was the state of Toi's face. The left side was swollen; bruised to the point where her left eye was almost closed.

Sarah rushed over and put her arm around her shoulders.

"What happened?"

"I, I walked into a door." Toi slowly replied head down, looking at the terracotta tiles. There was silence and an air of disbelief as the women stood there looking at her, half expecting her to continue, as everyone could see that her injuries couldn't have been caused by her walking into a door.

Karen walked over, stooped and now looking at Toi directly asked in a calm and gentle tone.

"Hasn't he taken you to the hospital?"

"No." said Toi shaking her head.

"He did this to you didn't he?"

Toi was silent, as she did not want to lie.

"Didn't he?" Karen repeated, this time sounding stern.

"He didn't mean it."

"Don't say that! Don't you ever say that!" Karen shouted, Toi stepping back clearly shocked by the outburst.

There was now a deathly silence as Karen looked around the room; all the women surprised by her outburst.

"They all say they're sorry when they're sober." Karen continued.

"It used to happen to me, but I got out." Said Debbie butting in.

"You've got to leave him, you cannot live like this." Said Karen.

There was general agreement from all the women, but Toi was afraid.

"Where will I live? They'll send me back."

"Don't worry about that, we'll sort it out." Jane replied.

"We will sort him out, but we need to get your face looked at first." Said Karen.

"You've got to go to the hospital."

It was clear to see that Toi was worried.

"No, no hospitals," she said shaking her head.

"You've got to." Said Sarah."

Karen held both of Toi's hands, stooped to look directly into her eyes and while nodding said, "Yes, we have to get you looked at."

Toi could not help but nod in unison with Karen and then replied.

"OK."

"Debbie, I want you to take her." Said Karen.

Toi and Sarah looked at each other, then at Karen.

Karen pre-empting what was about to come said.

"Sarah, I need you here, we're going to be down by two."

Sarah slowly but reluctantly nodded as she refocused on her responsibilities.

"Come on the rest of you," Karen continued, "we've got work to do."

Two of the women disappeared to various parts of the

kitchen leaving Toi, Jenny, Debbie and Karen.

"Come on Jenny," snapped Karen, "you're late, you'd better go and get changed and Debbie, you'd better hurry. Come on, get your coat, I'm going to need you back as soon as possible."

The women left the kitchen; Jenny following Debbie as they hurried down the corridor and entered the changing room.

Whilst inside, the creak of Debbie's locker opening before she picked out her coat filled the uncomfortable silence. Debbie then slammed the locker shut, turned the key then turned to face Jenny.

"What a bastard?" She said.

Jenny mustered a half smile, before looking at the floor and then mumbled.

"Yes, what a bastard."

Debbie seeing that Jenny didn't really want to chat decided that it was time to go.

"I'll see you later," She said before rushing out of the room.

Jenny watched as the door closed then said.

"Yes, I'll see you later," her voice reverberating off the walls.

As Jenny began to change into her whites, she thought, how it was that loved ones, it seemed, were the ones that hurt you the most. These thoughts magnified how she felt about her mother and father and before long was in floods of tears.

# CHAPTER 7

The usual sounds of chatter and laughter from the women above the noise of the kitchen was muted, as they worked in relative silence, clearly affected by what had happened.

When serving lunch, Jenny still red eyed and usually the most placid of the women snapped at one of the boys for taking a hand full of chips from her serving tray. The reprimand came as a surprise to the boy, as he'd usually done this when Jenny served and got away with it.

Thinking that he looked and acted like her younger brother when he was about the same age, she'd struck up a little rapport with him.

She immediately checked herself and apologised, then asked Karen if she could be moved back into the kitchen as what had happened to Toi that morning had clearly affected her. Karen agreed to let her work out the back for a short time, but warned that if it got busy she would have to return. Watery eyed, Jenny disappeared back inside leaving Jane to serve by herself.

The kitchen was usually busy on Mondays and today was no exception. With the kitchen staffing down by two, the women struggled to keep up and before long a queue formed, in which a scuffle broke out between two of the boys. The fight was broken up by the head master, one Mr James-Barton, an old school Harrow and Oxford educated man, who grabbed both boys and after giving them a ticking off, sent them to his office.

After looking around the dining room, he marched into the kitchen and called to Karen getting her attention. He straightened his green and oatmeal coloured tweed blazer before waving his finger in the direction of the corridor that led to the staff changing room. Quickly walking through the doorway, he politely held the door open letting Karen through before waiting for the door to slowly close on its hydraulic hinge. He stood silent for a few moments, increasing Karen's angst before asking.

"Why is the lunch queue so long today? Is there something wrong? Something I should know about?"

Karen and "JB", as the staff called him, did not get on; the tall, thin silver haired 60 year old was old school and preferred it when dinners were meat and two veg, served with gravy, followed by jam roly-poly or treacle pudding, rather than what was served up today; burger and chips and snacks from vending machines, which the boys preferred.

The company that ran the kitchen had tendered for the school contract and had come in cheaper than any of the others who had applied, which the school governors where happy to go with. Karen was the representative of that company in his school, and he now held a misguided belief that she represented all that was wrong in society. Loud women and burgers and chips "Just would not do," not in his school anyway. Karen believed him to be a male chauvinistic bigot and had a real dislike of him.

"Yes," Karen replied. "One of our women had an accident on the way to work."

JB looked concerned,

"On the way to work?" He asked.

Karen lied, "Yes, she slipped and hit her head and was badly bruised. I got Debbie to take her to the hospital."

Karen didn't know why she lied, but it just seemed to be the right thing to do. But JB was concerned, but for all the wrong reasons.

"So, that queue out there has been caused by something that has nothing to do with us. Nothing to do with the school I mean?"

He paused as if waiting for an answer and just as Karen opened her mouth.

"This is not good enough." He interrupted, "She should have made her own way to the hospital; could she not have taken a cab, or better still rang for an ambulance?"

Not surprised by his comments, Karen again about to reply was interrupted once more.

"I want that queue sorted out," He demanded. "And, I am going to report this to your line manager. We have a service level agreement and what's happening out there certainly does not meet it."

Like a scolded child, Karen stood there silent, head down, looking at the floor.

"Don't just stand there, get on with it!" He ordered.

Karen marched back into the kitchen and made her way to the back where Sarah knocking the excess oil off a basket of chips, saw some distress on Karen's face, and after catching sight of JB as he left the kitchen knew something was wrong.

"You OK?" She asked Karen

"Yes," then after a short pause, "can you please help out on the counter, we've got a queue." Karen replied abruptly.

"OK," said Sarah, surprised by Karen's sternness.

Karen's hardness did not mask the tears welling up in her eyes, and as it was clear that she didn't want to talk, Sarah went through to the counter where Jenny who had returned to help Jane were still struggling to reduce the queue.

* * *

It was nearing the end of lunch and within 15 minutes they had cleared the queue and were now cleaning trays and wiping tables. Jane as usual chatted to some boys at the far end of the restaurant, which prompted Sarah to shout over for her to get a move on.

Toi and Debbie got back from the hospital a little after 2:00pm and as they entered the kitchen, the other women rushed over to them. Toi's bruises looked a little better than they had been.

"So, what did they do?" Asked Sarah.

"Nothing," Debbie replied, before Toi had a chance to answer. "Bloody waste of time if you ask me."

"No," Toi interrupted, "they examined me and told me that nothing is broken, it just looks worse than it is."

"Did they ask how it happened?" Karen asked.

Toi was silent.

Karen sighed, before Debbie shaking her head jumped in again.

"They did ask and she told them that she walked into a door. I don't know why you didn't tell them the truth." She continued, forgetting how she'd been not so long ago.

"Alright," said Sarah. "Take it easy." Now coming to Toi's defence.

"OK. Let's just calm down," said Karen now turning to Toi. "What do you want to do? You can go to the women's shelter in town or you can go home. It's up to you."

"I don't know." Toi replied.

"The shelter's not that bad," said Debbie, "Sometimes there's a queue for the bathrooms and kitchens, but it's OK."

Toi thought for a second and to everyone's surprise.

"No, I'll go home." She said.

"But what if he does it again." Asked Jenny.

"He won't," said Karen. "Look," she continued turning to

Toi. "Go home if you want to, but if you do, you have to tell him that you've been to the hospital. If he knows that, he'll be less likely to do something like this again. Well, not until you're better I suppose. He can't risk you going back to the hospital; you know, just in case they get suspicious."

There was general agreement from the other women.

"We can sort out moving you to the shelter over the next few days if you want." Said Sarah.

Karen told Toi that she could have the rest of the day off, but Toi didn't want to go home and said that she would rather work, which was understandable.

At 3:15pm, most of the women had cleared up for the day and had gone home.

Debbie had given Toi a lift down to the canal, as she wanted to ensure that she got home safely, which was a bit ironic, as her problems originated at home, she thought, as Toi waved goodbye.

Sarah found herself alone in the kitchen, the air diffused with the smell of lemon disinfectant and the dull whirring sound of the extractor fans filling the background. It was nearly time for her to go and she hurried as she knew her children would be waiting. But where was Karen, she asked herself. When she'd finished mopping the floor and turned the extractors off, the silence now being a pleasure to her ears, she hurried along the now dark corridor to the changing room, where she thought Karen would be. Entering the changing room, she was surprised to find Karen crying.

She sat there, eyes red from where she'd cried so much.

"What's up?" Asked Sarah.

"Why does life have to be like this?" Karen replied.

Not knowing what Karen meant, Sarah asked.

"Like what? Do you mean like what happened to Toi?"

Sarah paused for a second waiting for an answer and when none came she continued.

"Come on Karen talk to me!" She demanded.

Karen felt that Sarah showed genuine interest and decided to go through what pained her while Sarah listened. In the back of Sarah's mind though, was the thought of her children waiting for her to pick them up and she now began regretting a little, that she'd asked Karen about her problems.

Karen explained that what had happened to Toi reminded her of her own marriage.

"The reason I divorced Hugh," she said, then correcting herself, "my ex, is because he hit me. I wanted to make a go of it, but it seemed like every time he got drunk, he took his frustrations out on me. I mean, he lost his job, then got into a rut and couldn't find work.

He's a labourer, or was a labourer. His drinking got worse and worse, and one day after getting drunk, he hit me. The next day, once he'd sobered up, he said that he didn't remember anything, but after seeing the bruise on my face, he knew that he'd done it. He said he was sorry and he even cried, but he carried on drinking and the beatings just got worse. In the end, I began to hate him and finally I left him, and the rest as they say, is history."

Sarah was surprised, as Karen came across as a bit of a hard woman, so it was strange to see her like this. *This must have been a particularly stressful day for her.*

Sarah hugged Karen, who began to sob uncontrollably. Through her sobs, she said that she was fed up with "men taking the piss" out of women and that, they had to see Toi's husband Graham.

"We have to sort him out. Today," She said.

"But what can we do?"

"I don't know, but we've just got to do something."

Sarah agreed.

* * *

A few minutes later, the women were outside where it was drizzling; though her eyes were still red, Karen now wore a smile as she hurriedly locked up.

*Getting some things off her chest seemed to have worked,* thought Sarah. In the changing room, Sarah offered a piece of advice that woke Karen up; it was one piece of information that had given Sarah herself real impetus to sort things out in her life.

So as soon as Karen heard it, she knew it; it was there all along and all she had to do was to act on it. It brought a smile to her face when Sarah told her and in that instant gave her a fresh outlook. They both left work that afternoon feeling good with themselves.

Karen waved goodbye, as like a mad woman, Sarah sped off; her children were waiting.

\* \* \*

The women arrived at the barge at 6pm. There was a break in the rain as the sun's brightness seemed to be breaking through the clouds and there was a slight but fresh breeze. As the women approached the barge, Karen saw that Sarah appeared worried.

"You OK." Karen asked.

"Yes." Sarah replied sheepishly.

"You sure, you don't look alright, you look worried."

"No, I'm fine."

"Look Sarah, if you're feeling uncomfortable with this, I'll do all the talking if you want.

"Are you sure?"

"Yes, I'm ready for him."

"OK," said Sarah, who now felt a little better about the situation.

They reached the barge and Karen knocked on the hatch, moments later Toi appeared.

"What do you want?" She whispered.

"We're here to see Graham." Said Sarah.

Toi put her finger to her mouth to quieten Sarah from talking too loudly and winced when her finger touched her bruised lips, which were still sore.

The three women were startled when Graham shouted from inside.

"Who is it?" Came his booming voice.

"Please go," whispered Toi.

"We have to see Graham," Karen replied loudly, hoping that Graham would hear.

"Shhh!" said Toi, now looking around nervously.

But it was too late; the women listened silently as Graham's heavy footsteps came shuffling up the steps before his head appeared through the hatch.

Slowly pushing his way past Toi, he now stood at the top, his intimidating facial expression filling both women with fear.

He was just what Karen and Sarah had expected; a big man with a beer potbelly, unkempt, an unshaven greying beard with signs of his last meal still in it, and wearing an old off white and baked bean stained vest. Sarah thought he looked awful, forgetting that she was trying to make a point of not prejudging people.

He looked at the pair, and from the look on their faces

guessed that they knew Toi and meant business. But, he couldn't help himself but treat them with the disrespect that he treated all women with, save his mother.

"What do you want?"

Over the following few minutes they were all taken aback by what Karen had to say. Karen read Graham the riot act as he stood there open mouthed, almost in a state of shock. Each time he tried to get a word in, Karen bombarded him with more. She amazingly talked for a full five minutes without a break and in the end finished with,

"And if she comes into work with so much as a scratch on her, the police are going to be all over you. I promise."

Sarah winked at Toi who was now standing behind Graham; she smiled back.

"Just mind your own business, go on, just piss off!"

Was all Graham could muster, before squeezing past Toi and disappearing back inside. He knew he'd been caught 'bang to rights', so there was nothing that he could say or do.

"I'll see you tomorrow," Toi whispered. "Thanks."

She then disappeared back inside, shutting the hatch behind her.

Karen had released the entire pent up tension that had accumulated throughout the day and now felt so much better. She thought that if she was able to deal with this man, she would be able to handle any man and from now on, she would give as good as she got. *So watch out head master.*

* * *

Earlier that day, in the changing room, Sarah had told Karen that she had become or thought like a victim and what she really needed to do was to take control of her life and the situations that she found herself in. Karen certainly controlled this situation and put what they had talked about into practice.

Karen smiled at Sarah as they walked back to her car and said.

"Well, that went well." Before they both burst into laughter.

# CHAPTER 8

All of the women met up at the local swimming baths the following Saturday, where Sarah and Karen agreed that between them they would teach Toi to swim, who now, following the confrontation with Graham, was now allowed to go out with her friends.

Sarah and Karen busied themselves in the pool, showing Toi what she should do with her arms and legs: Sarah supporting Toi's weight by holding her midriff buoyed by the surface water, Karen making over arm movements and Toi awkwardly trying to copy Karen's movements, while kicking her feet at the same time; it almost looking comical. Debbie and Jenny gossiped by the side of the pool while keeping an eye on Debbie's two children, who were splashing around in the shallow end, generally having fun. And Jane talked to one of the lifeguards, her body language giving away that she was flirting with him; her advances in return being warmly received.

Taking a break from the water and standing by the side of the pool, Sarah took some time to reflect. *This would never of happened a month ago, all of us having fun at the swimming pool.* She thought.

Things were so hostile then, but now, they had all become such good friends and the atmosphere in the kitchen was almost harmonious. Her thoughts were interrupted by Karen, who summoned her back into the water using her kitchen manager's voice,

"We've got work to do," she said, nodding in Toi's direction.

* * *

Karen had held a meeting with the kitchen staff on the Tuesday following the dressing down of Graham, telling the women that she wanted them to "Take Control" of their lives and not to become victims. Or, more precisely, rather than take everything at face value, challenge if necessary things that they believed were wrong or unjust. She wanted a renewed vigour in the kitchen, expressing the wish to work with empowered women. To this they may not have all believed, however they all agreed. In that week things were so different, there was a feeling of confidence and happiness.

The seeds that Sarah had planted, it seemed, had taken root, and she hoped this newly found confidence would flourish.

This confidence even seemed to have rubbed off on Toi, as during that week, she found enough courage to tell Graham that she'd bought a mobile phone and to her surprise, he didn't seem to mind. Now she was able to talk to Sarah much more and more importantly, she was able to speak to her countrywoman, her friend Abhasra, much more freely.

* * *

That evening after swimming the women met up at Sarah's house for dinner; a dinner which Toi cooked. She wanted the others to sample some real home cooked Thai cuisine and had promised them a meal for the kindness that they had shown to her over the past few weeks. Sarah agreed to hold the party at her home, as Graham said that he didn't want "those women," referring to Sarah and Karen, in his home.

All were surprised at the quality and taste of the food that Toi prepared and though none of them had ever eaten Thai cuisine before, there were no leftovers at the end of the meal.

As Sarah made coffee, the women sat chatting at the dining table.

"Toi, you've got to give me the recipe for that starter," said Jane, "those prawns were fantastic. They're my favourite."

"The green curry was good too," said Debbie. "Do you know I wasn't sure about coming tonight. But, I'm glad I did, I'm not too keen on Chinese food, but that was great. Thanks."

"Don't make me laugh," Karen chuckled, "For one thing this 'isn't Chinese food and secondly, fish and chips are more your style?"

The women laughed and then unanimously thanked Toi for doing the cooking, just as Sarah returned carrying a tray with the coffee.

"Ah! It's the teacher's pet back with the coffee." Said Debbie sarcastically, as Sarah entered the room.

Karen looked at Debbie clearly annoyed.

"I'm only joking,"

"I think she's had too much wine." Said Jenny.

"I'm only joking," repeated Debbie. "No seriously, thanks for having us round."

"That's Ok," Sarah replied.

All the women joined in and thanked Sarah for her hospitality,

"So," said Debbie, "How's your home life now?" Directing her question at Toi.

Toi looked down at the table, a little embarrassed to be in the spotlight.

"Debbie!" Jane interrupted, trying to highlight her insensitivity.

"You don't have to answer that." Said Sarah.

There was a momentary silence as the women, though concerned that Toi might be embarrassed, deep down really wanted to know what was happening in her life, but now seeing that she was embarrassed, Sarah came to the rescue.

"OK, I'll go first." She said.

Continuing to show her insensitivity Debbie butted in.

"Yes, but, I want to hear about."

"Leave it out Debbie!" Karen interrupted.

After another momentary silence, Sarah started, she gave a seemingly uninspiring update of things that were happening in her life and after a couple of minutes, seeing that the women had lost interest, wound her story up and knowing that Toi would be next, tried to deflect the women's attention.

"So Debbie." She said.

"Oh no," Debbie replied, "not me, you all know about me anyway, nothing new here." She said now looking at Jenny.

Knowing it was now her turn, Jenny sighed heavily, not really wanting to divulge anything.

"Come on Jenny," said Debbie, "give us the gossip."

Seeing Jenny's obvious discomfort, Toi butted in.

"OK, I'll tell you about me then."

"You don't have to." Said Sarah.

"I know, but here goes anyway. Well, things have changed a bit at home, Graham has changed." She continued, taking a sip of her coffee.

The women moved in closer and listened intently as Toi explained that she was now enjoying a newfound freedom and that Graham had not acted violently towards her over the past week or so. The women laughed when she referred to Karen and how she'd told him off; talking for five minutes.

"So, you reckon that he'll be alright now." Said Jane.

"No way," said Karen, "Once a bastard, always a bastard."

Her words making everyone laugh.

"Yeah, don't let him fool you." Said Debbie.

"No, said Toi, "I think he'll be OK now."

The feel from all the women was one of disbelief and after a short pause.

"So, you won't be going to the women's shelter then?" Asked Jane.

Toi paused for a second, as if in thought.

"No." She replied, much to Debbie's disappointment.

"I think I'll be alright at home now, I just wish we lived in a normal house."

"Oh, you still hate the water then?" Asked Jenny.

Toi nodded.

"But you did OK today." Jane continued, her words leading to an almost uncomfortable silence, which was broken by Toi.

"Well, I'd better be getting back."

"But it's only nine thirty." Said Jane, taking another sip from her wine glass.

"Can't you stay for another half hour?" Asked Karen.

"I can't" Toi replied gulping the last bit of her coffee. "I said I would be home by ten. But, I've got something for all of you."

She raised an eyebrow signalling to Sarah, who got up and disappeared into the hallway, leaving the women looking at each other with surprise and anticipation. Sarah reappeared a few seconds later with a white and red Woolworth's carrier bag, which she handed to Toi.

"I want to thank you all for helping me over the past few weeks," Said Toi. "So I've bought you all a gift, which I hope, will bring you good luck."

From the bag she produced a small expensive looking red and gold box, which she handed to Sarah and then another which she handed to Karen.

"You shouldn't have done that." Said Sarah, a sentiment mirrored by Karen.

Dipping into the bag once more she produced blue and gold coloured boxes, one for each of the other women.

"Go on then." She said, as the women sat there being polite and not wanting to open their particular box before all had been handed out.

The women slowly opened their boxes to reveal sand stone coloured amulets, with thin liquorice brown coloured ties.

"They are Luangpu Hong Promapunyo amulets, said Toi, where I come from, these are said to bring you long life and prosperity."

"Luangpu Hong, what?" Asked Karen, struggling with the pronunciation.

"Luangpu Hong Promapunyo." Toi repeated.

"They're beautiful." Said Jenny.

"You shouldn't have." Said Jane.

In her silence, Debbie thought how she'd been the instigator of most of the mistreatment Toi suffered in the kitchen over the past few months.

"Well, I'd better go." Said Toi, looking at Sarah, signalling to her that a lift was needed.

"Oh no!" Said Jane, "I want to give you my bit of gossip."

"Don't bother we know already that it's got something to do with a man. A new man perhaps?" Karen probed, to Jane's annoyance and to the amusement of the others.

"Alright girls," said Sarah, "I'm going to drop Toi home, I'll be back soon."

"I tell you what, I'm going home too." Said Debbie.

"You sure?" Asked Sarah, "I won't be long."

"No, it's getting late."

"OK." Said Sarah.

"I'm going to go too." Said Karen

"Me too." Said Jane.

Debbie wasn't the only one feeling guilty, that collective feeling beginning to swallow up the room. Though the feel was still jovial, there was a distinct dip in the atmosphere.

As the women left, they each hugged Toi, thanking her once again for the food and the gift. Debbie was particularly gracious, prolonging her hug and finally pulling away watery eyed.

As Karen and Debbie walked off through the front garden and then down the road, they argued.

"You crying?" Asked Karen.

"No," Debbie replied.

"Yes you are?"

"No, I'm not."

"You are, I can see the tears."

"I'm not bloody crying."

"Whatever, you say."

"What's that meant to mean...."

Toi looked at them puzzled, as the sound of their voices and heels echoed off the houses in the street, then dimmed and then disappeared.

"It's OK," said Sarah. "It's just the drink talking."

With the other women now gone, the house was quiet, only the sound of 'South Park' being heard seeping from beneath Carl's door.

"You OK." Asked Sarah as she quietly closed the front door.

"Yes," Toi replied, "but they didn't seem very happy with their gifts."

"They were happy with everything." Sarah replied. With a full understanding how the women must of felt.

"Are you sure?"

"Yes, and I think they'll treat you much better at work now."

\* \* \*

It was dark when the women arrived at the canal and

though it wasn't raining, it was overcast, the clouds obscuring the moon light. Sarah parked as close to the canal path as possible; underneath a yellow street lamp, which flickered on and off every few seconds.

"Are you going to be alright getting back?" She asked.

"I'll be fine." Toi replied with a smile.

"But it's pitch black out there."

"Pitch, black?" Said Toi, struggling to understand.

"Dark, it's very dark out there," said Sarah, "you sure you're going to be alright."

"Yes, I'll be fine, besides I've got this to protect me."

From beneath her coat and then her high-necked camisole Toi pulled out an amulet. An amulet very similar to the ones that she'd given out earlier.

They both smiled.

"OK," Said Sarah. "I'll see you at work, bye!"

* * *

From her car, Sarah watched as Toi disappeared into the darkness, and in the darkness Toi hurried along the canal path, minutes later arriving back at The Duck.

Quietly climbing aboard, she opened the hatch and tiptoed down the steps so as not to wake Graham. But in the distance she heard the sound of the TV and above that, the distinctive deep snoring sound that Graham made when he'd been drinking.

He was asleep in an armchair, snoring loudly when she entered the living room, with eleven empty beer cans lined up on the table in front of him. Now thinking that if she was quiet enough, she could go to bed without waking him, so switched off the TV and made her way to the bedroom.

Quietly going through her bedtime ritual, of taking off her jewellery, brushing her teeth and washing her face, she thought of the women, and what a wonderful evening they'd had. She now felt accepted by the people that she worked with: The people with which she spent most of her time. As she lay there, she said a prayer for all of her new friends, and then slowly drifted off to sleep.

Twenty minutes later, she was awoken by hands, rough groping hands and the smell of alcohol. Graham had woken up and had joined her in bed.

# CHAPTER 9

As the weather worsened over the few weeks that followed, it having been officially declared the wettest February on record, the mood in the kitchen continued to improve. The newfound optimism had positive effects on everyone and was illustrated when Karen had another run in with JB.

It was over something Jane had done that he'd mistakenly blamed Toi for and made derogatory comments about, which further highlighted to the women, the unwarranted prejudices which existed at the time.

Jane the youngest of the group: just 18 years old and of mixed race, African father, Irish Mother, beautiful and she knew it; was accused by the parents of a final year student of acting inappropriately towards him.

It was reported that one of the dinner ladies leant down to clean a table at which the young man sat, ensuring that he caught sight of a bit more than her cleavage, well quite a bit more, owing to her blouse purposely being unbuttoned quite low.

That evening whilst on the telephone, the boy was over heard by a tutor telling a fellow student about what he'd seen, a story, which he'd embellished; the whole thing got out of hand, was eventually escalated and got back to his parents.

Suffice to say, his parents were furious.

The following morning, Karen unaware of what had taken place, was summoned to the head masters office.

When she arrived, the school secretary asked her to wait outside his office and he would call her in, in due course.

As Karen waited, her mind wondered as she worried as to the reason why she had been summoned; feeling that she must have done something wrong, getting a sensation that brought her back to her school days: Waiting outside the head master's office, waiting for the punishment that he was bound to dole out, which brought on a feeling of dread to the pit of her stomach.

After waiting 5 minutes and now feeling annoyed, having being called away from her busy kitchen, Karen remembered that she had to take control. *Who does he think he is?* She thought. Also remembering that she had to be fearless.

Sarah had told the women that having a positive attitude could be difficult to obtain after leading a predominantly negative life: And that positivity or having a positive state of mine could be hard to achieve.

"It's something that you have to work on quite hard to begin with," She said, "And then it becomes easier. It does still require work, but in the end, it becomes second nature."

It was only now that Karen began to appreciate Sarah's words.

*Why am I frightened?* She asked herself. *I've done nothing wrong, so what can he do? And even if I have; still, what can he do? Nothing,* she thought.

Standing up Karen turned to the secretary and asked

"How long will he be?"

Without looking up from the head master's diary, she replied belligerently

"Mr James-Barton! Will take as long as it takes."

*Why the hostility?* Thought Karen shaking her head and now feeling a bit angry.

"Well, tell Mr James-Barton, that I've got work to do, and I don't want my time wasted so when he's ready to see me let me know. I'm going back to the kitchen."

As she turned to leave the office the secretary looked up from the diary, clearly taken aback.

"He has someone in with him at the moment." She said, this time in a more timid manner.

"Look in all seriousness I've got work to do, so I'll be in the Kitchen when he's ready for me." Karen replied, shrugging her shoulders.

The secretary got up from her desk now clearly annoyed.

"OK! Wait, I'll see if he is ready to see you." She said before heading off toward the head master's office door.

Karen's blank expression hid the smile she wore inside. *And why didn't you do that before?* She thought.

The secretary knocked, waited a second and then

disappeared behind a large dark oak stained door. A few seconds later, she reappeared.

"He's ready to see you now."

*Now that wasn't so hard was it?*

After thanking the secretary, Karen knocked on the door and on hearing a murmur from behind it entered the office.

Inside, he stood behind a large dark oak desk, dressed with an ink blotter, a few neatly positioned papers, a couple of crystal paperweights, and a gold pen and pencil stand. Behind him a large window presented what little light the grey morning had to offer, the trees outside being battered by the wind and rain.

A smartly dressed yet stern looking woman sat opposite holding a white china cup from which she took a sip and then slowly placed it on a saucer.

Turning to face Karen, without really paying attention, she perched the china precariously on the edge of the desk, swallowed the liquid and then forced out a smile, before turning to face JB, her unyielding expression returning once more.

"Ah! Karen, this is Mrs Mortimer; Mrs Mortimer, Karen O'Brien," JB introduced the two women, who nodded at each other in acknowledgment.

"Karen, I think we have a situation." JB continued while removing his blazer, revealing a smart brown lightly checked waistcoat.

"Oh!" Said Karen wearing a puzzled expression.

"Yes. Something to do with Toi, that woman you have working in the kitchen: Mrs Mortimer's son Brian reported it to us."

Karen turned to Mrs Mortimer as JB began to tell Brian's story: He painted Toi in a very bad light. He said that she'd purposely revealed herself to the student, and continued on to say that what she'd done was unacceptable and would not be tolerated. Karen remained silent while he talked, all the while couldn't help noticing the way JB showed off in front of the parent, strutting around behind his desk, gesturing like some old eighteenth century Shakespearian actor.

As he continued, his gist suggested that he wanted Toi out, fired, Karen standing there, all the while thinking to herself

'Take Control, Take Control."

JB finally completed the story and while Karen gathered her thoughts, Mrs Mortimer wore an almost worried expression, while JB, waited in an almost baited breath fashion for what Karen had to say.

She made a tentative start.

"It's all well and good you accusing Toi of doing something like this, but that's not Toi, she wouldn't, she just wouldn't do something like that."

"Well, I don't know." He said, briefly smiling at Mrs

Mortimer and then turning back to Karen.

"Why would the boy make something like that up?"

Karen made a face, shrugged her shoulders and said sarcastically. "Because he's a boy, and that's what boys do?"

She was amazed by JB's attitude; his willingness to sacrifice a member of staff to look good in front of one of the parents, or that is what it seemed. But, she was determined that this was not going to happen, well at least without a fight.

"Do you have any evidence, you know, evidence that she did what you're accusing her of?" Karen asked.

Mrs Mortimer stood up looking clearly upset.

"Now see here, my son, does not lie and I take exception to the insinuation." She said, now glaring at JB, trying to summon his support.

"Those SORTS of women should not be working in this school." She continued, now turning to face the headmaster, who came to her aid.

"Agreed, and in light of what has taken place, her position here is now untenable."

Karen now feeling isolated told herself to be strong and stood there for a second almost shell shocked, trying to think what to say in response. After taking a deep breath, she blurted out

"What sort of women?"

"Well," Said JB slowly, "she's a Thai woman isn't she?"

"What are you trying to say?" Karen replied and now clearly taken aback at the remarks

"Well," he said hesitantly, "we all know what those Thai women get up to, don't we."

"NO we don't." Replied Karen angrily now turning to see even a shocked expression on Mrs Mortimer's face.

"So you think I should sack a member of my team, without first getting proof that she's done anything wrong? Whatever happened to innocent until proven guilty?" Asked Karen before pausing for a second and then continuing,

"If you think Toi loosened her blouse and deliberately leaned down in front of the boy, I say let's get her in here to explain herself."

Mrs Mortimer, butted in, as she turned to face JB.

"No, It wasn't a Thai woman, It was a young mixed race girl"

"Oh! You mean Jane." Said Karen. "Well, it makes no difference, get her in here, let's see what she's got to say."

Karen continued to gamble that JB wouldn't be man enough to confront Jane himself.

There was a momentary silence; it was JB's turn to take the centre stage and as he began to blush, he stuttered out.

"Well I, well we."

He was clearly in a panic, and seeing her opportunity, Karen pounced. She interrupted him, turned to Mrs Mortimer and offered her the opportunity to speak to Jane. As expected, she too was reluctant to do so, telling Karen that it wasn't her responsibility to talk to school staff, before taking her seat once more and again looking to JB for support.

"Jane is a hard working member of my team, who I want to keep. After listening to you two, you would think that she was stripping off in front of the boys in the middle of the restaurant."

"No, I wasn't saying that." He blurted out.

Once again, Karen interrupted, glancing at Mrs Mortimer for a second for inspiration, then turning back to face JB; she played on the comment that Mrs Mortimer had made earlier.

"She is an 18 year old girl and I'm sure her parents wouldn't like to hear the 'SORT' of girl that you're making her out to be."

"No she didn't mean it like that." JB interrupted, now eager to distance himself from the comments.

"How do you know what she meant, you're not a mind reader." Said Karen, who was now beginning to enjoy herself, but in the back of her mind thought she'd started to sound a bit rude.

Shaking her head she continued,

"And I'm not sure what the news papers would think of your thoughts on Thai women, because frankly what you just insinuated is just sexist, no racist to say the least."

JB and Mrs Mortimer were silent and Karen now realising that she had the upper hand checked herself, thinking that it was time to calm the situation down.

"Look, I'll ask Jane about what happened, if anything, and deal with her if I find that she has been doing what you've said. But I'm sure there's been some misunderstanding; I'll let you know what I find out."

"Alright, please let me know." JB replied with a distinct look of relief written across his face.

He turned to Mrs Mortimer who blushed with embarrassment.

"I WILL get to the bottom of this." He said.

*Will you now,* thought Karen.

He turned to address Karen once more. "I wasn't trying to be racist, I just think that people from that country."

Karen interrupted by putting one finger in front of her lips and shaking her head, as if to shush him.

"I wouldn't." she said.

To which JB stopped talking.

Karen left the office wearing a smile and winked at the secretary as she walked through the office, who rolled her eyes disapprovingly.

As she slowly made her way back to the kitchen, she thought that had gone quite well and that she'd taken control of the situation and won. Never again would he belittle me, she thought.

* * *

On her return to the kitchen, Karen called Jane over to a quiet corner, where they talked privately. She noted that Jane's kitchen white coat and under blouse was opened quite low and on speaking to her found out, that there was a boy that she liked and that she frequently lowered or opened the buttons on her blouse when cleaning his table. 'To give him a flash.'

Karen explained that she'd been reported to the head master and that she should now behave herself, as he would be watching her.

"I'm not going to do anything, but you have to behave yourself."

"But he's so fit." Jane replied, not recognising the gravity of the situation.

"Jane!" Karen replied, giving her a stern look. "I'm serious."

"OK, OK, but Sarah did tell me that, because I'm young, I shouldn't waste any of my life; if I see something that I want; you know, in life, I should grab it, and make the most of it."

Karen paused and thought for a moment before saying.

"OK, but you're trying too hard. Look, you're a beautiful young woman and I think he would have noticed you anyway. Just promise me you'll behave."

Jane Smiled, "OK, I'll behave."

"You'd better."

They smiled at each other for a moment, before Karen continued.

"Go on, you'd better get back to work.

Karen now had no intention of telling JB what she'd found out. She'd taken care of what she thought was a very small, youthful and naive misdemeanour and did not intend to give him any form of satisfaction.

\* \* \*

At the end of the day, before they went home, Karen and Sarah were as usual the last to leave and were in the changing room getting ready to depart. Karen took the opportunity to tell Sarah what had happened that morning.

Sarah showed concern that the head master harboured such prejudices and was openly willing to put them out into the public domain and especially to parents. But they both laughed when Karen explained about the look on JB's face when she mentioned Jane's parents and when she winked at the secretary on her way out of the office.

"It feels so good, to get one over on them." She said.

# CHAPTER 10

For four weeks in a row the women met up at the local baths and though Toi could only manage one width of the pool, they all thought she was making good progress, given her fear of water.

She also began to take the lessons that Graham had paid for, which she decided to take on Tuesday evenings directly after finishing work, and though she held on to the belief that she was not cut out for swimming, with encouragement from the others she pressed on.

After one of her Tuesday swimming lessons, Toi telephoned Sarah, wanting to talk about something that worried her. With some trepidation she told Sarah that Graham had planned a trip to Northampton over the Easter holiday, which was that weekend.

"He wants to see his mother." Said Toi.

Sarah paused for a second to let Toi continue, but Toi silently waited for Sarah to answer.

"Yes, I know, haven't you booked Thursday off for that?" Sarah asked breaking the silence.

"Yes." Replied Toi in a long and drawn out way.

"So what's wrong with that? Don't you want to go?"

"Haven't you heard? There's been a bad weather and flood warning for this week and weekend. The forecast is for high winds and lots of rain and we're meant to be going on

Thursday morning."

Sarah now understood, they were going to Northampton on the barge.

"Yes, I did hear something on the news, didn't they say that you shouldn't travel unless really necessary and wasn't that up north somewhere?"

"They said in the Northampton and Peterborough area."

"OK, but he knows that the weathers going to be bad, doesn't he?"

"Yes, we talked about it earlier tonight when I got home from swimming. I asked him if we could take the train."

"Oh yes, how did your swimming lesson go?" Asked Sarah, changing the subject.

"It was OK." Toi replied, frustration now heard in her voice and then quickly going into the reason why she'd called.

"Sarah, I'm scared, I don't want to go. I just think something's going to happen."

Taking Toi more seriously, Sarah asked.

"What did he say when you asked about the train?"

"He said everything would be OK."

"Everything would be OK? Well that's good, isn't it?" Asked Sarah now trying to reassure Toi.

"Does he seem confident?" She continued.

"Yes, he said all that happens is, the rivers and canals just rise, but we should be fine: And that he's travelled many times when there's been flood warnings. He even joked about me being a strong swimmer now and that I should be able to swim to the bank if anything happens; but that just frightened me."

"You see, he knows you're not a strong swimmer; and if he's showing that amount of confidence, then you should have nothing to worry about. Remember what I told you about visualisation." Sarah continued. "Just visualise yourself sitting calmly inside Graham's mother's house, talking to his family, or just imagine yourself at work on Tuesday, telling us what a good trip you've had."

"I can't, I'm too scared to imagine anything good, I just keep thinking of my sister drowning and then imagining it's me in the water."

"Don't say that!" Sarah snapped. "You've got to stay positive and everything will be alright."

"Yes, I know." Toi replied unconvincingly.

Realising that she may have been a bit harsh, Sarah said with a chuckle

"You'll be fine, I'll visualise for you. You'll be at work on Tuesday telling us what a good time you've had and that you're no longer afraid of water."

Toi laughed, "You're such a good friend."

"Look," said Sarah, "if you really don't want to go, you could stay at my house over the weekend."

Toi thought for a second.

"I'll see. I'll ask him and let you know tomorrow, but I think he'll be grumpy if I don't go."

"Look, you've got to do what's best for you, so if you don't want to go, there's always room for you here."

"Thanks."

The women talked for twenty minutes about things in general, work, swimming and men. During which time Sarah realised how good Toi's use of English had become.

After the call, Sarah thought about work and how the women now instead of ridiculing Toi for her bad use of English, were helping by correcting her and were also speaking much more slowly, allowing her to take more in.

She thought that things in general at the kitchen were the best that it had ever been, as there seemed to be more laughter and a lighter and more positive atmosphere. She was beginning to like working there; indeed, she was beginning to enjoy being a dinner lady.

* * *

At work the following day, Toi again voiced her concerns and as most of the women had seen the weather reports on the morning news, they were also concerned, but they all gave her reassurances that things would be fine. During the morning, Sarah remembered that she'd offered Toi a room for the weekend.

"So, what did Graham say?" She asked.

"About what?" Toi replied.

And by that reaction, Sarah figured that she hadn't spoken to Graham.

"You didn't ask if you could stay over at my house did you?"

Like a naughty schoolgirl, Toi looked down at the floor, giving no answer.

"Toi, it's OK, just be safe and enjoy the Easter Break." Said Sarah with a reassuring smile.

\* \* \*

Later, in the changing room, from a carrier bag Toi produced an unusual looking parcel, wrapped in brown paper and tied with blue ribbon.

On Easter Monday, it was Karen's Birthday; a fact that she'd only mentioned once in Toi's presence, so was therefore surprised that Toi had remembered.

"This is for you," said Toi handing Karen the parcel.

"What is it?"

"It's for your birthday."

Jane and Sarah, also in the room took note; they had no intention of buying a present and were put to shame as Karen took the parcel and began to blush.

"You didn't have to."

Toi smiled.

"Don't open it until Monday." She said.

That afternoon, the women said their goodbyes; Sarah hugging Toi, telling her that all would be fine and to enjoy the bank holiday even though the weather forecast predicted rain for the entire weekend.

* * *

At home later, Sarah watched the evening news reports, as they again predicted floods and gave bad weather warnings for various parts of the country, which included Northampton and Peterborough. They predicted the worst weather to hit the British Isles in years and advised members of the public to stay at home.

A special weather programme followed the news report, that gave a breakdown of how bad weather formed, and went into high and low pressure conditions, isobars, and things that were lost on her; but it only served to worry her.

Thinking that she should have paid more attention to the mornings news reports, she now felt annoyed with herself. If she'd known how bad it was really going to be, she would have insisted that Toi stayed at her house.

* * *

The reports were not wrong and the weather was fierce during the night, which, seemed to bring some calm the following morning.

The day started bright and the streets were unusually

clean, as the dark grey city grime that usually clung to the urban roads and buildings had succumbed to the wind and rain that had fallen. The brightness of the red and terracotta coloured house fronts on Sarah's road, glistened in the sunlight, as tufts of moss dislodged from the gutters blew about the pavement in the light breeze.

Sarah watched as the morning news flicked between various parts of the country, showing the sad faces of people leaving their sodden homes and possessions behind after being rescued by the emergency services.

She listened when the report focused on the devastation caused when a river: The river Nene in Northampton burst its banks in the early hours, but not being quite sure of where Toi had travelled to and being pretty sure that the barge couldn't have possibly reached Northampton in one day, believed that Toi and Graham were sure to be fine.

At work, the women broke for the Easter break; looking forward to spending time with their families.

## CHAPTER 11

Sarah spent the following day at her parent's house; her father, a builder who couldn't work owing to the weather, asked that she bring the children round.

She was surprised at the Sunday lunchtime news, as it reported that the body of a third victim of the floods had been found. She had no idea that people had lost their lives, so turned the volume up on the TV and asked the children to quieten down while she listened.

"Two people were killed and two more, including a 14-year-old boy, are feared drowned as torrential rain and flooding swept Britain. The body of a middle-aged man was recovered from a flooded caravan park on the banks of the Avon near Evesham, Worcestershire. The body of a woman was also found in a house in Northampton."

"Police in Warwickshire also fear the worst after a van was swept from a flooded road into a ditch near Leamington Spa."

"Rescue teams with dogs are searching for a 14-year-old boy who was a passenger in the van, but it is feared he has drowned."

"And hopes are fading for a 33-year-old woman believed to have fallen from a narrow-boat on a flooded river in Northampton."

On hearing this, Sarah snapped at her children whose

volume had begun to rise once more.

"Come on you two, I'm trying to listen to this!" She snapped.

The report continued.

"**The woman, who lived on the boat moored on the River Nene with her 57-year-old husband, was reported on Friday night.**"

"**About 60 officers and a helicopter have been searching for her without success as the river was put on a red flood alert**".

"**Police and fire fighters have been carrying out several rescue operations in the Midlands, Buckinghamshire and Oxfordshire as the number of people stranded or evacuated from their homes continues to rise...**"

As the news droned on in the background, Sarah began to ask herself about that 33 year old woman. *But, Toi's in her twenties isn't she?* She thought, now unsure. Toi had never divulged her age to anyone. But, the 57-year-old man, was about the right age for Graham.

She now worried and considered telephoning but stopped herself, instead going with the belief that she should be more positive, should have more faith and that Toi would be fine. *Besides, Graham knew what he was doing, didn't he?*

The report was repeated later on that evening, which prompted her into trying to visualise a happy Toi arriving to work on Tuesday morning. However, she found it hard, her vision appearing clouded, no matter how hard she tried.

* * *

Happy to be back at work on Tuesday morning, Sarah arrived earlier than usual.

Shielding herself from the rain with her umbrella, she waited by the kitchen entrance for Toi to arrive, greeting the women one by one as they arrived for work, chatting a little to each of them as they came in.

"Happy Birthday," She said when Karen arrived, a little later than usual, "did you have a good weekend?"

"Yes, not bad, but did you see the weather up north? Those poor people."

"Yeah, pretty bad eh."

"Is Toi in yet?"

"No, not yet. I'm just waiting for her." Sarah replied now wearing a worried expression.

"I'm going in to get changed, don't be late." Said Karen, glancing at her watch, then back at Sarah, before disappearing into the kitchen.

At 8:55am, Toi had still not arrived, so Sarah decided that she would get changed; passing the other women in the corridor that led to the kitchen before entering the changing room. She found Jenny sitting on the bench that faced the door, her eyes red as if she'd been crying.

"You OK?" Asked Sarah.

"Yes." Jenny sniffed.

Sarah opened her locker, reached inside and produced a small packet of tissues.

"Here you go." She said, trying to catch Jenny's attention, who stared at the floor, fully engrossed and focused on her own issues.

Sarah threw the packet to her.

"Keep them."

"Thanks." Jenny replied, before pulling open the packet, taking out a tissue and blowing long and hard into it.

"You sure you're OK?"

"Yes, I'll be fine," replied Jenny, blowing her nose once more. "I'll see you in there," she continued, before getting up to leave the room. As she reached the door she asked.

"Hasn't Toi arrived?"

"No."

"Hmm." Jenny groaned, before rushing off through the doorway.

\* \* \*

Toi didn't turn in for work that morning and there was no telephone call to say that she wouldn't be in, prompting speculation from the women as to why she'd not turned up.

As lunchtime approached, Sarah now torn between

phoning her or not, wanted to remain positive in the belief that Toi would be fine, but on the other hand, was eager to ensure that her friend was OK.

In the end, she decided that she would call, which was the general consensus and as she pulled out her mobile phone the kitchen came to a standstill as the other women waited to find out what had become of their friend.

Sarah trembled as she dialled the number, now fearing the possible outcome of the call. Only the sound of the extractor fans could be heard as the kitchen fell silent, the women waiting in anticipation.

Sarah held the phone to her ear.

"Hello, oh sorry."

She'd dialled the wrong number and hung up after hearing the person she'd just dialled wasn't Toi. She began to dial again, hands still trembling; Karen grabbed hold of the hand with which Sarah used to press the buttons.

"Calm down."

Sarah looked at her for a second, before nodding and then tapping in the numbers much slower than she'd done before. She put the phone to her ear and hung up after 20 seconds.

"It just rang off." She said, now looking worried.

"Try again." Said Jenny.

"You sure you've got the right number, or put it in right?" Karen asked.

"Yes, Yes" Sarah replied, as she quickly redialled the number, then putting the telephone to her ear once more.

"Same thing," she said after about 20 seconds.

"OK, back to work." Karen ordered. "We'll deal with this later, but right now we've got work to do."

The women hurried back to work and the bustle of the kitchen began once more; the difference this time being that the women worked relatively silently and only communicated about work matters. With little thought to what they were doing, they worked largely on autopilot, while the majority of their thoughts were of Toi.

In the changing room later on, Karen suggested that Sarah and herself go down to the canal after work to see why Toi had not come in, which Sarah agreed to do.

* * *

It was 5pm when the two women reached the canal where The Duck was usually moored.

It had just stopped raining and there was a quiet lull in the squalid weather that had dogged the day so far.

They were surprised, as The Duck wasn't moored in its usual place and quickly looked up and down the moorings to find that it wasn't there.

Sarah pulled out her mobile phone from her bag and called Toi's phone once more, again there was no answer.

"Now, I'm really worried." She said.

"So am I," said Karen, "but the weather's been so bad, perhaps they've just been delayed in getting back."

"Yeah, but, I just know that Toi was frightened; she just didn't want to go."

"Yeah, I know," said Karen, putting her umbrella up as it began to drizzle. "Look, if she doesn't come in tomorrow, we'll try again tomorrow evening. If they're not back we'll call the police or something."

"OK," said Sarah while looking up at the dark clouds, now wishing that she'd taken her umbrella from the car.

The women made their way along the bank, back to the car and headed for home.

\* \* \*

Once more, that evening the news report gave footage of the devastation caused by the bad weather.

**"The body of a 14-year-old boy has been found in Warwickshire, bringing the death toll up to three in the floods that have caused havoc across large areas of the UK"**

**"Searches are continuing for a 33-year-old woman who is feared drowned."**

**"The boy was washed out of a milkman's delivery van when it was swept off the road at Eathorpe, near Leamington Spa in Warwickshire, on Friday."**

**"The boy was earning extra pocket money during his school holiday."**

"The driver managed to clamber to safety and was treated for hypothermia."

"But paramedics could not reach the submerged van, and police launched a search for the Coventry teenager on Friday."

"The search, which was joined by the Army and sniffer dogs, was called off at nightfall and resumed at dawn on Saturday."

"On Friday, an elderly woman was found dead inside a flooded house in Northampton. She is believed to have drowned as floodwaters overwhelmed her as she slept."

"The body of a middle-aged man was also recovered from a caravan site that flooded near Evesham in Worcestershire."

"But hopes are fading for the 33-year-old woman believed to have fallen from a narrow boat into a flooded river in Northampton. The woman, who lived on the boat moored on the river Nene with her husband, was reported missing on Thursday night."

"Thousands of people were evacuated from their homes after the equivalent of one month's rain fell in 24 hours."

"There are still 30 rivers on red flood warnings, while 40 more have amber warnings, mainly across central and eastern England...."

Again Sarah worried, so decided to call Karen to let her know what she'd heard. However, Karen having seen the news appeared calm.

"Look, it can't be them; the news said that the woman went missing on Thursday. Didn't they go on Thursday?" She asked.

"Yes," Sarah replied. "But they said Friday night on yesterday's news."

"There's no way they'd get up there in one day, even two days for that matter. I just think that they couldn't get back. Remember what you are always saying to us," she said, referring to the other women in the kitchen.

"Be positive!"

## CHAPTER 12

For a second day Toi didn't turn up for work and the women spent the morning worrying, prompting Sarah into driving down to the canal during her break time. She was very surprised to see that The Duck was back, moored in its usual place. *So why was Toi not in then?*

She toyed with the idea of knocking, but thought that she may in some way be intruding, and perhaps she would return later after work. Nevertheless, she was glad to see that The Duck had returned, as were the other women when they heard the news.

Like her they speculated as to why Toi had not turned up for work and after a short discussion agreed that after work, Sarah and Karen should go to see Toi, to find out what was going on.

\* \* \*

The two women arrived down on the canal at 6:30pm, and as they walked towards The Duck Karen asked.

"Why didn't you knock earlier?"

"Oh, I didn't want to intrude." Sarah replied, before pausing for thought.

"If the truth be known, I was frightened." She said, "I told you the other day that fear makes you do funny things, like stopping you doing the things you know you should do. I was frightened about what I may have found, if I'd knocked. You know, if she had bad news. So I told myself that I may be intruding if I knock."

"So, even you, the person that keeps on telling us to be positive, and that we have nothing to fear, is human and is just like us after all."

Sarah chuckled, "Human. Yes, I'm still learning this stuff, so there's going to be times when I feel fear and fail to act. Hopefully that won't be too often."

When they arrived at The Duck, Sarah noticed that it looked different; much of the junk that was on deck the last time she saw it had gone and it looked cleaner, as if it had been given a good scrub. *The weather has certainly made a difference.*

The women stood in front of the barge.

"Frightened?" Karen asked.

"Yes." Sarah replied her voice a bit trembley. "But let's do this."

Tentatively they climbed aboard and knocked on the hatch, and a few moments later Graham appeared, his face wearing a half smile, almost inviting, which made the women feel a bit better.

"We're here to see Toi." Said Karen.

"You'd better come in." He replied.

Now with some suspicion, the women went down through the hatch and inside, Graham leading them into the living room and then turning to face them. Standing in the middle of the room looking at the pair, mouth ajar; he struggled to find the right words. The women scanned the room; '*no Toi*', then turned back to Graham, the sight of his obvious nervousness making their anxiety build once more.

"What's going on? Where's Toi?" Karen asked.

With a grim expression on his face, "Toi is missing," He replied.

"What? What do you mean missing?" Asked Sarah.

"Well, I warned her, I told her that we shouldn't go."

"What are you talking about?" Sarah replied angrily.

"Well, I wanted to go to Northampton to see my mother, but because there was a flood warning, I changed my mind and decided to take the train. But, she wanted to go up on the barge. She begged me to take the barge."

"Graham, what are you talking about?" Asked Sarah frowning.

"My trip, our trip, to see my mother." He replied. "She loved the water; and was such a good swimmer."

A feeling of dread now rose within the women, as Graham now obviously nervous, appeared apprehensive and talked about Toi in the past tense, and was talking a load of nonsense.

Sarah sat down, as if in a state of shock.

"What are you saying? Asked Karen.

"She's missing."

"What do you mean, how is she missing?" Karen Replied.

He carried on with his story and conveyed that because there was so much rain, and the river levels were so high, that they got stuck under a bridge near Northampton.

"We were trying to move the barge off the walls of a bridge, one minute she was there, the next she'd gone, I looked everywhere, but she wasn't on board. She must have fallen in, I couldn't find her anywhere. She's missing, haven't you seen the news reports?" He asked.

The speechless Sarah stood up joining Karen as a strange silence filled the room, them both not knowing what to say, still trying to take in what Graham talked about.

Sarah deep in thought and shaking her head, stared down at his coffee table; her attention then broken by Karen.

"Yes we have. You obviously mean about the 33 year old woman?"

He nodded.

"But you don't seem very worried." Said Karen noting his calm.

Graham didn't respond.

Surely, she was wearing a life jacket?" She asked.

Graham's eyes motioned to the entrance of the barge where the life jackets were stored. Karen suspiciously followed his eye movement, wondering what he was looking at.

"She didn't need one, she was a strong swimmer." He said.

As Sarah regained her focus, she recognised that she was staring at a self-help book lying on his coffee table. The moment was surreal, as the book was the one that first inspired her: The one that made her first think about taking control of her life.

It now reminded her that some control was needed here, as parts of Graham's story didn't make sense. *Toi hated the water and the barge; she definitely wasn't a good swimmer. What's he up to?* She thought.

"Hang on a minute," She said, "Toi hated the water; you know that?"

Graham was silent and wearing a almost nervous smile.

"And she wasn't a good swimmer either, she was taking lessons and you know that too; and she told me that you paid for some of her lessons for her." She continued.

"We were giving her lessons." Said Karen.

Sarah could no longer contain her thoughts and after a short pause.

"Graham what are you up to? What have you done?" She demanded.

"I've told you what happened."

"I don't believe you," she said angrily. "She hated the water and this barge!"

Now looking flustered and with his eyes fixed on Sarah, he responded.

"What are you saying? Eh? What are you accusing me of? I told you what happened, and it wasn't my fault."

He didn't notice that Karen had picked up his book from the coffee table and was now flicking through its pages.

"She told me that she was a strong swimmer now. How was I to know that she wasn't?" He growled, hoping to intimidate the women.

"What, after four weeks and eight lessons or something like that?" Sarah asked. "And if you knew the weather was going to be as bad as it has been you shouldn't have gone. And she should have been wearing a life jacket."

Now seeing that he'd not intimidated the women, he asked them to leave.

"Look, I don't have to take this, I've invited you into my home and this is how you treat me: Look you'd better go." He said, now noticing that Karen had started looking through his book.

"PUT THAT DOWN! That's my book." He shouted, startling the women.

As he quickly rushed towards Karen she dropped the book back onto the coffee table and took up a defensive stance, head held high and in an almost boxing pose.

He grabbed the book from the table.

"It's mine," he said once more, holding it close to his chest. "Look you'd better go." He repeated, breathing heavily.

With her heart still racing, Karen slowly relaxed her pose and gave Sarah a puzzled look before turning towards the door.

"I don't know what you've done, but you haven't heard the last of this." Said Karen.

Now angry with herself, for getting angry with Graham, Sarah tried to calm things down.

"Look, I'm sorry, I'm not accusing you, but you must understand that we're worried about her."

"Well that's it, I can't tell you anymore." He said, now wanting to end the conversation and edging towards the hallway that led to the hatch, his body language giving an unmistakable indication that he wanted them to leave.

"I'm her husband how do you think I feel?"

"OK," said Sarah, "I'm sorry, but I just need to know what, if any, are the chances of finding her alive."

Graham shrugged his shoulders, as if he didn't really care.

"I don't know." He replied.

"Don't you care?" Asked Karen.

"Look, you'd better go!" He repeated.

The women glanced at each other and Karen nodded, before they headed down the hallway towards the hatch.

"I hope they find her." Said Sarah.

"Hmm, I'll get fifty thousand if they don't." He mumbled, now wishing that he'd never opened his mouth.

"What?" Said Sarah.

"Nothing."

Sarah glared at him, puzzled. *Fifty thousand, Fifty thousand* she thought and then remembering the letter that she'd posted to the insurance company a few weeks earlier, she turned to Graham, now angry once more and with nothing but foul language in her mind. Opening her mouth to speak, she was interrupted by Karen who sensed her anger.

"Come on, let's go." She said.

Sarah looked a Karen but ignored her words.

"Come on you can't really mean that." Said Sarah, now turning to face him.

Not answering, he looked a bit embarrassed, knowing that he'd said the wrong thing while saying it, but just couldn't stop himself.

"Just make sure you tell us if you hear anything." Sarah growled through clenched teeth.

He watched as the women climbed out onto the deck and then onto solid ground, before in defiance shouting over to them.

"If you know someone who wants some jewellery or some clothes, I've got some for sale.

The women looked back at him.

"Bastard!" Karen shouted.

They walked slowly along the path back towards the car.

"He's done something to her. I know it."

"I know, but what can we do?" Karen replied.

* * *

There was silence in the car on the way home as both women deep in thought played what had just happened over and over in their minds.

It began to rain once more, the droning sound of the droplets against the car having a calming effect on them both.

"We're here." Said Karen breaking the silence.

They had reached Sarah's house.

Sarah still feeling annoyed got out and said goodbye. Karen told her not to worry; Sarah nodded and sighed heavily as she walked towards her door and waved as Karen drove away.

Thinking the worst, Sarah spent the evening doing exactly the opposite of what Karen had asked her to do. She couldn't shake the feeling of being somehow responsible for what had happened.

*Toi is probably dead,* she thought, *drowned and after all the reassurances I gave her.*

That evening she snapped at Carl over something quite trivial, then realised that the situation had affected her more than she'd thought, so decided to go to bed. Though retiring early, she still didn't sleep well and was restless as visions of Toi laying somewhere out there, alone, cold, in the wind and rain, plagued her mind. Before long an hour went by, then two and soon it was 5am; only an hour and a half before she had to be up for work. Quite tired now, she closed her eyes and drifted away.

# CHAPTER 13

The mood the following day was sombre after Karen held a meeting, telling the other women of the news. When they heard what Graham had said about Toi's swimming and the part of his story where he reported that she pestered him to go on the trip, made things worse, as they all knew how she felt about water. There was also the question about the life insurance that he'd just taken out, which in her anger, Sarah had told everyone. The sombre feeling quickly turned to anger, as things just seem to point to Graham having done something underhand.

"We've got to do something." Said Sarah.

The group was silent, waiting, as if Sarah had not finished her sentence, waiting for her to continue, so she duly obliged.

"I'm going to the police." She said

"But there's nothing to report," Said Karen, "Toi is missing and could be anywhere. She could have hit her head and lost her memory."

"But," said Sarah, about to start a sentence.

"We don't know what he's done" Karen interrupted. "He may be telling the truth for all we know."

"After what I've heard, I think we should go to the police." Jane interrupted.

There was unity amongst the other women, as Sarah looked on at Karen in defiance, her expression seem to be saying, 'see, I told you'.

"Look, if we've not heard anything by Monday." Karen replied,

"Monday!" Jane interrupted once more.

"Yes Monday. Look, there's nothing to report yet and they may find her. If nothing happens by then, we'll get the police involved."

Again and for a second time there was silence as the group waited for Sarah to reply.

"OK, Monday," she said reluctantly agreeing, but finally seeing Karen's argument. "If we haven't heard anything by then, I'm going to the police."

"Alright." Karen replied.

She then reminded the women that they were at work

"We've got a thousand boys to feed; c'mon it's time to get some work done."

* * *

As the week passed so did their hopes, that Toi might be found alive. By Wednesday the mood in the kitchen had become highly charged and before long the old bickering returned, the women eventually taking their frustrations out on each other.

It was clear, but not surprising that they had let the situation have a negative effect on them, the situation coming to a head when Sarah broke up an argument between Jane and

Jenny over something quite trivial.

Karen decided to hold a short meeting at mid morning break time; wanting Sarah to speak to the group, hoping that she would have a calming effect on them. And as it happens, the meeting turned in to a mini counselling session, where Sarah got the women to try to talk about how they felt about what had happened, as with everything out in the open, they would have a chance to deal with all the issues.

It turned out that there was a lot of pent up anger towards Graham, which was spilling out into the workplace. Sarah put her feelings to one side and spoke about trying to be positive and striving to generate good thoughts.

"Look, Karen was right, we don't know what's happened to Toi, for all we know, she's sat at home right now having a hot cup of tea."

"What! Are you talking about? We all know that he's done away with her." Jane snapped.

"We don't know what's happened to her, all we know is that she is missing." Sarah replied calmly.

"Yes and I'm sure none of you want to put the mockers on her getting back to us safely." Said Karen.

"We want her back as much as anyone." Debbie replied.

"We know and this is why we want you to be positive with your thoughts." Said Sarah.

Debbie responded after a long sigh.

"Come on be serious, I don't know about anyone else, but that isn't what I want to hear right now."

For a moment, the room fell silent as the women sensed aggression in Debbie's tone.

"Yeah!. Why are we having this meeting anyway? Look, Toi is probably dead." Said Jenny.

She then paused taking a breath, waiting for reaction from the others, which was not going to come, as knowing Jenny, they were all shocked that she'd even opened her mouth; and when no reaction came back, she continued.

"Erm, yeah, she is probably dead and all you want to talk about is some positive mumbo jumbo. She's not at home having a cup of tea. Come on just be real. This is the real world!" She raved.

There was a pause while everyone took in what was just said, and then Sarah in a controlled and calm tone responded,

"Jenny, you and Jane were arguing about an apron earlier, why is that?"

Jenny looked on awkwardly and then down towards the floor, not giving an answer. Sarah then turned to Jane.

"Well Jane?" She asked.

Jane also sat silently.

"Can't you see that you are blaming Graham and the now pent up anger you have for him is making you bitter?"

There was no reaction from the women as they sat in

silence.

"You all know what a bitter person is." Sarah continued

They all nodded.

"Well your bitterness towards Graham is affecting your emotions; the anger you have for him is spilling out here. Normally there is no way you two would be fighting over an apron?"

Jenny and Jane nodded in agreement.

One by one, the penny was dropping as the women began to understand. Karen smiled as she saw that Sarah was finally getting through to them.

"I say be positive: And yes, sometimes it's hard, but if you're not positive then you'll find it really hard to be happy. And that's what we all want isn't it? To be happy. I believe that Toi is alright and will believe that until I hear otherwise. It means that I'm not going to feel anger towards Graham, and that means that I'm more likely to be happy and not start fights at work or at home."

"But we're not you." Said Debbie. "You've been doing this for ages and I don't know about anyone else, but I find it hard not to feel this way, you know, angry with that bastard. How can I stop him making me feel like this?"

"Look, he's not making you feel the way you feel. You are. You look after your feelings don't you?" Sarah replied.

"What do you mean?" Debbie asked, pulling a face,

shrugging her shoulders and then looking around the room as if to summon support from the others.

"You look after your own feelings." Sarah repeated. "If you want to cry, you cry, if you want to laugh, you laugh. No one makes you do those things, only you can."

The women looked puzzled.

"Let me put it like this, often we say, I'll be happy if I win a million pounds on the lottery; does this mean that we'll never be happy unless we win a million pounds?"

Seeing that the women still didn't understand Sarah continued.

"Look, what I'm saying is that you don't have to wait for a million pounds to be happy. I mean. most of the time we're happy, even without interacting with other people, without that million pounds, without having a new car, a new dress and so on. Can't you see that we make our own happiness, so look after our own feelings?"

After a momentary silence

"Does that make sense?" Sarah asked.

After a moment pondering Sarah's words.

"Oh yeah, I'm with you now," said Debbie, "I've never thought of it like that."

Sarah smiled and said,

"OK, now for Graham, there is only one way you're going to get rid of the feeling of anger you have towards him and that is to tell yourself that you like him, or even love him."

The expression that appeared on Debbie's face made everyone laugh.

"Well you don't have to love him," Sarah continued, "but tell yourself that he's blameless; you like him; that he's harmless and poses no threat and things will change, you know, you'll be less likely to feel anger towards him or anyone else."

Debbie slowly nodded, then with a smirk said.

"Love him and I'll be happy? I don't think so."

All the women burst into laughter, apart from Jane who was still a bit puzzled.

"I don't get it; tell me that happy thing again."

Karen rolled her eyes as the women laughed once more.

"OK, OK, you lot," said Karen. "So no more arguing, c'mon back to work. Toi will be fine."

Sensing the lift in the mood as they left the changing room, Sarah reached down, tapped Jenny's hand and raised her eyebrows signalling she wanted a private chat. The two women, waited in the corridor for the last of the other staff to disappear behind the kitchen door, before Sarah started.

"That was good."

Silent, Jenny looked worried, not really understanding what Sarah was referring to.

"You know, what you said in there, you really spoke your

mind."

"Oh, yes." Jenny replied, before raising her eyebrows and shrugging her shoulders, which gave Sarah a cue to say why they were really standing in the corridor.

"Look, the reason I want to speak to you alone is because I've notice that you've seemed to be a bit unhappy or." Sarah paused for a moment, "well a bit withdrawn just recently. Is everything all right? I mean at home."

Jenny nodded nervously, biting her bottom lip. Sarah seeing Jenny's nervousness and not wanting to start her off crying ended the conversation.

"All I wanted to say is that, if you ever need to talk, about anything, I'm here."

Jenny nodded once more before moving off towards the kitchen with Sarah following behind.

"You don't have to speak to me, you could get counselling." Said Sarah, Jenny's back now facing her.

"I'm OK." Jenny replied, as she hurriedly burst through into the kitchen.

\* \* \*

Though Toi's fate still played on the women's mind, the mood in the kitchen improved; it was almost back, to what it was before Toi's disappearance. Karen was impressed, and now understood how it was possible to manage her feelings. Sarah also felt better within herself; she'd given herself the therapy that she'd needed, and stopped blaming Graham for Toi's disappearance, at least for the time being.

* * *

The week seemed to last a lifetime, but the weekend did come and there was still no news.

On the Friday as the women said their goodbyes there was positive talk of Toi's return on the following Monday, though deep down they believed that their friend would not be found alive.

# CHAPTER 14

The following day, Sarah watched the television as the afternoon news reported that, all of the people that had gone missing during the flood in the east of the country were now found. The reporter braving the conditions and being buffeted by the wind said that:

"The Eastern parts of the country are now recovering from what is now being described by locals as the Great Flood."

"Several inches of rain fell over the bank holiday weekend, making several rivers burst their banks, flooding parts of Northamptonshire, Bedfordshire, Warwickshire and Lincolnshire and many areas still remain underwater; bringing misery to homes and businesses.

"But many locals count themselves lucky, as the body of a woman, who still hasn't been named, was found in the river Nene. The body is believed to be that of a 33 year old woman who was reported missing just over a week ago."

"The woman, a strong swimmer, who was on holiday, was said to have been swept overboard and was pulled under by strong currents and is believed to have drowned.

Three other people lost their lives; however, others who were reported missing have now been accounted for."

"A spokesman for the Police said that, the loss of four lives is tragic and is four lives too many; and could have

**been avoided."**

**"Officials maintain that flood and bad weather warnings were not taken seriously enough, which has led to several hundred people being hospitalised."**

**"It is believed that the cost of the clean up process will run into millions and some people are now blaming the government....."**

Sarah stared at the television, her numbness turning to fear as she began to question herself. Was the body found that of her friend? Things became hazy as her breath quickened and fear took hold. Now panicking she wasn't thinking straight. *Toi was not a strong swimmer, so this can't be her.* Not knowing what to do, doubt began to take hold. *Can this be Toi?* She asked herself once more before whispering.

"Be strong, be positive."

Though worried she reminded herself that fear shouldn't stop her from doing what she knew she must do and decided to take some action.

Seeing that it had stopped raining, she began to get a good feeling as she continuously told herself that Toi would be fine.

The sun broke through the grey clouds, and the sky brightened up as she left the house, driving down to the canal, and still unwilling to accept that her friend had gone.

*Toi must be back now* she thought as she hurried along the wet canal path, breathing in the earthy yet sweet smell of the wet blossom, while the pinks and blues magnified by droplets that still clung to the early spring flowers shimmered in the afternoon sunlight; *spring's finally arrived.*

Approaching The Duck, she found Graham untying the barge from its moorings and as she reached him he looked up, glancing at her before carrying on untying the barge.

"They've found her." He said, still not looking up.

"How is she?" Said Sarah excitedly and still refusing to see the obvious.

There was a long pause, before the look on Grahams face began to tell the full story; and in those moments a feeling of dread washed over her, butterflies in the pit of her stomach, a sickly feeling, and a momentary weakness of her knees; she knew what was to come next.

"No, No," She groaned.

Graham now made no eye contact and just stared down at the deck.

"What happened?" Said Sarah, already knowing what the answer would be.

"She drowned. They phoned me today, I've got to go to identify the body."

She sighed, as though she somehow expected the worst, his words were like a punch to her stomach.

"The current was too strong," He continued. "It pulled her down and she drowned."

Sarah, now silent, shocked and numb shook her head.

"She was a good swimmer, but not strong enough." He continued.

"What are you talking about?" Sarah snapped, the feeling of dread now turning to anger,

"You know that she couldn't swim, you know that she didn't want to go; why are you lying?"

Graham continued looking at the deck trying to avoid Sarah's gaze.

"Graham, what's going on?" She asked, putting him on the spot. "WHAT IS GOING ON?"

"Nothing's going on! I told you what happened!" he replied angrily.

She sighed and shook her head once more.

"Why wasn't she wearing a life jacket? Why?" She said before waiting for an answer that did not come.

"What happens now?" She said impatiently. "What are you going to do now?"

He thought for a second and then came out with something that took her by surprise.

"I'm going to be rich and I'm going to do the barge up."

Sarah looked at him puzzled for a split second and then a disbelieving expression appeared, eyes wide and mouth open as she'd expected him to talk about the funeral.

"You know; the money from the insurance." His words

tailing off slowly as he finished the sentence.

Like a few days earlier, he knew he'd said the wrong thing as the words left his mouth and now embarrassed by his blunder he turned and carried on untying The Duck from its moorings.

"Is that all you care about?"

Ignoring the question, he continued making ready to go as she stood there silently, watching him, wondering what she could do. *He can't be allowed to get away with this,* she thought, as he quickly made his way to the wheel room and turned the engine over.

As it coughed and spluttered in to life, spewing out puffs of soot into the afternoon sunlight, she still was lost for words, the shock of the news still sinking in.

The barge slowly moved off from its mooring, and as he made his four mile an hour getaway he couldn't resist showing his defiance, shouting to her.

"Anyway, there's plenty more in Thailand, I'll just go and get another one." His comment breaking Sarah's train of thought.

"What?" She replied angrily.

She stood there for a second, shocked and thinking how she could get him. Appalled by his words, she was now lost in rage, forgetting her positive views on life and returning to the human realm, which most of us inhabit:

And after seeing Graham's defiance, she scanned the canal path to see if there was anything laying around; something that she could throw at him, but found nothing.

Completely deflated and tears beginning to well up, she turned to go, but he had not finished, it was time to get his own back for the hard time Karen had given him weeks earlier.

"What do you care anyway?" He shouted.

Ignoring his question, Sarah turned to him.

"You bastard; she wasn't a strong swimmer, I know that she wasn't." She shouted back.

"She was." he replied, and as if to rub it in, he mimicked Sarah's last sentence. "I know she was."

"Well we'll see what the police say."

Head tilted, he smiled, gestured and shrugged his shoulders as the barge moved out into the middle of the canal and glided off, gently caressing the waters of the Grand Union.

As she walked back to her car, she felt sick; in her mind he had murdered her friend and concocted a lie. *He can't be allowed to get away with this.*

By the time she got home, she had to run to the front door to avoid being soaked, as it had begun to rain once more. Going straight to her bedroom, she burst into tears. *Why was this happening? Why must the good die and people like Graham survive?* She thought. There was a knock on her door and she quickly dried her eyes, knowing that it would be one of the children.

"Come in."

The door slowly opened, it was Louise.

"Mum, are you OK?"

Sarah stretched out her arms and they hugged.

"I am now." She replied.

# CHAPTER 15

Unsure of what to do next and not wanting to rush into anything, Sarah decided that she would get the children sorted first, before speaking to Karen.

After dinner she sat by the window watching the rain, trying to replay what had happened down by the canal. *Did he really kill her? Or is he just an obnoxious, chauvinistic so and so,* she thought, now worrying about reporting him to the police. *Accusing someone of murder is pretty serious: And what if I'm wrong, what if Toi just fell in like he said, I'll look such an idiot.*

With the weight of the decision she on her mind, she found it hard to focus, as images of Toi swirled around in her head, continuously breaking her train of thought.

Feeling a bit flustered and a headache coming on, she took a couple of paracetamol and went to her bedroom to lie down. As she laid there, eyes closed, beginning to relax, she focused on her breathing, *'slow, deep and steady,'* and soon drifted off.

* * *

In her mind's eye she appeared back on the canal path, but this time as a spectator; watching as the conversation with Graham unfolded; the arrogant smile as he sailed off and his words *"There's plenty more in Thailand, I'll just go and get another."*

Again, she felt the fear, anger then anguish as the entire conversation replayed itself; it all felt so real.

Minutes later, she awoke taking a sharp intake of breath, as if startled. Tears rolled down her cheeks, which were quickly dried as she regained full consciousness, now relaxed and headache gone. Feeling a little embarrassed, she smiled when recalling how angry she had been and how she'd looked around the canal path for something to throw at him for being so arrogant.

She knew that she had to somehow detach herself from the situation to become more focused. *If he is responsible for Toi's death then he must be held to account.*

Knowing what had to be done, she picked up the phone, paused for a second and then took a deep breath before dialling; a few seconds later.

"Karen, I've got some bad news."

Having seen the news report, Karen had a feeling of what was to come, but was silent as Sarah began.

"Toi is dead, she drowned and I think Graham had something to do with it."

She paused before saying.

"I think we should go to the police and report him. I mean," she said now rushing to get her words out. "I think anyone that knows anything should report it to the police. I think he killed her. I really think he may have killed Toi."

"OK, OK, but slow down. I saw the news report as well. I mean, how do you know that it was Toi? And are you OK?"

Karen replied, sensing something different about Sarah's voice.

"Yeah, I'm OK, but I'm not, if you know what I mean." She replied, before slowly recanting the conversation she'd had with Graham earlier.

Throughout, Karen noted that Sarah sounded a bit abrupt with a distinct lack of emotion and as Sarah finished she said.

"Bastard, I told her that they don't change, he killed her, the bloody sod's killed her. But, are you OK, well, you know what I mean. You sound a bit..."

Karen paused, giving Sarah a chance to respond.

"Yes, I'm trying to stay calm, positive and objective."

"Objective!" Karen replied angrily. "We both know that that bastard killed her and you're trying to stay objective?"

"No we don't. I mean don't know for sure. All we know is that her body's been found. We need to get all of our facts straight and then go to the police; perhaps they can prove that he killed her."

Now sounding frustrated. "How the hell can you be so calm at a time like this?" Asked Karen

"Karen, if I get angry about what's happened, I'll start to blame people, get angry and get upset; all negative things that I want to avoid. I've had my cry and think it's time to move on."

"You see! All you seem to want to talk about is that

positive stuff, all the time. And being positive didn't save Toi's life, did it?"

After a momentary silence and feeling the tension that she felt earlier beginning to return, Sarah said.

"Karen, being positive has helped you just recently, so why are you knocking it?"

After a momentary pause she continued.

"Look, I don't want to argue about being positive, but it's the way I'm choosing to live my life, so let's just move on. Toi's dead, let's get that bastard sorted out."

"No! Karen replied voice raised, then feeling the anger she had inside and remembering Sarah's words checked herself.

"No," she continued, this time her voice returning to normal. "Look, I can't move forward until I get this off my chest."

"Get what off your chest?"

"He had one of your books; I mean, when we went to see Graham last week, I saw, on his table, a book that I know that you've read. You know, one of your positive thinking books.

"So." Sarah replied. 'Where's she going with this.'.

"I mean, how can you read a book like that and then kill someone. And you can't tell me that killing someone is positive."

There was a pause as Sarah thought about how to answer, wanting to put this argument to bed as soon as possible, now realising that by saying that she didn't want an argument, just served to draw one.

"C'mon Karen, we haven't got time for this, our friend has just died. Let's just move on; let's just call the police."

"No," Karen replied, now feeling smug with herself and thinking, *let's see you talk you way out of this one*. The old rivalry was back.

"You're always banging on about being positive and I believed you, we all believed you and look, it didn't help Toi did it." She continued.

Sarah sighed and then in an attempt to placate Karen replied.

"Do you know, a person can be positive and commit acts of carnage, or what would usually be perceived morally wrong or negative? I'm not saying that he did, but Graham could have read that book. And yes I did see it: And he could have taken a lot from it, but it doesn't make the book bad."

"But," Karen tried to interrupt.

"Come on, let me finish."

After a short pause, Sarah continued.

"So hypothetically, let's say that he read the book, which told him to visualise what he wanted. In his case, his barge being fixed up. To take the necessary steps to get there, he would have to get the money, from the insurance policy. And to do that, he would have to"

She paused for a second, knowing that what she was about to say could prove to be inflammatory.

"Kill Toi." She mumbled.

Being more interested in the argument Karen just continued.

"But you haven't answered the question. How! Can killing someone be positive?"

"If you'll let me finish." Sarah repeated.

"I didn't say killing someone is positive, but as you've asked; if someone had killed Hitler during the war, would that have been positive? After all, millions of lives would have been saved. And if Hitler had been killed as a child, even more lives would have been saved, so what do you say now?

Karen now silent knew Sarah had a point.

"Hitler's goal was to create an Arian race and in his eyes he was taking positive steps to get there."

"What, by killing millions?"

"By whatever means." Sarah replied.

"What I'm saying is this, being positive is a state of mind. I mean planning and then committing murder is called premeditated murder. Premeditation is thinking, planning and even visualising an act: And then you take positive steps to complete the act."

Karen understood but still could not accept that murder could be positive.

"But murder?" She said.

"OK," Sarah replied, "say it's baking a cake then; If you bake a cake, you'll have a vision of the cake, I mean, what it should look and taste like, you'll plan making it, then follow the steps to get the end results, you know, buying the ingredients, the right baking tin and so on. And in the end if you have the cake you visualised. That would have been a positive process."

"Oh, now you're comparing murder with baking a cake." Said Karen sarcastically.

Sarah sighed once more; it seemed as though Karen just didn't want to get it, or did get it but just wanted to argue. Sarah now looked for another angle to allow her to put the argument to bed.

"Look," she said, "We successfully feed one thousand boys at the school every day and that is down to your planning or, premeditation if you like. You plan what you want, then achieve a positive outcome every day. Would I be right in saying that?" She asked.

"Yes," Karen replied, now wondering where Sarah planned to go with the argument.

"Say you wanted for some reason; to feed none of the boys, you would plan that too. And probably not make any food and again achieve a positive outcome, your goal, not to feed anyone. Do you see what I mean now?" Sarah asked, now exhausted.

Karen had to admit to herself that Sarah was right, and no longer argued; Sarah continued, just to ram the argument home.

"Look, the saying one man's freedom fighter and all that. Both sides would see the positives in killing each other in order to achieve their goals."

Karen was now silent, as Sarah, eager to end the augment continued.

"It can be difficult to explain, but I'd rather be positive than negative, what about you?"

"Yes." Karen replied, not really giving a proper answer.

After a momentary pause Sarah continued once more.

"All I'm saying is that, I'm going to try to stay focused. So it doesn't matter what Graham reads, I'm going to report him to the police."

"OK," said Karen, now conceding defeat and changing tact.

"I think we should meet up to sort our story out before going to see them."

"Yes, you're right. I'll come to you shall I?"

"Err, yes." Karen replied. "At about seven thirty, we can go from here.

"OK, I'll see you then."

The women said their goodbyes and hung up.

*What was that all about?* Thought Sarah. *An argument about being positive?* It was then that she thought she knew what was going on in Karen's head.

She thought that just like many people in this world, not only did Karen live in a blame culture; she also lived the blame culture. *It's part of who she is.* Years of conditioning had made her who she was and it would take some time for her to see past that conditioning. In the end, Karen wanted to blame someone or something for Toi's death and picked on Sarah, or more precisely her positive side, trying to show her that living life optimistically was, in some way flawed.

*Oh well, Pandora's Box is well and truly open, let's see what happens now.*

# CHAPTER 16

It was still raining when Sarah arrived at Karen's house, which had become the norm and was a full illustration of the term April showers.

Though the women greeted each other warmly, there was an awkward tension in their body language, as the discussion they'd had earlier still filled their minds.

While Karen made them both a cup of tea, Sarah sat down at the dining room table, in front of her lay a copy of the same book that they had discussed earlier. *Oh, so that's why she questioned the book* she thought, *she's reading it herself.*

Wanting to put an end to the tension and tackle their differences before they got down to business, Sarah prepared herself by visioning an amicable outcome to the meeting.

A couple of minutes later Karen brought their tea in, resting the cups in front of Sarah then sitting opposite. Sarah looked at the book and then back at Karen who felt Sarah's questioning eyes.

"I'm 37 and still trying to find my way," said Karen, "and seeing it in that bastard's house the other day just got me questioning this whole positive thing, you know?"

Sarah nodded and now understood that she'd been quick to pre-judge and that all Karen wanted were answers; there was no need to go back to the discussion from their earlier encounter, as they both felt that the tension had already dissipated.

For a moment they smiled at each other, however, this was quickly replaced by sterner expressions as it was now time to get down to business.

"I can't believe she's gone." Said Karen.

"Yes, I know."

"We were just having dinner last week, and that present she gave me for my birthday."

They both stared into space for a moment, both sighing heavily.

"OK, said Sarah, breaking the silence. "We need to make a list of things that we think will be relevant. And maybe order them into things that are fact, you know things that we can prove and then things that we can't but have a good idea about."

"OK, let me just get a pen and some paper." Said Karen, before getting up, disappearing into the kitchen, and then returning a minute later with a pen and a pad of pink writing paper.

"I haven't got any other paper." She said looking at the half smile expression on Sarah's face.

They thought for a while, then began to make a list of things they thought were relevant.

1.    **He acted violently towards Toi in the past - She was hospitalised a few weeks ago. (Hospital should have records)**

2.     He had recently sent a letter to a life insurer - (Sun Alliance) (He said that he stood to gain 50k)

3.     Toi didn't want to go to Northampton on the barge, as she was frightened of the water. (We are witnesses to that)

4.     The news reports and Graham said that Toi was a very strong swimmer when she was clearly taking swimming lessons. (The baths should have records of that)

5.   He offered us her jewellery and clothes before it came out that she had died. (We are witnesses to that)

"Anything else?" Sarah asked.

"Yes, he's an obnoxious bastard!" Karen chuckled.

"C'mon Karen, anything that we can use."

"I know, I know." Karen sighed, "I just can't believe that she's really gone," she continued, pulling out her amulet from behind her cardigan and holding it tightly.

Wanting to ensure that they had covered everything, the women thought for a little longer and after thirty seconds.

"Just think," said Sarah breaking the silence, "there's no way we would have gone swimming together if it wasn't for her."

"Yeah and the meal the other day, that would have never happened. Can you imagine Debbie eating Thai food before that?" Karen chuckled once more.

The women laughed.

"I don't know how I'm going to tell them." Said Karen,

"You know, the girls. I don't handle death very well. What do I say to them?"

"I'll do it if you want," said Sarah, "but I think you'll be fine. I know we all handle death in different ways, just be yourself."

Karen nodded.

"Come on, we'd better get going." She said before pausing. "You sure about this?"

"Fear again?" Asked Sarah.

Karen smiled, "Yes, come on lets go,"

\* \* \*

They arrived at the police station at 9pm, entering through the toughened glass sliding doors, into a light blue coloured foyer.

With an air of the dramatics, Sarah addressed the desk sergeant.

"I want to report a murder."

"What, you've seen someone murdered?" Asked the officer surprised.

"Err, no, we want to report what we think is evidence to a murder." She replied, now feeling a bit silly.

"So, you have some evidence of what could be a murder?" The officer repeated back.

They both nodded.

"Yes," said Sarah.

The Sergeant paused for a second, not knowing what to make of the pair, but he saw that they were serious.

"OK, just take a seat," he said nodding to the waiting area behind them. "I'll get someone to come down to speak to you."

\* \* \*

The women sat silently in the waiting area, both trying to take their minds off Toi's death; Sarah scanning the raft of anti crime posters on the notice board, thinking how negative they sounded; 'Don't do this and don't do that,' while Karen stared at the floor, thinking about work and the menu that they would be preparing tomorrow. Her thoughts moved onto the premeditation argument that they'd had earlier, and then in the end got butterflies in the pit of her stomach as she remembered that she had to break the bad news to the other women.

The desk sergeant returned a few minutes later and to their surprise, said,

"OK, come on through."

Pushing a large green button, he released the security door, which buzzed, signalling to the women that the door had opened. He then pushed the heavy metal and glass door open, letting them into the station offices.

"The person you need to see is in one of the back offices, this way." He said, before pulling the security door, ensuring it was properly closed then leading the way.

He led the women through a quiet seventies styled open planned office, the two men occupying the space glancing up from their work, eyeing the women as they passed.

They went through a set of brown double doors at the end of the office and then down a narrow brown formica and frosted glass fitted corridor, reminiscent of some seventies cop show. They stopped at an office where the sergeant knocked on the door and not waiting for an answer, immediately opened it; and while holding it open he motioned with a nod of his head for the women to go in.

"Detective Sergeant Kirkland." He said introducing the only occupant of the room.

From behind a replica light oak finished desk, a tall, dark man stood up. The rings around his eyes, the 5 O'clock shadow, and thinning mousy brown greying dishevelled hair added ten years to his thirty something. His cheap ruffled charcoal grey suit, and lime green half Windsor knotted tie, which hung three inches lower than his collar revealed an unhealthy relationship with his job.

"These are the women," Said the sergeant.

"Thanks Jim." Said DS Kirkland.

The sergeant nodded and then closed the door.

"OK." Said the detective, "what can I do for you ladies." Looking them both up and down, his attention focusing on

Sarah's blond hair and northern European looks.

It wasn't long before the women were telling their story; it took an hour, and he seemed to be very interested in what they had to say. In the end, they both shook hands with the detective and were told that someone would contact them in due course. They left feeling pleased with what they had done and now felt that Graham wouldn't get away if he were responsible for Toi's death.

# CHAPTER 17

At work on Monday there wasn't a dry eye when Karen broke the news to the other women, and although they had all thought the worst, Toi's passing still came as a shock.

At 10am that morning a reporter from the local news paper turned up having heard the news reports and now wanted a story.

\* \* \*

"I went to see her husband Mr Morton," he said, "but he didn't really want to talk about it, which I suppose is not surprising. But he did tell me she worked here and I thought... Anyway," he continued, "Mr Morton's' in his fifties and Mrs Morton was in her thirties and I believe she was from Thailand, so what's the story there?"

"Look! I know what you're thinking!" Said Karen, "But it wasn't like that! She's a, I mean was a decent woman and if you've come here to dish the dirt, then you'd better go."

"No, No, I wasn't trying to insinuate anything."

"No, it didn't sound like it," said Sarah sarcastically. "Look! If you want a story then you'll get one, but it won't be smutty."

The reporter blushed with embarrassment as Karen started.

"I'm not surprised he didn't want to talk, he was a complete bastard to her."

"What do you mean?"

The other women and the reporter listened as Karen gave the interview, giving as much information as possible; not only telling him what a wonderful person Toi was, but laying out the evidence against Graham, which seemed to be so clear-cut, that, even the other women were taken a back with what they heard.

"So you're saying that he bumped her off?" Asked the reporter, once Karen had finished.

"Make of it what you will," she replied, "but that's what we think happened."

"Look, said Sarah, he's got a motive and he had the time, you know, the opportunity and the way he use to treat her, nothing would surprise me. I mean, who would go on holiday, on a barge, knowing the weather was going to be that bad? He's definitely done something. I know it."

There was general agreement from around the group.

"So you're going to print this then?" Asked Jane.

The reporter paused for a moment.

"For legal reasons, I'm not sure if we can report this." He replied.

"Why?" Jane asked.

"Well, for a start, I'm only hearing once side of the story. I'm not saying that you're lying." He hastened, "But, Mr Morton should have a chance to give his side. To say nothing about it being libellous: Have you spoken to the police?" He asked.

"Yes," Karen replied, "they're looking into it."

"OK," he said", "I'll speak to the police in a few days, to see what they've got to say; in the mean time, I'll try Mr Morton again. I can't promise that we'll print anything, it's not up to me, but what I will say is that, Toi sounded like a really nice person and if we do print something, it will be good."

"It had better be." Said Sarah.

* * *

In the days that followed, the women grieved the loss of their friend, however, by Friday; their grief had again turned to anger.

Today Karen had to go to the doctor for a check-up, leaving Sarah in charge.

At the end of her shift, she hurried along the dimly lit corridor and entered the changing room where Debbie, Jenny and Jane were deep in conversation. No sooner as the women saw the door open, they fell silent, giving away that they were up to something.

Now looking round the room, Sarah sensed that something was not right.

"Come on then," she said smiling, "What is it? What are you up to?"

The women remained silent, all trying to avoid making eye contact with Sarah, herself staring at Jane, who now could no longer contain herself.

"We've got to sort Graham out!" Jane blurted.

Annoyed, Debbie glared at Jane, lightly shaking her head, trying to indicate for Jane to keep her mouth shut.

"What do you mean?" Said Sarah, the smile now disappearing from her face.

"What do you mean?" She repeated, this time voice raised when no reply came back.

"Well." Said Jane hesitantly; not really wanting to speak.

Shaking her head, Debbie came to her rescue,

"That bastard murdered her and we're going to make sure that he pays."

"Pays?" Sarah replied. Now realising who and what the women were talking about.

"How are you going to do that?" She continued.

After another pause Debbie continued.

"Well. My brother."

"Your brother!" Sarah interrupted. "Your brother has just got out and you want to get him involved?"

"Well the police aren't doing anything and that bloody man should be banged up."

The other women agreed, their body language showing that they seemed to be drawing strength from each other.

"My brother is going to go round and sort him out." Debbie continued.

"So what's your brother going to do? Eh, kill him?"

The room fell silent once more.

"Just have a think about what you're doing; what you're planning to do. You're plotting to either hurt or kill someone. Do you want something like that on your conscience? Can you live with that?"

Sarah turned to Jenny, "Can you?"

"What about you?" She said now turning to Jane.

There was no answer.

Sarah sat down on a bench, thought for a second and then sighed.

"I'm going to tell you something, but take it or leave it, the choice is yours. You all got to know Toi and I'd like to think that you all became good friends with her; in fact I know you did. You wouldn't be plotting to hurt someone if you hadn't been. But do you think Toi would want this? I knew Toi and I know that she wouldn't have wanted this."

The silence was broken by Jenny's sniffing; she'd started crying and was using a hanky to dry her tears.

"She wouldn't want this." Sarah repeated.

"You're letting your anger get the better of you and if you do this, it makes you no better than Graham."

"Look, there is a thing called karma." She continued.

Annoyed, Debbie opened her mouth to interrupt.

Debbie! Let me finish" said Sarah firmly. "Let me put it this way, what goes around comes around, I know you all understand that, well that's no difference to the karma I'm talking about."

Jane nodded.

"There is a balance to things in this world and if he's responsible for what happened to Toi, believe me, it will catch up with him. I'm certain of that."

"But nothing seems to be happening; he seems to be getting away with it." Debbie growled.

"Karma: What goes around comes around," Sarah replied. "Look, even if he gets away with it now, in the grand scheme of things, it will catch up with him, believe me it will. The reality is that you only want to hurt him to try to make yourselves feel better, but once you've done it, you'll be carrying that guilt around and as I said, what goes around comes around."

By now, Debbie was fuming, she'd heard enough.

"I've got to collect my kids." She said shaking her head before standing up.

"OK I've talked enough, just think about what I've said." Said Sarah. "Just try to enjoy the weekend."

Debbie stormed off, trying to slam the changing room door, which slowly closed on its hydraulic hinge.

The other women said their goodbyes and left.

Sarah couldn't believe that these were the same women,

that only six weeks earlier referred to Toi as a whore and now wanted to kill for her. *See what you've done* she thought, silently talking to Toi, *you bring us together, then you go and die on us.*

# CHAPTER 18

A few days earlier, DS Kirkland had started to make his enquiries. Now he sat in the mishmash of his office lent back on a blue fabric coloured swivel chair, staring at the ceiling as he talked to an old friend.

Mike Tomlinson; DS Tomlinson, a friend and colleague who he'd known for years: Having gone through Hendon at the same time and both working at the MET back in the late eighties, before going their separate ways.

"It's been manic." Said Mike.

"I can imagine." Kirkland replied.

"Can you?" Mike sighed. "You don't know the half of it.: The worst thing about this flood was the shite. I've never seen anything like it. You were there waste deep in shit, you know, stinking raw sewage, trying to get these bloody people out of their houses, so they don't drown in it and all they do is complain about their possessions and what the government's doing about it. I tell you it's unbelievable. And I tell you what, I need to move back."

Kirkland chuckled. "A good life, or was that a better quality of life, you said?

After thinking about the question for a few moments.

"No, I love it here really," Mike replied changing his mind. "Green and fresh air most of the time; but when things like this happen," he sighed. "Anyway, I got your email: So what's your interest."

"Well, a couple of women came to see me the other day; they seemed to think that the husband may have had something to do with her death."

"Yeah, well I know the officer who interviewed him and from what I can gather he was pretty shook up, I mean who wouldn't be; seeing your wife go overboard like that and not being able to do anything about it."

"Hmmm, so she drowned then?"

"It definitely looks like a drowning, but saying that, the body had been in the water for some time, so we'll have to see. There's going to be a post mortem within the next couple of days. So I'll let you know what happens."

"Yeah, that would be good; the women said that there had been some domestic violence, so, if you could let me know if you find anything that would be great."

"OK, I'll let you know: There's already a conspiracy theory as to why the floods happened."

"Oh yeah. What's that then," Kirkland replied sarcastically, "Aliens had something to do with it?" He chuckled.

"No, I'm serious, something to do with the water companies not being able to cope with the amount of rain that fell. People are saying that they mistakenly opened a flood barrier or sluice gate or something like that..."

\* \* \*

Thinking that he may have been making a wasted trip given the information he'd gathered from the Northamptonshire constabulary, still, Kirkland made is way down to the canal to see Graham. It was 3pm on another grey spring afternoon and though it wasn't cold, it looked as though it was about to start raining.

As Kirkland trudged along the canal path, Mike's words ringing in his ears "he was pretty shook u*p." Maybe it's a bit too soon to quiz this guy,* he thought. *But I'm here now and besides, going by what the women said, this guy sounds a bit dodgy, may as well check him out.*

Minutes later, he reached The Duck, climbed on-board and knocked on the hatch. For a while, nothing happened, so he knocked again, this time a little harder. Now hearing movement inside he knew someone was in, and after a short time Graham appeared, popping his head through the hatch.

"Yes," he said, looking Kirkland up and down.

"Mr Morton? Mr Graham Morton?"

"Yes," Graham replied suspiciously.

"DS Kirkland, Wattsford." Kirkland replied, taking his warrant card out from his inside jacket pocket and waving it close to Graham's face.

"I know this might be a bad time for you, but, I'm here about your wife, Mrs Morton."

"I've been through all of this with Northampton police."

Said Graham, still examining Kirkland's warrant card.

"I know Mr Morton," replied Kirkland pausing for a second and feeling a bit guilty, "but some accusations have been made surrounding the circumstances of your wife's death, which I am investigating."

"Accusations? What accusations? But she drowned, I've already told the police, she fell overboard and drowned. What accusations?"

It now began to drizzle.

"Can I come in?" Kirkland asked.

"What for?"

"Mr Morton," said Kirkland, pulling up the collar of his jacket and squinting as the rain began falling heavier.

"Some serious allegations have been made about you in relation to your wife's death, I'm sure we can have them cleared up in a few minutes. But..." Kirkland paused and looked up at the grey that covered the sky, then back at Graham.

"Oh you'd better come in then."

The men walked down the steps into the barge, Graham leading Kirkland through the passageway into the living area. As they passed through the passageway, Kirkland felt that they were not alone; sensing another presence from behind one of the closed doors.

"So you and Mrs Morton lived here alone?" He asked.

Graham hesitated.

"Err, Yes." He replied, his gaze now shifting towards the passageway, giving away that someone else was onboard.

"And children, do you have any, children?" Kirkland asked, finding himself now looking towards the passageway.

Graham shook his head and then looked at the floor.

"No, I couldn't have any." Then in an attempt to change the subject said speculatively. "So who's been making allegations then? I bet it's those women."

*What is he hiding*? Thought Kirkland.

"For now, it doesn't matter, who's made the allegations; I just need for you to answer a few questions, if that's OK?"

Graham nodded and Kirkland produced a small black book from his inside jacket pocket as outside the heavens opened up, the rain beating hard down onto the roof and deck of the barge, making it difficult for the men to hear.

"So," said Kirkland, voice raised, "your wife came from Thailand…"

## CHAPTER 19

The following Monday during morning break, Debbie called Sarah into the changing room. Standing in the middle of the room, she tried to summon up enough courage to admit she'd been wrong when last they spoke.

"Look," she said hesitantly, "I just want to thank you for stopping us from doing what… You know; what we wanted to do, you know to Graham, on Friday."

"It's OK." Sarah replied.

Debbie's brother, a violent career criminal, who'd just been released from prison after serving two and a half years for aggravated burglary, had agreed to, 'sort Graham out.'

"It isn't OK. If my brother had got hold of him, he would have killed him and I know that if I'd been caught up in the whole thing, I dread to think what could have happened: I could have got banged up myself and what would happen to my kids then?"

"Really, it's OK we caught it in time didn't we?"

"Yeah, just as well; I know I don't think sometimes. Anyway, I just thought, I'd thank you."

"That's fine, how are your kids anyway?" Asked Sarah now changing the subject.

"They're OK, but Charlie, the little bugger's playing up at school; I don't know what to do with him."

"I'm sure he'll be fine. My Carl was the same at his age."

Debbie nodded as an awkward momentary silence ensued. Sarah again playing the agony aunt wanted to ask about Debbie's well being, however, felt a bit awkward given their recent history. *What the hell,* she thought.

"Anyway, so, how are you," She asked.

Debbie, a bit suspicious replied.

"Yeah, I'm fine."

Sarah nodded before saying.

"Have you ever thought about managing this place? I mean being in charge?"

"What are you talking about?" Debbie replied with a frown

"I mean, being the manager of this place."

"Why? Do you know something I don't? Are you and Karen leaving?" Debbie replied with a chuckle.

"No," Sarah replied now smiling. "I just think you'll be kitchen manager one day, that's all."

Again, Debbie looked at Sarah, this time a bit puzzled.

"I mean I'm not trying to be patronising, but I just believe that you will be in charge of this kitchen." She repeated.

Again, there was a momentary silence as Debbie thought about how to reply and to Sarah's surprise said.

"Do you think so?"

"Yes, I just think you need to sort your personal life out and things will start happening for you."

Debbie now taken aback, her expression changed to one of

anger.

"No, I mean, look," Sarah blurted out. Now feeling that she may have said a bit too much. "I know it's none of my business."

"No it isn't." Debbie replied.

"All I'm saying is that you spend so much time worrying about men, that it takes up time you could spend doing other things."

Debbie seemed to be fuming now, as Sarah tried to talk her way out of the hole she seemed to have no control over digging.

"Come on Debbie, all I'm trying to be is truthful; we all know that you've had problems with the men in your life.

Debbie's expression changed, now knowing that Sarah was right; she'd had a feeling that all the other women in the kitchen knew about her current situation and unlike Sarah, were afraid to approach her for gossip. She now looked down at the floor as her face flushed with embarrassment, but still thinking Sarah was *a nosey cow*.

"All I'm saying is this, you don't need a man to be happy, so stop chasing them. Try to be content with what you've got, your children, your job, your health and concentrate on getting the job here. You know, the kitchen manager's job and you'll probably get it.

Now sounding a bit pretentious she continued:

"And with it more money, and more of the things you want in life."

After a short pause.

"Believe in yourself and men will be chasing you."

Debbie found it hard to believe that of all the women in the kitchen, it was Sarah; the one whom she liked the least, was the one that was bold enough to talk to her about her problems, well at least tried.

Though she'd done little of the talking during the exchange, she felt somehow that a weight had been lifted from her mind and that someone cared and actually believed in her.

"Anyway." Said Debbie, still blushing and now changing the subject, "Thanks for, you know, stopping me from doing...

Sarah nodded and smiled.

"But, it's not about me now," Debbie continued. "It's about Toi and doing right by her. We've got to get some justice for her."

* * *

In the days that followed, though the women were miserable, there was a strange tinge of excitement in the air. They believed that they were in the middle of some scandal and maybe they would be called as witnesses in a murder trial. Sarah however, wanted them to take things more seriously and couldn't help thinking that they were dishonouring Toi's memory by making light of the situation.

* * *

A week went by, then ten days, then two weeks, and the police had still not contacted Sarah or Karen, so they decided to wait no longer. That evening, after work, Karen met Sarah at her home, where they had planned to contact DS Kirkland.

With some apprehension Sarah made the call and after being connected asked an operator if she could speak to the detective.

Moments later,

"Hello, DS Kirkland,"

Sarah answered, "Hello, my name is Mrs Braithwaite, I came in two weeks ago to report a murder: Err, I mean, to give evidence about a death."

"Yes I remember you," said Kirkland, "I meant to call you."

The call had surprised Kirkland, as he'd not quite finished his investigation; more precisely his friend Mike had not got back to him with the pathology report.

However, with what was likely to come back from the post-mortem and the statement he'd taken from Graham, Kirkland had already formed an opinion.

"Oh." Replied Sarah.

"Yes and please accept my apologies for not getting back to you before now. I've just been a bit snowed under."

"Yes I can imagine," she replied sarcastically, now eagerly wanting him to hurry up and get down to the nitty-gritty.

"Well Mrs Braithwaite, I can say that we've found nothing suspicious.

Sarah, sighed heavily.

"We've interviewed Mr Morton and from what we can gather, Mrs Morton was a strong swimmer; unfortunately she took her life into her own hands when she ignored the flood warnings."

Sarah wanting to interrupt barely got a word out before Kirkland continued.

"Look, I don't want to go into the detail, as I know she was your friend, but take it from me it was a tragic accident".

As Kirkland paused, Sarah took her chance to respond.

"It wasn't an accident and she couldn't swim that well, and she was taking lessons." She blurted.

To her annoyance he interrupted once more.

"I'm afraid it was."

Sarah realised that she'd begun to feel flustered and could now feel an element of fear.

*Why am I frightened? I've got nothing to fear,* she thought trying to reassure herself, then quickly regaining her composure.

"Mr Kirkland, I was teaching Toi, I mean Mrs Morton, how to swim and I can tell you, that she was not a strong swimmer.

She was also getting lessons that Mr Morton had paid for, she told me. Did you check with the baths?"

"Yes, we checked and there were no records of her ever attending lessons there."

"I don't believe this." She replied angrily. "What's going on?"

"What do you mean?" Kirkland replied surprised at Sarah's tone.

Sarah feeling the anger rising once more checked herself.

"Listen, I've personally been teaching, Mrs Morton how to swim and I've got five witnesses to that."

Kirkland now silent began to realise that he had not done a thorough enough investigation and perhaps he'd hastily formed an opinion.

"Five witnesses." He replied.

Yes, five witnesses; the people I work with. We've all been to Waterfields swimming baths with her. We all knew, or should I say, saw, that she couldn't swim. And I suppose he told you that she wanted to go on that trip?"

*Waterfields'* Thought Kirkland.

"Well, yes," he replied. "He said that she really wanted to go."

"She did, but not on the barge, she told me, so I offered to put her up at my house."

"Look," said Kirkland now on the back foot, "I don't know how you can prove that, at the moment this is all hearsay. We've spoken to the police in Northampton who've conducted a full investigation themselves and they say that."

He  paused for a second before continuing.

"Look, I didn't want to go into detail but, as you were friends: She was in a pretty bad state when they pulled her from the water.

He paused once more, trying to remember what Graham had told him, *'she must have slipped and fell in, one minute she was there the next she was gone'. Hang on a second!'. 'Mike said that Morton saw her fall in.'*

He now continued trying to be confident, but knowing something was wrong.

 "One minute she was there and the next she'd gone;  she slipped and fell in, she stood no chance".

Pausing again once more, he tried to remember exactly what Graham had told him.

"Her body caught on some wire that was dumped into the canal and that's why it took as long as it did to find her". He continued.

"Barbed wire! But, he had a roll of barbed wire on is barge, a big roll of it." Sarah replied.

Again, Kirkland paused. *'Barbed wire eh.'*

"That doesn't really prove anything." He said.

"But he could have used that to weight her down or something like that."

"Even if he did, have barbed wire like you say, it could

have just fallen off the barge due to the bad weather; as I say, it doesn't prove anything.

Sarah thought for a second.

"What about the insurance then, he said that he would get fifty thousand. And he was selling off her jewellery and clothes before she was even found."

"Yes, yes, I've asked him about his insurance but you'll understand that it's something I can't really speak to you about, but I can say, that everything is above board: and as for the clothing; Mr and Mrs Morton had agreed to sell some of her clothing and jewellery to raise money for a holiday in Thailand.

*He's bloody got an answer to everything,* thought Sarah.

"OK, we told you that he abused her, he beat her up what about that."

"Yes, I did ask Mr Morton about that; he said that they had a fiery relationship, which from time to time did end in blows, but he said, she gave as good as she got."

That sounded wrong and Kirkland knew it.

"What? She is; was, a small woman." Said Sarah, frustration creeping into her voice. "There's no way that she could have stood up to him. Whatever he's told you, he's lying."

"You don't like him much, do you?" Kirkland asked.

"No I don't, but whether I like him or not is neither here

nor there; a woman's been killed and I want you to take this seriously!" Sarah snapped.

"Mrs Braithwaite, I can assure you that we take all crime seriously! In this case we've exhausted our investigation and there is nothing more we can do." He replied, taken aback by Sarah's tone.

"What?" Sarah replied now wishing that she'd not antagonised him.

"Yes, it's over, there is nothing more to investigate I'm afraid."

Sarah sighed once more; the conversation was going nowhere as Kirkland didn't seem to be interested and now seemed to be on the defensive, but knowing that she had to do something else she tried another tact.

"Look, I want to take this further because I'm not satisfied with the answers I'm getting. Is there anyone else I can speak to?" She asked.

"Yes, but I'm not sure if it'll get you anywhere."

"Please just tell me who I can speak to."

"Well, DCI Thornton is the person to speak to; he's on annual leave at the moment, but he'll be back tomorrow."

"DCI Thornton," Sarah repeated back. "OK, I'll call back. Oh! One other thing, she wasn't wearing a life jacket; Toi I mean, perhaps you can ask Graham why."

Sarah thanked the DS and hung up.

She was shocked by what she'd just heard; *nothing more would be done about Graham,* so if he did have something to do with Toi's death, then he'd got away with it.

Karen sat silently knowing the call didn't go well.

"Well, that's that then." Said Sarah

"No," Karen replied, "What goes around, comes around. Remember, you said that. He'll get his comeuppance."

The women felt deflated and for a while sat talking about the whole experience and needed to; they both wept, but drew comfort from each other.

# CHAPTER 20

Kirkland sat at his desk knowing that he'd not done enough and now had more questions that needed answering, which were added to when he called Mike that evening.

Mike told him that Toi had drowned, not before being crushed between a bridge and the barge itself; *'she stood no chance and would have died given the head injuries that she had received.'*

* * *

"Could her head injuries have been caused by, say someone hitting her." Asked Kirkland.

"Well I suppose they could have," Mike replied, "but she was in the water for some time, so there's no real way of telling."

"Hmmm," Said Kirkland.

"Why, do you know something I don't?" Mike asked suspiciously.

"No, it's just a thought."

"Come on Trev, don't give me that, what are you up to?"

"It's just something that I'm looking into."

"Well?" Mike inquired once more.

Kirkland thought for a second and then continued.

"OK, before I say anything, just one more question."

"OK."

"Did Mr Morton say that he saw Mrs Morton fall off the

barge?"

Mike thought for a moment.

"Yes, I think he did. Why?"

"Are you sure?"

"Pretty sure, look, just hang on a second."

Kirkland, listened as in the background Mike spoke to an officer on another telephone and asked the same question. Then *"great; are you sure, OK."* Mike was now back.

"I don't know if you heard any of that. But the answer is yes, in his statement, Morton said that he saw his wife go overboard and could do nothing as the current was too strong, she was pulled under very quickly, or so he said. So what's going on?" Mike asked once more.

Kirkland took a deep breath.

"What would you say if I said, that I think he hit her over the head and then threw her overboard?"

"You serious?" Asked Mike. "What evidence have you got?"

Kirkland ran through what the women had told him; how apprehensive Graham had acted when he had to see him and how persistent Sarah had been earlier that day.

"So what do you think?" Asked Kirkland once he'd finished.

"Wow, well, there's a lot there and it's compelling, but it's all circumstantial. I can see him doing it. But unless you get him to confess, I'm not sure if you'll get anything to stick. I mean, he could say that he made a mistake and didn't see her go overboard, you know one minute she was there and the next he saw her in the water. It's not a giant leap."

"I know, and a lot of it's hearsay, and now with the pathology report, it's looking less likely that we'll get him. Saying that, I am going to see him again, just to be sure."

"Well good luck. I think you'll need it. But if I can help in any way, let me know."

"I will," said Kirkland, "don't worry about that. Well, anyway, how's it going now, the last time we spoke, you were wading through crap?"

Mike sighed. "No, I count myself lucky mate, after seeing what some people have gone through, what they've lost."

"Yeah, but it's all insured isn't it.?

"Yes, I know, I just feel a bit stupid for complaining, you know, people rely on me and if the job requires that I help people when something like that happens, then that's what I have to do."

"Bloody hell what's come over you?" Asked Kirkland.

After a short pause, Mike replied.

"Nothing, a few people lost their lives; I'm just putting my woes into perspective I suppose..."

* * *

As twilight encroached, Kirkland stood in his shadowy

office as the ensuing darkness slowly engulfed the room.

He stared out of the window, watching as the offices opposite emptied, the workforce streaming out onto the already packed exhaust fume filled streets near to the train station, which was only a stone's throw away. *A Better quality of life,* he thought, remembering why Mike had moved to the country.

He envied the people in the streets as they were heading home for the evening; he still had work to do and after switching on the lights which flickered into life, he sat down, leant back in his chair and stretched.

Picking up the phone, he called Waterfields swimming Centre; he'd forgotten that the town had more than one swimming pool and never thought to ask when the women told him that they were giving Toi swimming lessons. He'd automatically assumed that they used the old swimming baths at the top of the town; the swimming baths that he'd used as a child. *You're getting sloppy.* He told himself.

After a conversation with the centre manager who confirmed that Toi had been taking lessons, he decided that he would go to the canal to see Graham once more. He first flicked through his address book and finding the number that he wanted, dialled.

* * *

After Karen had gone home, Sarah spent an hour and a half

locked away in her bedroom, trying to read her new book. She couldn't get past reading the first four pages and now for the fourth time started the book from the beginning of chapter one. Finding it hard to concentrate; owing to her earlier encounter with DS Kirkland still fresh in her mind, she found it difficult to assimilate the information from the pages.

While the phone rang in the background, she first stared at the words on the page and then into space. *Why can't he see that Graham has done something?*

"Mum, it's for you!" Carl shouted from behind her bedroom door.

"MUM! Telephone," he repeated when Sarah didn't reply the first time.

"OK!" Sarah answered.

She picked up her extension.

"Mum," said Carl from the downstairs extension, checking that his mother had picked up.

"I've got it," she replied. "Hello."

"Hello, Mrs Braithwaite, its DS Kirkland."

Sarah had a feeling of butterflies in her stomach as she recognised the voice before the name registered.

"Oh, DS Kirkland."

"Yes," he began now sounding a bit sheepish, "I thought I would call back to tell you that."

He paused for a moment before.

"There are some inconsistencies with Mr Morton's story and I'm going to re-interview him."

There was another slight pause as Kirkland waited for a response.

"So why are you telling me?" Sarah snapped, still feeling angry about their last encounter.

"I just thought that you'd want to know."

She began to realise that he didn't have to tell her anything and was just probably trying to be helpful. Of course, she was glad that he'd decided to carry on with the investigation and perhaps, if Graham was guilty, he would be brought to book.

So why have you changed your mind? I mean, I thought that you said that was it."

"Well," he replied, "I just need to be certain about a few things, I'm not saying that things will change, but, as I say, I want to check a few things with him."

"OK, so what now?"

"I'll let you know what happens within a couple of days. I mean, obviously if this becomes a criminal investigation, the information I'll be able to give you will become limited, however, I'll let you know what I can, but in the mean time, I would ask you to keep this conversation between us confidential."

"OK, and I take it, that it means I won't have to speak to DCI Thornton then?"

"No, not for now, I'll get back to you by Friday."

"Please do."

"OK," he replied, "I'll talk to you then."

\* \* \*

*Dam rain!* Thought Kirkland, as he sat in his car waiting for a break in the weather. He'd got down to the canal at 8pm; now it was eight thirty and there was still no let up.

A man dressed in dark clothes walked on the pavement towards the car as Kirkland peered at him through a small patch that he'd wiped from the heavy condensation, which formed on the inside of the windscreen. As the man walked passed and then disappeared up the road, Kirkland noticed that the rain had let up a little. *I'd better get going.*

The dim yellow street lamp flickered; the time it spent in darkness now becoming more prolonged, leaving the area around the car in almost total darkness, only the light pollution from the houses 150 metres away challenging the gloom.

He got out, and though not cold, pulled the collar of his jacket up around his neck and then hurried along the canal path, trying to make the best of the break in the weather.

Reaching the moorings, he found that The Duck wasn't where it had been moored before, so continued on to see if it was moored further up. *Shit, I should have come earlier...*

But finding that the barge had gone, he slowly walked back

to his car and went home.

## CHAPTER 21

The sun shone, with its warmth trying to break through the early morning mist when Jane arrived for work the following day.

There was going to be a big change in the weather, or so it was reported in the news. Summer was finally here! And a mini heat wave, where temperatures were set to reach a scorching 80 degrees had been forecast.

Jane arrived slightly later than usual, as it had been a late night for her, as well as her new boyfriend. She arrived to find the women quietly huddled around a workbench, the quiet low hum of the extractor fans filling the room.

"What's going on?" She asked as she entered the kitchen and breaking the silence.

All of the women looked up from the workbench.

"We're in the news." Debbie replied.

"In the news? " Jane asked puzzled.

"Yes," said Jenny, "in the Observer."

Jane hurried over to join the huddle; on the workbench in front of them lay a copy of this week's Observer. Now feeling that all eyes were on her and sensing that everyone waited for her to read the report aloud to confirm what they had already read, she duly obliged.

On the front page, taking up about one fifth of the page a bold headline read:

"Body discovered on river bank"

Hesitantly Jane continued.

"Police have found the body of Toi Morton, the woman who went missing after she was swept overboard from her boat three weeks ago, has been found. Mrs Morton 33, fell overboard during the floods in Southbridge Northampton. She had been on holiday with her husband when the accident happened."

"Police say her body was discovered on a bank on the River Nene on Bank Holiday Monday. A Northampton police spokes-man said: 'the body that has been formally identified is that of Toi Morton.'"

"Mrs Morton lived with her husband on the boat, which was usually moored in Croxten."

"She was a kitchen assistant at the International Boys School. The kitchen manager Karen O'Brian said 'Toi was a lovely person. She cared and was always thinking of everyone. She gave more than she received. We used to go out as a group every now and then.'"

"Mrs O'Brian said Mrs Morton had been learning to swim at Waterfields. She said, 'She went swimming at 8am in the morning and would come into work after that. Sometimes she would complain that the pool was closed. It's very sad. Before she went on holiday, she gave me a present and asked me not to open it until Bank Holiday Monday. She was thoughtful like that. We are all pretty upset.'"

There was silence when Jane finished, Sarah clearly upset hurried over to the sink area where she tore off a piece of blue roll kitchen paper from a dispenser and dried her eyes. Karen went over and put an arm around Sarah's shoulders, comforting her.

"Come on you lot," She said, "We've got work to do." Her words not having their usual gusto, just sounding synthetic and dreary.

\* \* \*

Jane dashed off to the changing room to get ready for work, words ringing in her ears, *'She gave more than she received.'* Only a few weeks ago Toi had loaned Jane fifty pounds to pay a catalogue bill that had been sent to a collection agency. She felt guilty, as she'd come into some money and could have paid the loan back a week before Toi went missing, but instead, chose to use the money to pay for a couple of drunken nights out with her girlfriends and using the remainder last night, on her new boyfriend.

After changing into her whites, she hurried back towards the kitchen, where in the corridor between the kitchen and changing room Sarah and Karen talked, their voices lowered. As Jane approached, the women fell silent and watched as Jane passed them pulling open the kitchen door.

"Err, Jane, I want you to fill up the vending machines, OK." Said Karen, before producing a bunch of keys from her coat pocket.

Jane turned and nodded.

"Here," she said throwing the keys to Jane. "Make sure you lock the store cupboard and all the machines as you fill them."

"OK." Jane replied.

As the kitchen door slowly closed on its hydraulic hinge, Sarah and Karen continued

Sarah now with total disregard to the discreetness that was asked for, filled Karen in on her conversation with DS Kirkland.

* * *

That afternoon Kirkland returned to the canal.

Taking off his jacket and rolling up his shirt sleeves, *Bloody weather,* He thought. *One minute it's raining and the next...*

In stark contrast to the past few weeks, the world was warm and bright, if only a few degrees warmer than it had been.

There it was, 'The Duck' moored in its usual place. As Kirkland approached, Graham appeared; coming through the hatch carrying several beer bottles and behind him a woman, or more like a girl; a girl in her late teens, also carrying several beer bottles, and a couple precariously squeezed under her arms. Graham lined his bottles against the side of the barge, before catching sight of DS Kirkland, his face now displaying an obvious alarm.

"Mr Morton." Said Kirkland.

"Yes," Graham nervously replied, now turning to the woman and waving her back inside.

"Yes, I've told you everything." He continued.

"Yes I know Mr Morton, but there are a couple of things that I need clearing up, can I come in?"

"No," Graham replied sternly, "Look, I don't know what you want, but you can't come in. I don't let people in."

"Mr Morton, have you got something to hide?"

Backing off, Graham didn't answer, only slowly edging towards the hatch.

"Mr Morton," Kirkland continued, "we can either do this here, or down at the station, the choice is yours."

Graham froze. "What do you want?"

"Shall we go inside?" Kirkland asked once more, before dodging two cyclists, one whizzing passed his front and the other his back."

"No, whatever you've got to ask me, you can ask me here."

Kirkland, increasingly suspicious said,

"OK suit yourself," before reaching into his jacket pocket and pulling out a black leather covered note pad.

"OK. In your statement to the Northamptonshire police you said that you saw your wife go over the side and get dragged down by the current."

Graham, eager to get the interview over and done with,

jumped in.

"Yes, that's what I told them"

Kirkland smiled.

"OK, well you told me that one minute she was there and the next she had gone. Now what is it, did you see her go over or… "

"I, I…" Graham was now flustered. "Look my wife had just gone over the side." He continued.

"So you saw her go over then?" Kirkland interjected.

"No," said Graham, "One minute she was there and the next she'd gone."

"So why did you tell Northants."

Graham butted in once more.

"I was in shock; I didn't know what I was saying."

"OK, Mr Morton, Said Kirkland, writing a note into his note pad. "We'll come back to that."

And after a short pause, he continued.

"OK, in your statement you said that Mrs Morton was a strong swimmer, but she was taking swimming lessons at Waterfields, surely you knew that."

Graham, unable to contain himself any longer said.

"Those bloody women put you up to this didn't they? My wife has just died; they have no respect."

"Mr Morton, please stay calm, I'm just trying to clear up some loose ends. Now, did you know if Mrs Morton was taking swimming lessons, yes or no?"

"No,"

"No?" Kirkland asked, "But, weren't you paying for her lessons."

"No!" Graham snapped. "Who told you that? She was paying for her own," he said before stopping abruptly, knowing that he'd put his foot in it.

"Continue Mr Morton; she was paying for what?"

In the ensuing silence, beads of sweat began to appear on Graham's forehead and now Kirkland had heard enough.

"Mr Morton, I think we should carry on with this conversation down at the police station."

"My wife has just died," said Graham, now backing off, "how about showing some respect."

"Mr Morton, please get your coat." Kirkland replied sternly.

# CHAPTER 22

It was late afternoon; Kirkland and DCI Thornton stood in a dark viewing room behind a two way glass. On the other side Graham sat at a table in a dimly lit grey windowless interview room, opposite a heavy blue door. Kirkland tried to convince DCI Thornton that Graham was hiding something and that it was quite possible that he could have murdered his wife. But Thornton was less than convinced, instead agreeing with Graham, that so close after the loss of a loved one, it was likely that anyone would quite easily give an incoherent statement, especially if in a state of shock.

"Gov, I want a warrant to search his place; he's hiding something, I know it."

"No way" Thornton replied, "Can you imagine what the press would say. They'd have a field day, and you know what relations are like between them and us. Look, his wife has just died for God's sake."

"Gov, he did it." Kirkland replied, with an almost pleading expression.

"Look Trev, everything that you've got is circumstantial and the only reason he's still here, is that he's taken out that insurance policy. That's the only thing that we can prove and even that's not illegal, but I agree that there may be something there."

"Yes, but it gives him motive. Look, he's got the motive

and had the opportunity, he could have done it."

Thornton thought for a second, then:

"But where's the physical evidence? Where is it? I know what you're trying to do. You're trying to bully a confession out of him. Look, you've got half an hour; if you don't get anything out of him, then I want him out of here: And remember his wife's just died so take it easy; and by the book OK? And I want Shrives in there with you."

"Shrives!" Kirkland droned before tutting and rolling his eyes.

\* \* \*

DC Carol Shrives, a graduate from Oxford, had been fast tracked through the system and in the higher echelons of the force had been earmarked for a future top job; Chief Superintendent or something like that.

She believed that Kirkland's' detection, interview techniques and general attitude were throwbacks to the dark days of the seventies, when men were supposedly men, which made him in her mind, a dinosaur.

Kirkland, along with many of his fellow male colleagues believed that, it wasn't just her intellectual capabilities that made her stand out. Rather, her blue eyes, long sweeping blond hair, and shapely body playing a big part in her rise to stardom. In her own mind, she denied using her femininity to further her career; however, it was clear to see by everyone else, that she used the tools that were available to her to get where she wanted to go.

\* \* \*

"It's either that or nothing." Said Thornton.

"OK," Kirkland replied reluctantly.

After leaving the viewing room, Kirkland appeared moments later on the other side of the glass in interview room 2 carrying a folder and was followed in by DC Shrives. They both sat down at the table opposite Graham, Kirkland resting the green folder on the table then introducing DC Shrives.

"OK, what's this about?" Asked Graham, staring at DC Shrives, his admiring gaze then being interrupted by Kirkland.

"Mr Morton, as I said earlier, I have a few things to clear up in relation to your wife's death. Now I just want to make you aware that you are not under arrest: you've been asked here to assist us with our enquiries. Do you understand?"

Graham nodded, nervously moving his hands from underneath the table where they had rested on his knees, folding his arms across his chest and then moving his hands back underneath the table, interlocking his fingers, trying to appear calm.

"OK, said Kirkland. "Please run through the events leading up to Mrs Morton being swept off the barge."

"She wasn't swept off the barge, she fell," Said Graham.

He went on to repeat what he'd told Kirkland when they

were at the canal.

"OK," said Kirkland, "so one minute she was there and the next she was gone? Yes."

"Yes," "That's what I said."

"OK" said Kirkland seemingly satisfied. "So tell me about the swimming lessons, how long had she been swimming?"

"I don't know."

"What! A week, two weeks, a month, surely you must have some idea?" Kirkland asked in disbelief.

After a short pause, "Yes, I think about six weeks." Graham replied.

"But you told me that you didn't know that she was taking swimming lessons, why was that?"

"I was confused. You make me confused," Graham complained.

"I'm sorry Mr Morton, I don't mean to confuse you, but this won't take long. So, six weeks? You told Northants that she was a strong swimmer. Is it likely that she could have been a strong swimmer after just six weeks?"

"Well I don't know, but she did go twice a week."

"So, say she had twelve lessons, even after that would you say that she was a strong swimmer?"

"I don't know," said Graham seeming annoyed. "How would I know, I'm not a swimming instructor." He said, a tinge of sarcasm appearing.

"No, you're not, but I've checked with Waterfields and I can tell you that she had been taking lessons, but only for four weeks.

Graham shrugged his shoulders.

"Well did you or did you not tell Northants that Mrs Morton was a strong swimmer." Kirkland demanded.

"Yes, but I thought she was."

"OK," said Kirkland, shaking his head and now changing the subject; "Was Mrs Morton wearing a life jacket?"

"No, she was a strong swim..." Graham failed to complete the sentence and corrected himself, and just said. "No."

"Why was that? Asked Kirkland sarcastically. "Don't tell me, she was a strong swimmer! There was a storm, the water was high, there were flood warnings, and she wasn't wearing a life jacket?"

Now speculating and again changing the subject once more.

"And what about the insurance?" Kirkland asked.

"What about it. Look, I've had enough of this. I don't want to carry on with this interview."

"Well I did say that you weren't under arrest, but you know what it'll look like if you walk out now: don't you?"

After a moments silence while Graham pondered Kirkland's words.

"So, what about the insurance," Kirkland repeated. "Even

you, have to admit that it looks a bit suspicious."

"Not really, all I did was increase the level of our life insurance; there's nothing illegal about that is there?"

"But why? Why did you increase your level of insurance?"

"Look, it was as much for her as it was for me. I'm getting on, I'm 57 years old and I thought if anything happened to me, she would have got fifty grand.

"Yes," Said Kirkland, smiling, "but surprise surprise; it's you whose ended up getting it, isn't that right? He asked shaking his head."

The interview wasn't going well. *Can't prove anything here.* Thought Kirkland. *Move on.*

You were selling her clothes and jewellery before you knew she'd drowned, weren't you.

"I don't know what you're talking about."

"I beg your pardon." Said Kirkland sounding very surprised. "I asked you about that when I saw you on your boat. Look"

Kirkland flipped through the pages of his note pad and then put it down on the desk flipping it round to show Graham the note.

"Look, it says that you were selling her clothes and jewellery to raise money for a holiday."

"No I didn't." Graham replied, now looking at DC Shrives, subconsciously trying to summon her support. "I did not say that, I don't know what you're talking about."

"You know what I'm talking about Mr Morton, you knew that she wasn't coming back, so you started to sell her possessions, didn't you? I've got it documented in my note book."

"No, no; where are you getting all this from, they're lies, they're all lies."

DC Shrives leant over and whispered into Kirkland's ear. Kirkland nodded and then looked at his watch.

"OK, Mr Morton, he said, "just a couple more questions: Did you ever have a large roll of barbed wire on your boat."

"Barge, it's called a barge and I did have a roll, I think it got swept overboard in the storm."

"You think." Replied Kirkland. "Did it or didn't it?"

Graham's face had began to lose its colour, turning a shade of grey, as beads of sweat started to appear on his brow and around his mouth.

"Yes. It did, One minute…"

Kirkland interrupted. "Don't tell me, one minute it was there and the next…"

He now found it hard to contain his frustration.

"Mr Morton," he continued, "do you realise that your wife's body had snagged on a large roll of barbed wire?"

"Well, I knew that. But that had nothing to do with me." Graham replied shrugging his shoulders.

"You already know?" Kirkland enquired.

"Yes, I had to go to Northampton the other day to identify her body; she's been released; I mean her body's been released. And I've already arranged for the funeral."

Kirkland put his head in his hands and shook his head. Mike didn't tell him that the body had been released and now with some urgency he continued.

"Look, Mr Morton, I want you to tell me why Mrs Morton wasn't wearing a life jacket?

You knew she was taking lessons and weren't you paying for them?" he asked, now probing with some of the information that Sarah had given to him.

"She was a strong swimmer, or that's what she told me."

"Come on Mr Morton! She was still taking swimming lessons."

"I wasn't paying for them either" Graham replied, before standing up.

DC Shrives again lent over and whispered into Kirkland's ear, to which he gave her a stern look, then shook his head and then sighed.

"Please sit down Mr Morton." He said.

"No, I know what you're trying to do, but it won't work."

"Mr Morton, sit down!"

"No, you said that I wasn't under arrest, so you can't keep me here."

"Please Mr Morton, DC Shrives interrupted, "please sit down: This interview is over," she continued, before glancing at Kirkland, who sighed, then lent back in his seat, now beginning to realise just how flimsy the evidence against Graham was.

And after a short pause, DC Shrives said. "I'll get someone to drop you home."

Once Graham had sat down, frustrated, Kirkland lent forward and said.

"I know you've done something and I'm going to get you."

"OK! OK, that's where we'll leave it." DC Shrives interrupted giving Kirkland another stern look. "Come on Mr Morton, I'll sort you out a lift."

Graham smiled at Kirkland as he stood up, while Kirkland glared back, now in full belief that there was a very strong possibility that Graham had murdered his wife; he just couldn't prove it.

Graham and DC Shrives left the room, leaving Kirkland hunched, in front of the table, palms down, staring at the green folder and lost in his thoughts.

\* \* \*

Two hours later, he sat in his office; he'd done nothing more that day, apart from repeatedly playing the interview over in his mind, thinking how it could have gone better. DC Shrives entered and silently, without acknowledgement, walked across the office, sat at her desk and opened a folder, taking out the paper work.

The two sat in silence for about five minutes, both thinking about what had happened earlier, all the while Kirkland getting more and more frustrated.

"Go on then," he blurted out, unable to contain himself.

DC Shrives looked up from her paper work.

"Go on then, what?" She asked.

"Look, I know you want to say something about that interview."

She said nothing and carried on working, head down staring at the paperwork.

"Look I think he's murdered his wife!" He said voice raised.

"Trevor, I know what you think, but the way you've gone about it, is all wrong. I mean what real, and I mean, concrete evidence do you have?"

Kirkland didn't answer and just sighed.

"See, all you have is speculation and hearsay, or a gut feeling. This poor man has just lost his wife. I mean, yes he may have been a little misguided by chancing a trip when the weather was going to be bad."

"A little misguided!" Kirkland interrupted.

"Listen, it's not against the law to not heed flood warnings," DC Shrives continued. "If it was, we'd have a lot of

Graham Mortons in prison."

"I know, I know," said Kirkland, now sounding as if conceding. "But her friends talk of her in such high regard; she was a lovely woman, by all accounts."

"Trevor, just listen to yourself. What are you always telling me? "'Don't get emotionally involved.'"

"I know, but did you see his face in there."

"Look, you're emotionally involved," DC Shrives replied, "Just let it go. If you go after this guy, it's going to look like harassment, especially after a completed investigation from Northants and with his wife just being killed. What do you think the press will make of it?"

"I suppose so." He replied, raising his eyebrows. "Always the voice of reason aren't you?"

"Just give it a few days; look at it afresh and take it from there."

"Yeah." Kirkland replied as he stood up. "I'm going to the machine, do you want a coffee?"

"No, I'm OK."

Kirkland left the office and headed down the corridor to get his drink, feeling that he'd lost.

# CHAPTER 23

Sarah waited for the expected call from DC Kirkland and as the evening drew on she became more agitated, believing that he'd forgotten.

She was in bed reading when the phone rang; It was Abhasra: Toi had given her Sarah's number as back up, to use just in case she couldn't get hold of Toi.

She had been trying to contact Toi for the past week and had begun to worry, so called to find out if everything was OK. This left Sarah having to break the news, something that she did not relish.

Abhasra listened as Sarah ran through the story, and when Sarah had finished, Abhasra surprisingly didn't seem stunned or shocked; quite emotionless really.

"This happens to us all the time," she said. "We try to get away to find a better life and many of us are exploited, it's unfortunate, but we know the risks."

Sarah was shocked by the way in which Abhasra took the news.

"But she was your friend." Sarah replied.

"I know, but what can I do. I mean, I look at the news from my country every week and every week they say that more and more girls go missing. Last week they said there were about five thousand women missing from the country."

"What! Five thousand?" Sarah gasped, in disbelief.

"Yes, the government thinks, no, they know, that the girls have been taken by gangs, who use them for prostitution. Or they are sold by parents, husbands, brothers, and so on, for brides in China, Japan and India, or end up working in brothels in Bangkok, Tokyo, and now in the countries in Europe."

"Sold by their parents? But, what's being done about it, surely the government, your government is doing something about this?"

"I don't know, so many things happen and it seems like nobody cares. Do you know, in China where they can only have one baby; if people have girls they sell them, and I've heard that many boy babies are stolen and sold. And now there's about ten thousand babies missing."

"Ten thousand?" Asked Sarah again in disbelief.

"Yes, I suppose I was lucky, usually the men who want brides, take girls of thirteen, fourteen or fifteen, not older women like me. But I suppose we know the risks. Well the older women like me, we know the risks."

Abhasra was almost emotionless, as emotionless as Sarah, when she'd given Karen the news a few days earlier and she now understood how Karen must have felt. Though angry that Abhasra showed little to no emotion, Sarah kept herself in check.

Abhasra asked when Toi's funeral was going to be held,

which was something that the women had not really thought about. The reality was that no one knew when or where it was going to take place.

"I'll try to contact Toi's family back home," said Abhasra, "I have an idea of where they live. I'll get my cousin to speak to them. But please let me know where and when it's going to be; I want to pay my respects."

"OK, I'll let you know."

* * *

The women said their goodbyes and no sooner had Sarah hung up, the phone rang once more.

"Hello." She answered.

"Hello, is that Mrs Braithwaite? It's DS Kirkland," came back the reply, his voice droning off as the sentence ended.

She could tell by the manner of his tone that his news wasn't going to be good.

"Thanks for calling back."

"That's Ok."

Then after taking a deep breath he said.

"Well this is how things stand at the moment. I'm sorry to say that we don't have enough evidence to charge Mr Morton with anything."

Sarah sighed,

"What about!"

"I know," Kirkland interrupted. "I know what you're going

to say, but everything that we have is circumstantial."

"But she wasn't a strong swimmer and she wasn't wearing a life jacket."

"Yes I know, I know."

"You know?" Sarah asked, surprised,

"Yes, I also know she was taking lessons, which she paid for."

"No," said Sarah, "he paid; Toi told me that he paid."

"Well, I checked with Waterfields and they said that she paid cash; so, maybe he gave her the money, but she definitely paid. You see that's like all of the evidence we have on him. It's all hearsay and very easy for him to defend. So I'm not sure if we can do anything more."

Sarah sighed. "What, the swimming lessons, him saying that she was a strong swimmer, then selling her clothes and jewellery before she was found, her not wearing a life jacket, going on holiday in the middle of a storm?" She reeled off.

"Yes, none of which is illegal. Look, I'm sorry Mrs Braithwaite, but I'm not sure what else I can do."

"Nothing by the sounds of it!" She replied angrily, before apologising. "Oh I'm sorry. I'm sure it's not your fault and you've done your best."

*I should have done better*. He thought.

"Yeah," sighed Kirkland, "Anyway, look, I'll have a look at it in a few days, to see if I've missed anything. Anyway I've got to go."

"OK, let me know if anything else happens, bye and thanks for calling."

* * *

Sarah sat in bed trying to come up with a way to trap Graham, but in the end had to concede that they'd come to the end of the road. *Without a confession, the bastard's got away with it.*

* * *

The following afternoon and with some reluctance, Sarah decided that she would go to see Graham, as she needed to find out when and where Toi's funeral was to be held. Unsure of how she would react to him, she made a conscious decision to be as positive and calm as possible.

Arriving down on the canal at about 2:30pm, she admired the early afternoon; the sun set in a brilliant blue sky and the fragrant, brightly coloured flowers, swayed in the warm early summer breeze. The persistent rain over the past few weeks had promoted the growth of lush green vegetation, leaving the canal path over grown, but full of life, *beautiful* she thought. But, there it was "The Duck", sat in its usual place, the one thing that didn't belong, the thing that spoiled the beauty and serenity of her image.

As she reached the barge, she paused before knocking; shaking her head when she saw a new set of twenty or so empty beer bottles that had been placed in a neat row along the side of the barge, as it was when Toi was alive. *Perhaps he was drunk when Toi went overboard* she thought, still trying to find a reason to why her friend had died.

She knocked on the hatch and didn't have to wait long before, to her surprise a woman answered, another Thai woman who looked a bit like Toi.

"I'm here to see Graham." She said, sharply, already forgetting that she was meant to be trying to stay calm.

The woman nodded, but said nothing and quickly disappeared back inside. Sarah figured that she'd gone to get Graham and a few moments later he appeared at the hatch, his mouth half full, still eating his lunch.

"What do you want?" He mumbled rudely.

"When's Toi's funeral?"

He said nothing for a few moments while he chewed and then swallowed the food that he ate, before moving his tongue over his teeth and round his mouth to remove the remnants.

"I've already done it." He said, smiling smugly. "She was buried last week at the cemetery in the town."

Surprised, Sarah asked "What? You've already buried her?"

"That's what I said."

*When I thought there was nothing more he could shock me with.* She thought shaking her head.

"Why didn't you let us know?" She said angrily.

In that second Sarah knew, she would get into an argument if she carried on.

"Do you know what, forget it." She said as she turned to leave in disgust.

"Well you had the police round here and I don't appreciate that."

"I said forget it."

She stopped and turned.

"Her body isn't even cold and you've got her replacement?"

With his new woman standing behind him, Graham smiled,

"I told you there were plenty more."

It was then that Sarah knew that he had killed Toi, she didn't know how she knew; it may have been his body language, the smile on his face, or the look in his eyes. Nevertheless, she knew.

Turning to the Thai woman, "Watch him, he's a bad man." She said before turning to go.

The woman seemed puzzled by her comments.

Still smiling first Graham, disappeared back through the hatch and back inside

"Come on!" he shouted to the woman, who promptly followed.

As she walked slowly back along the canal path, Sarah at first felt quite angry, but as the sunlight warmed her face, she reminded herself of what a kind, giving and forgiving person Toi was: Now instead of feeling anger she began to feel some peace.

\* \* \*

She got to the cemetery in town, just catching the Vicar as he closed up for the day. From him she found out that he'd performed six burials in the past week and because of her unusual name, remembered Toi and where she had been buried.

"She's over in the western corner, plot E35." He said, "It has a marker on it."

Sarah nodded.

"A friend was she?" He asked.

"Yes, a good friend."

"You weren't at the burial were you? I don't remember seeing you there."

"No, I wasn't sure when it was going to be held, were there many people there then?"

"No unfortunately; just one man."

*What? That bastard came to admire his work then.* She thought with a puzzled expression.

"Yes, as I recall, one tall man, grey suit, in his forties. Said he was a friend."

*Forties? That couldn't have been Graham. Hmm, I wonder who that was?*

"Anyway, my condolences; plot E35, western corner." He said before turning to go.

"OK, thanks." Sarah replied, before making her way across to the grave.

In the cemetery, the shade of the oak trees dropped the temperature by a couple of degrees and now feeling the chill, she swung the pink cardigan that she carried, over her shoulders and continued over to the western corner.

She arrived at two fresh mounds when she got to what she thought was the western corner and had to stoop down, and squint to read the plot numbers, which were scribbled in black marker pen onto two posts that looked like really large ice-lolly sticks. Plot E35 lay on the left in the shadow of a large oak tree, leaves of which cast crescent shaped shadows that danced about on the yellowy patch of clay, as the branches swayed about in the breeze.

She laid four lilies beside the post, then stood up. *At least your resting place is beautiful, s*he thought as she looked around the cemetery, then at the grave, now thinking how out of place the lilies looked laid on the fresh clay.

# CHAPTER 24

"DS Kirkland please."

"I'll try his extension." Replied the operator.

Sarah called Kirkland when she arrived home, wanting to tell him about Graham's new woman, more precisely, that he'd already found another woman; this being only a few weeks after Toi's death, which may have had some significance.

Seconds later, "putting you through." Said the operator.

"Hello. DS Kirkland."

"Ah yes," said Sarah, "It's Mrs Braithwaite."

"Oh, Mrs Braithwaite, Hi, what can I do for you?"

\* \* \*

"That doesn't surprise me." Said Kirkland, after Sarah told him about Graham's new woman.

"An Asian woman you say?"

"Yes she looks Thai and much younger than Toi." Sarah replied.

"Yeah, I saw her the other day; I thought it might be one of Toi's friends or family. Or something like that."

"No, Toi's got no family over here, well, apart from Graham, if you can call him that: And us at work; but she did have one other friend. A friend who lives in Surrey."

"I see, but, again, he's doing nothing illegal, so we can't really do anything."

"Yeah, but I can see him doing the same thing when he's finished with this one and we can't let that happen."

"Well, perhaps I'll go and check, I'll find an excuse to go to see him and let him know that I'm going to be watching him from now on."

There was a moments silence, before Kirkland sighed.

"Well, Mrs Braithwaite, like I said the other day, I'll let you know if anything turns up."

"Sarah, you can call me Sarah. She replied.

"OK Sarah, I'll let you know."

There was a strange silence as Kirkland thought for a moment, before they both began talking at the same time, then politely stopping to let the other continue. Then, on both hearing the silence started talking, then stopping again.

"You first." Said Sarah

"No you, I insist."

"Oh, thanks, all I was going to say is goodbye." She chuckled.

"Oh OK," He replied slowly.

"Now you."

"Oh, it was nothing."

"Come on," She said. "I told you what I had to say."

"Oh." He said hesitantly. "I just wondered, if." Then he paused, a little too long for Sarah's patients.

"If what?" she asked, now voice raised.

"Oh nothing. It doesn't matter."

"What the bloody hell was it?" She barked, almost in anger. After a short pause.

"I just wondered if you'd like to go for a drink, sometime." He said, his words speeding up and then tapering off as he came to the end of the sentence.

There was an awkward silence as Sarah with the feeling of butterflies in her stomach and one of apprehension, thought about what she'd just heard.

"YES, yes" She blurted out. "Yes, that would be nice." She said now regaining her composure and not wanting to seem too eager. "But do you always ask your witnesses out."

"No," Kirkland chuckled, "Just the good looking ones." He replied sarcastically.

\* \* \*

A few minutes later Kirkland readied himself to get off home, *just one more thing to do.*

He picked up his receiver, dialled a number and after a few moments.

"Hi Mike, it's Trevor. Rang you on the off chance that you might be in. How's it going mate?"

Kirkland went through what had gone on since the day of their chat.

"Well don't sound so disappointed." Said Mike. "I did say that it would be hard to get him."

"Yeah well, I just thought I'd be able to get the old so and so. It's at times like these that makes me ask, is it worth it.

Then after a short pause.

"I think I've taken it personally," he continued. "I even went to the funeral."

"Bloody hell, it's unlike you to take it like that."

"I know, but she sounded like a really nice person and the worst thing about it is, no one else turned up at the funeral. No one," his voice now sounding shaky, as if about to burst into tears.

"You did," Mike replied. "Look mate, I was there once and you know what I did."

Clearing the tears from his eyes, Kirkland replied. "Don't tell me, I've heard it all before," emotion clearly heard in his voice.

"Yeah, but don't knock it until you've tried it.

Then after a moments silence.

"You know what it did for me and I couldn't be happier." Mike continued.

* * *

Five years earlier, Mike's life looked as though it was going down the pan; after a couple of high profile mistakes at work where he spent the majority of his days, things started to look bad. This had a knock on effect in his personal life, which lead to alcohol taking the place of what a loving family had once provided.

His wife finally threatened to divorce him if he didn't get help, which he did; and it was whilst attending Alcoholics Anonymous, that he got talking to another attendee, who introduced him to self-help. He was introduced to a book, which he believes changed his life. It talked about time bound goal setting, visualisation techniques and what he really found useful; documenting the steps needed to achieve goals. Within a year, he and his family had moved to Northampton, he started a new job with Northants police and has never looked back.

\* \* \*

"Trev, I think you need to do something," Mike continued. "You've been sounding down just recently. Look, I'll text you the name of the book."

"Yeah," Kirkland droned.

*I can't be doing this.* He thought, thinking how reading some funny old book was really going to help.

"Look, I know there's a job coming up, here soon; well soon meaning later this year, or early next year. I know that it might seem a long way off, but perhaps a change in scenery would do you some good."

"I don't know." Kirkland droned once more.

"Come on! Wouldn't it be great for us to work together again?"

"I suppose so. But, one thing at a time. Let me have the name of that book and we'll take it from there."

"Good, that's the spirit; I'll text it over after this. Anyway, you got any gossip, is that DCI of yours; you know, Thornton. Is he still, you know, seeing to that Shrives woman?"...

# CHAPTER 25

Mike was right; a change was what Kirkland needed, as Toi's death only served to highlight how unhappy he'd been over the past few years.

After first reading the book that Mike suggested and then putting into action what he took from it, Kirkland's life took on new significance.

With the emphasis on, *'a better quality of life,'* within nine months, Kirkland had moved to a small village in Northamptonshire and took up a roll in Northants police, where he found the pace slower than that of the city and all together much more enjoyable. Where there was once cynicism and disbelief, there was now openness and appreciation, as Kirkland now took the time to recognise and appreciate beauty in all things and was not so quick to jump to conclusions.

His work colleagues saw him as an old wise head and respected him, which was something that he'd rarely experienced back in Wattsford.

During his first few months away, he kept in contact with Sarah, and although, *'how to trap Graham,'* was the main topic of conversation, for the most part, there was a deeper connection between them; their need for companionship blossoming into a relationship, which was doomed from the start, given their distance apart and their lifestyles.

Sarah chose to put her two young children first, while Kirkland continually cancelling their engagements opted instead to establish himself in his new role. This brought on an inevitability, that saw them grow apart and in the end, a reluctant, but mutually agreed end to the fledgling relationship; both putting its break down, down to, *'Bad timing,'* though they agreed to stay friends and keep in touch.

Though things were better with Kirkland, he still carried a nagging feeling; the circumstances surrounding Toi's death leading him to view Graham as the one that got away. This feeling was compounded when in the following spring, he took a trip to see some friends from the old constabulary.

After lunching with DCI Thornton and the now 'DS' Shrives, in a calculated move, Kirkland invited them to walk back to the station via the canal.

Unbeknown to his colleagues, he hoped to see Graham, or more precisely, that Graham would see him, as he wanted Graham to know that he still had an eye on him.

Unfortunately, Thornton declined, as he had to prepare for a meeting that he had to attend that afternoon, but DS Shrives eager to get some sun onto her winter white skin thought the walk back to the station would do her some good.

The weather had been mild and fairly dry since the beginning of the year and today, even the breeze was warm. The mildness brought out an abundance of deep green coloured foliage, along with bright lightly coloured hog weed and a mixture of pink and pale green oak, apple and sycamore blossom which covered parts of the canal path

As the pair walk slowly up the path, DS Shrives's chatter fell on deaf ears, as Kirkland miles away, thought about what he would say if he saw Graham, afraid about how he would react. *What if I don't see him,* he thought and fearing what the outcome might be.

"Trevor, Trevor!" said DS Shrives voice raised, "you OK. You don't seem to be all here."

"I'm fine, "Kirkland replied. "I've just got something on my mind."

DS Shrives smiled,

"Penny for your thoughts," she said.

Her smile and genuine interest encouraged him to feel less apprehensive.

Now without the burden of competition for the attentions of the Detective Inspector and limited promotion opportunities, Kirkland began to see her in a different light. *This woman is beautiful,* he thought, in that moment his eyes displaying a lustful desire, which made her blush.

"Well." She said red faced, looking down at the path,

"OK," said Kirkland, regaining his focus. "Look, you may not like what I'm about to say, but I need to get this of my chest."

"Try me?" She said, with an eagerness that played itself out in her body language: The subtle, but distinct movement of her hips, her broadening smile and fluttering lashes, showing that she'd become receptive to him.

"Well, you know that guy we interviewed last year."

DS Shrives thought for a second,

"What guy?" She asked, almost disappointed that his question wasn't of a more personal nature.

"That old geezer, the one that I thought. But I really know, murdered his wife."

She thought again then shook her head.

"Vaguely," she replied. Stopping to think once more. "About a year ago?" She asked, shaking her head once more.

"OK," said Kirkland, "Well this woman fell off her barge last Easter."

"Oh, I remember now," she interrupted, as if just awakened. "I seem to remember that you gave him a hard time."

"Do you also remember giving me a hard time?"

"Yeah, but you were a bit of a dinosaur back then. Plus, Thornton didn't want the potential publicity, I seem to remember."

Kirkland looked at her, shaking his head and then smiled, subconsciously trying to remind her that there were sordid rumours involving her circulating at that time.

"And no, it wasn't like that! ." She continued, picking up on his unspoken insinuation.

"But I thought, we thought, I mean everyone thought that."

"I know what you all thought;" she interrupted angrily. "One drink, just one drink and nothing else happened. It's the same old thing with you men and your dirty little minds. You think all good looking women all use their bodies to get."

Now trying to defuse the situation Kirkland interrupted.

"Good looking! What good looking woman." He said, sarcastically grinning broadly, causing them both to burst into laughter.

"OK, ok, sorry about that, I just thought." He chuckled.

"So, tell me about this guy then." She replied now eager to change the subject...

* * *

Sunisa, a 21-year-old Thai woman, who Graham had met before Toi's death and married soon after, had only been in the country just over a year.

Graham found her through the use of one of his contacts, meeting her in a special singles bar in London; the special being that it dealt in supplying illegally smuggled in girls, as young as 13, and young women for London's sex trade, as well as for men who were willing to pay for brides.

Sunisa had paid the equivalent of one thousand pounds for passage to the UK and on arrival was told that she owed more than double that amount for her passage, which now amounted to more than three thousand pounds.

After the smugglers threatened to harm her family back home, she agreed to work as an escort at a London bar to pay off what she owed.

Graham "saved" her, by paying her debt off and reminded her of that every time he beat her for any minor infraction. Her situation was compounded, as she had not found legitimate work in the time that she'd spent in the UK, which frustrated Graham, as the insurance money that he'd received following Toi's death had started to dwindle. He now constantly told Sunisa that he would get rid of her and "find someone else."

\* \* \*

Today Sunisa was out on deck, where she'd been for most of the morning, cleaning the cabin windows and new brass fittings.

An old trebly sounding radio crackled in the background and she hummed and sometimes mouthed the words of the songs. With her long jet-black coloured hair tied back, she wore a knee length pale green floral patterned cotton dress, with a fitted bodice and loose skirt, which flapped about in the warm breeze; her yellow dirt stained rubber gloves spoiling this picture of beauty.

Mr Jenkins, the owner of the neighbouring barge, had been sitting, watching Sunisa from his wheelhouse for about fifteen minutes, his eyes slowly feeling their way around her body as she cleaned. He wondered how a man like Graham could possibly attract such a beauty, as he played out an erotic fantasy in his mind, briefly looking over at the barge and then double taking when she caught him staring at her.

She gave him the briefest of acknowledgement in the form of a smile before being startled, jumping when Graham shouted.

"Haven't you finished yet?" as he walked up the stairs to the top of the hatch, "I want something to eat. What's for lunch?"

As if just been caught, the guilty looking Mr Jenkins skulked off and disappeared inside, not before forcing out a smile and nodding at Graham as they glanced at each other.

"Nearly." She replied.

"What was he doing?" Asked Graham.

Sunisa didn't answer and seemed puzzled.

"I saw him looking at you, what were you doing?" He growled.

Staring at the deck the now frightened Sunisa tried not to make eye contact with him and just had the chance to say.

"Nothing, I didn't do anything,"

Before he gave her a backhand, the force of which sent her stumbling into the side of the wheelhouse before falling onto the deck.

As Sunisa looked up at him, nursing the right side of her face, and with tears in her eyes,

"I paid for you," he growled, "I paid for you; do you want me to send you back?"

She hunched and tensed her body, bracing herself for impact as he raised his hand once more, but was surprised when one didn't come

.

"What do you think you're doing?" Said a voice from behind.

DS Shrives had grabbed Grahams arm, stopping him from delivering the blow.

* * *

Kirkland had run through Toi's story with DS Shrives, who was now intrigued; though the evidence was flimsy, or as she diplomatically put it, "incomplete," she saw how a crime could have been committed and couldn't believe that she didn't listen to Kirkland a year ago. *I must of had my head up my arse back then*. She thought.

As they approached The Duck she suggested to Kirkland that they go onboard.

"Just to have a look," she said. "If he had another woman, he could have done the same thing to her. If he asks what we're doing onboard, we can say, that there's been a couple of burglaries reported."

* * *

"You," said Graham looking at Kirkland. "What are you doing here, this is private property."

"There's been a spate of burglaries," Said DS Shrives and after taking a second to realise that she no longer had to lie said.

"You were assaulting this woman."

Graham watched in silence as Kirkland pushed passed him, knelt down and taking her by the arm, helped Sunisa back to her feet.

"Back to your old tricks then?" DS Shrives continued.

"Old Tricks, what old tricks, what are you talking about?"

"I'll take her in to get a statement," said Kirkland, as he pushed his way pass Graham once more, glaring at him as he led Sunisa back to the hatch.

"What are you doing, you can't go in there!" Said Graham.

"We saw what you did, said DS Shrives, "now, you need to stay calm, or we'll be doing this down the station."

Kirkland and Sunisa climbed down through the hatch and down the stairs. *What a transformation*, thought Kirkland. From the outside, it was clear to see that the barge had been refurbished; a polished pine stained deck, giving way to an oak wheelhouse, where most of the once rusting metal fittings were now brightly polished brass. Hanging flower baskets adorned the deck and the duck mascot had been given a new lick of green, brown and yellow paint.

Inside had a contemporary look and feel to it; in the lounge area the once seventies drab gave way to magnolia washed cabin walls, newly refurbished green and red seating and a flat screen TV. Only the coffee table had been kept, a reminder of an earlier time and it stood out like a sore thumb.

Sunisa, still holding her face, sat down.

"Can I get you anything," said Kirkland, as he scanned the room. "Something to drink?" He asked.

Shaking her head she just stared down at the floor.

"What's your name?"

"Sunisa." She replied slowly.

"Sunisa. Well, Sunisa what's been going on?"

"Are you the police?" She asked with a trembling voice.

\* \* \*

Up on deck, DS Shrives quizzed Graham.

"What's going on? Why were you hitting her.? Who is she anyway?"

"Well, I wasn't hitting her."

The police officers had not actually seen him hit Sunisa, so DS Shrives fished for some kind of confession.

"Why was she holding her face then?"

"The clumsy mare tripped and fell against the side of the wheelhouse. I was helping her up. And she's my wife, if you must know."

*Clumsy mare!*

"Your wife?" She replied in disbelief, "Well, I had to stop you from hitting her."

"I wasn't hitting her." He repeated.

"Well that's what it looked like to me: Shall we wait to see what your wife says then?"

"Look, I wasn't hitting her, you'll see." Graham replied smugly, now with his arms folded across his chest, in the full knowledge that Sunisa wouldn't say anything to incriminate him.

A moment later, showing his impatience he said.

"Look you can't keep me here and, I've asked you not to go into my barge and you've ignored me. I'm going to complain about this."

"Just calm down. We believed a crime was being committed."

"I thought you said there had been a spate of burglaries." He replied. "I know what you're up to."

*Rumbled!*

"Well there has been." She said now less convincingly.

Graham turned and headed back towards the hatch,

"Look, I want you off my barge now!" he ordered.

DS Shrives followed Graham as he went through the hatch, down the steps and in to the living area. There, Kirkland still talked to Sunisa and in his right hand, as if about to open it,

Graham's self help book, which had been resting on the old coffee table.

"Give me that!" said Graham, snatching the book from Kirkland's hand. "I want you off this barge now, or I'm going to make a complaint. This is harassment."

Kirkland looked over to DS Shrives who raised her eyebrows and shrugged her shoulders.

"Come on, I want you out of here."

"You were going to hit her weren't you?" Asked Kirkland

Graham's eyes widened on hearing Kirkland's words, as he now knew that they had not seen him do anything.

"Prove it." He said belligerently.

Kirkland glanced at Sunisa, who turned to look at the floor once more.

I'll be watching you." Said Kirkland, before heading towards the hatch.

Graham glared at Sunisa before following the detectives up through the hatch and watched in the warm sunlight, as they made their way off the barge and walked slowly up the canal path towards the town.

Inside, Sunisa smoothed out a crumpled business card that she'd held tightly in her hand and then tucked away into her bodice.

\* \* \*

"Well," said DS Shrives, "what did she say?"

Kirkland sighed, "Not a lot," he replied, "She's shit scared of him, I'm not even sure if she's legal."

"I think she is, he told me that she's his wife."

Kirkland sighed once more

"Yes, I know." Said DS Shrives. "What makes a beautiful young girl take up with a slob like that?"

"Look, I'm not going to judge him." Replied Kirkland. "I just want her to be safe and not to end up like his last wife."

"Yeah, I know what you mean now. But I think it may be too late to do anything about his last wife."

"I have a friend who lives nearby, I'll get her to keep an eye on things." Said Kirkland. "If you can get the beat officers just to keep an eye out, perhaps he'll think twice before trying anything."

Painfully, it seemed as though Graham had won again, but the pair made the most of the sunshine and slowly made their way to the police station; finally getting to know each other.

* * *

On the barge, with his book held under an armpit, Graham had a clamp-like grip on both of Sunisa's arms.

"What did you tell him?" he asked, while he shook her.

"Nothing" Sunisa whined, "I didn't tell him anything."

"You'd better not have," he said, relaxing his grip a little. "Remember, I bought you and without me, they'll send you back; understand?"

Sunisa nodded.

"Do you understand?" He growled.

"Yes, Yes." She replied, the strain on her shoulders beginning to burn.

He released his grip, embraced her tightly and grinned, his yellowy brown tea stained teeth making Sunisa reel slightly.

"Do something nice for lunch."

As Sunisa disappeared into the galley he sat down, noticing that he was still holding the self-help book.

Looking up at the highly glossed finished ceiling as if in thought, he then stood up and headed off to the bedroom, on entering pushing the door to near closed, which slowly swung back to half open on its dodgy hinge.

Kneeling down on his side of the bed, he pushed the self-help book in to a slit in the mattress; a hidden pocket where he kept his most intimate of items, while through the crack between the door and the doorframe, Sunisa silently watched.

# CHAPTER 26

The warm spring made way for a hot summer; one of the hottest ever recorded and for the first time talk of global warming filled the news. The summer months soon gave way to the usual British weather and by late September the country was gripped by spates of autumn showers, where flood warnings were issued for various parts of the country.

Karen sat in her dimly lit dressing room in front of a dressing table, going through a list written in the back of a book.

Putting the book down on to the table, she glanced at herself in the mirror forcing out a smile, then a broad grin, revealing her teeth, then back to a smile. She moved her tongue over her teeth, then leaning forward she picked up a large pink powder puff and dabbed her forehead, then tutting and rolling her eyes, remembering that when she got out onto set, a makeup artist would probably want to re-apply her makeup.

She had just finished rehearsing lines for a television soap in which she played a major role and used the book she now read to remind herself of why she'd made such big changes to her life.

The book offered a few pages at the back to allow the reader to list desires, goals, objectives and a path that could be taken to reach them; which she'd done a couple of weeks after buying the book some eighteen months earlier.

A knock at the dressing room door made her jump.

"Yes, come in."

A production assistant, a small Indonesian woman came in.

"You're on in ten." The production assistant said. "Is there anything I can get you Mrs O'Brian?"

"Hi Arti. No thanks, I'm OK; actually, I feel a bit of a headache coming on, if you could get me some paracetamol that would be great."

"OK, I'll be back in a second." Replied Arti, bowing her head slightly before leaving the room.

In that moment, Karen got a strong feeling of déjà vou; Arti's mannerisms somehow reminded her of Toi, which made her think about what had happened all those months ago. A few minutes later there was another knock at the door, it was Arti, back with the paracetamol.

"Here you go." She said, handing Karen the pills. "You're on in five."

Karen smiled and thanked Arti who then left the room.

\* \* \*

An hour later, after completing her filming, Karen returned to the dressing room where she poured herself a large glass of red wine and while she sipped it, thought about the women who she'd left behind in the kitchen.

\* \* \*

Following Toi's death, she finished reading her book, after which she made her list of desires; one of which, was to *'Become an Actress:'* Which is something she went all out to do; and after nine months of doing adverts and bit parts, landed a role in one of the major soaps and now appeared on the television every couple of days.

\* \* \*

As she ran through the events leading up to and after Toi's death, she realised though they all knew Toi, there was one other thing that linked Sarah, Graham and herself.

*The Book. He was reading the same book, there is just something about it.* She thought.

It was one thing that had always played on her mind and now reminded her of the conversation that she'd had with Sarah on the day that they found out that Toi had died. Sarah's words now came flooding back. *"A person can be positive and commit acts of carnage."* With an understanding how this could be, she continued staring at the book on the table.

Moments later, a revelation; she was hit by an idea and quickly reached over and picked up her mobile, which rested on the dresser.

Excited, she called Sarah, but there was no answer, so hung up, then dialled another number, this time getting Sarah's mobile answer phone, so left a message.

"Sarah, give me a call, It's about Toi and Graham, I need to talk to you. Make sure you call back when you get this."

* * *

The rain lashed down on to The Duck, which was moored on the canal at Croxten. In the bedroom Graham, out of breath and sweaty, grunted and then rolled over.

Underneath him lay Sunisa, also trying to catch her breath and feeling disgusted with herself. After rolling over onto his back, he stared at the ceiling, breathing heavily with an almost half smile on his face.

"That was good wasn't it?"

"Yes." Sunisa replied, trying to muster a smile.

Getting up, he picked up his trousers and underpants from the floor and grabbed a copy of yesterday's newspaper from the dresser, before heading for the toilet.

The bedroom door did its usual thing on the dodgy hinge, leaving the door ajar. Sunisa lay there for a second trying to get the taste and smell of his sweaty body from her mouth and nostrils, before getting up and staring at her naked body in the dresser mirror.

The feeling of disgust rose within her once more, but this time with herself, for getting in to the situation in which she found herself.

Reaching for the box of tissues that rested on the dresser, she pulled one out then wiped Graham's fluid from herself before sitting back down on the bed. Now staring into space, she wished that she was back home in Samut Prakan, her Thailand home, where the grass definitely began to seem greener.

Sitting on his side of the bed, she took a welcomed and pleasurable respite from Graham's continuous nagging, groping and beating; feeling relief, as if in that moment, a weight had been lifted from her. As her mind wondered, she remembered his stash hidden in the mattress.

Often having thought about taking a peek on several occasions and now feeling a rush of excitement, owing to a belief that he was definitely going to be out of the room for some time, she let her inquisitiveness get the better of her.

After getting down on all fours on his side of the bed, she slid her hand into the slit in the mattress, first pulling out the self help book, which she rested on the bed. Out next came a couple of gold rings, an old gold chain, a mobile phone, and a roll of money, which she held aloft as if to examine it almost in disbelief, as he always complained about how much money he didn't have. She placed all the items on the bed and notice that one thing stood out from the rest. The book, *what is so precious about this,* she thought. Picking it up, she first flicked through its pages, then held it by its spine, shaking it, waiting for something to fall out.

Like mist, outside the bedroom porthole, the rain seemed to steam up the glass as it fell heavier.

The noise of the droplets hitting the deck began to sound quite loud and woke Graham who after his exertions had fallen asleep on the toilet.

Inside the bedroom Sunisa, still interested in this seemingly valuable but uninteresting book again flicked through its pages once more. Coming towards its end, she came across some writing scrawled on the last few pages and not being able to read English very well couldn't make out what the scribble read.

Suddenly, she heard the toilet flush, *He must have finished.* Her excitement quickly turned to fear as she heard the toilet door close. Quickly she gathered up the items, fell to the floor, then stuffed them back into the mattress, quickly getting to her feet as Graham entered the room.

"What are you doing?"  He asked seeing that Sunisa stood on his side of the bed.

"Nothing." She replied, sheepishly.

After slowly walking over to her, he forced her to back up into the gap between the bed and the two walls in the corner of the room. Then staring intensely into her eyes he grabbed her left hand causing her to jump and then forced it open. On seeing nothing, he did the same thing with her right.

He nodded, then looked at her naked body then smiled.

"OK, I believe you; you'd better get some dinner on." He said now backing off, letting her out of the corner and allowing her to grab a nightgown before leaving the room.

As he sat down on the bed, his large frame making it creak under his weight, something shiny caught his eye, something just sticking out from under the quilt. Looking down he found one of his gold rings. *What are you doing here,* he thought, already knowing the answer to the question. He'd been standing watching Sunisa through the crack in the door, while she stuffed his valuables back into the mattress.

After putting the ring back through the slit, he rummaged around for a second before pulling the book out, immediately turning to the pages at the back. He then read a couple of sentences, and then stared into space, as if deep in thought, now realising what had to be done.

Later on, the rain stopped, but the wind still blustered around outside. Inside Graham and Sunisa were able to relax without the noise of rain noisily beating down on the deck.

After dinner, they sat in the lounge area, Sunisa nervously looking at the TV, while having an eye on Graham. He sat next to her reading from his book, every so often stopping to think, and occasionally making a note in the back of it.

She caught him staring at her a couple of times; him smiling at her then his face disappearing back into the book. *Does he know that I've been through his things?*

She suspiciously thought it uncanny that on the day she'd gathered enough courage to see what he'd hidden in the mattress, was the same day that he decided to start reading this book and now he was acting unusually nice.

\* \* \*

"We certainly now know the meaning of autumn showers." A voice from the television said.

Graham lent forward, his attention now completely taken up by the evening weather report.

"It is expected to be very wet for the next week across many parts of the country." The report continued. "The MET office has issued a severe weather warning; and warns of localised flooding.

"Experts say that this is destined to be one of the wettest Octobers on record and believe that some areas, especially those in the south east could see storms rivalling those of Easter 1998, where four people lost their lives in Northamptonshire and Warwickshire."

"The public are advised to take extra care over the next few days."

Once the report had finished, Graham lent back into his seat and now showing less concern smiled at Sunisa, before burying his head back into the book.

\* \* \*

The following day, from an expensive looking hotel room, Karen lay in the middle of a king size four-poster bed talking to Sarah.

"Sorry it's taken this long to get back to you," said Sarah, "I got your message, but I was up the hospital with Carl. He did his hamstring yesterday, playing football.

"Oh, poor thing. Is he alright now?"

"Yes, he's fine. So what's this about Toi and Graham?"

"Well…" Karen replied.

Karen explained her version of what could have happened leading up to Toi's death and now half believed that Graham had incriminated himself.

"I can't believe he would have been so stupid as to do something like that." Said Sarah once Karen had finished.

"I do. Remember how arrogant he was, nothing would surprise me about that man. And didn't you say that he had another woman? What's to say he hasn't done the same thing to her?"

"Yeah, you're right, Sarah replied, her voice droning off to almost silence. "I tried to put the whole thing behind me: I mean we all put the whole thing behind us. I'd almost forgotten what a horrible slob he was, and yes, the last time I saw him, he'd already got Toi's replacement in."

"Well what do you think?" Karen asked.

"I'll call the police," Sarah replied. "I think I've got a card knocking about somewhere, of that detective who was looking into the case; you know the one."

"Kirkman?" asked Karen.

"No Kirkland."

"Oh yes, I knew it was something like that."

"I've got to go," Said Sarah, "I can hear Carl calling; I'll let you know what happens."

# CHAPTER 27

It was early evening and as predicted it was cold; the clouds taking on a greyish blue complexion such was the colour of the encroaching darkness and of course, it was raining.

After her conversation with Karen, Sarah grew more and more concerned, so decided to go to The Duck.

She'd only been down to the canal on a few occasions following Toi's death and had only done so within the past few months, owing to a request that Kirkland had made, which was to keep an eye on Graham and his new woman. But, every time she'd reluctantly dragged herself down to the moorings, the barge had not been there. But now feeling that she'd not done enough, she had to see if Graham's new woman was all right.

Speeding along, almost jogging as the rain began to fall heavier, her concentration firmly fixed on the canal path, she twice almost ran into cyclists who didn't avoid displaying their annoyance.

With only her racing green coloured hooded waterproof coat for protection, she squinted as the rain from time to time lashed against her face, obscuring her vision, and that coupled with The Ducks new condition, made her race past its moorings. Not finding the barge further up the path, and thinking that Graham may have taken a trip, she stopped and slowly walked back.

Then seeing a familiar site; beer bottles lined up along the side of a barge, and squinting as the natural light diminished, she caught sight of The Duck's mascot. *So that's what he's done with the insurance money* she thought, on seeing the way in which the barge had been decorated.

Standing there in front of the hatch, she now felt fear and was increasingly unsure if knocking would be the right thing to do. But remembering that she had done that just before she found out Toi had died, told herself to *be strong, be positive, everything will be fine.*

She moved down the path and peered through the rear starboard porthole and saw part of the living room area. Two people were sitting, or more precisely two sets of legs were positioned as if two people were sitting down.

*OK, so she's still alive, perhaps I'm over reacting.* Relieved, she stepped back and again considered knocking once more, but instead turned to go, but was startled when she heard the hatch opening. Like a frightened animal, she backed off in to the shadow of the bushes, squinting, silently straining to see who would appear.

She watched as a hooded figure appeared and saw from their frame that it could not have been Graham. The person held four beer bottles and slowly shuffled toward the bottles that were already lined up. Now was her opportunity.

"Hello," Sarah called out.

The person carried on as if they had not heard and placed the bottles in a line at the side of the barge.

"Hello." She called out once more, this time stepping out of the bushes.

The person stopped, looked over, and started to slowly back away. As the person turned to go, Sarah realised that she must have frightened them.

"Hey, it's OK, it's OK!" She called.

Sunisa thought that she recognised the voice and then stopped.

"It's OK," Sarah repeated. "I just want to talk, just talk."

As Sarah drew closer, Sunisa recognised her face and for a moment the two women stood looking at each other, squinting as the rain continued to fall, each waiting for the other to begin talking.

"I know you." Said Sunisa, trying to produce a smile.

"Yes," replied Sarah, nodding. "We met last year, when you were first here."

"Yes, I remember," said Sunisa, glancing at the hatch. "What do you want?"

"Well, I was just out for a walk and passed and saw you."

*What are you doing you stupid woman.* Sarah thought to herself. *What would anyone be doing out in this weather?* She checked herself and then came clean.

"I came to see you; I want to know if you are alright."

Nervous, Sunisa again glanced at the hatch; the half smile disappearing and now looking down at the deck nodded.

"I'm OK," she said unconvincingly.

"Are you sure?"

"Yes, look you'd better go." Sunisa replied nervously.

Unconvinced Sarah said. "Look, whatever's going on, you don't have to put up with it. Just leave him. I can help if you want."

"Look, you'd better go." Sunisa repeated and now backing off towards the hatch.

Just then, the hatch opened and Graham shouted through. "What are you doing out there?"

"I'm coming." Sunisa replied.

Turning to Sarah she whispered, "I've got to go. You've got to go."

Sarah pulled a piece of paper from her coat pocket and shoved it into Sunisa's hand.

"This is my number, call me."

Sunisa looked at the hatch once more and then at the piece of paper in her hand, the rainwater beginning to soak it and almost in a panic said.

"I've got to go."

"Call me," said Sarah, closing Sunisa's hand. "Promise that you'll call."

Sunisa pulled her hand away and nodded, just as Graham pushed his head through the hatch, squinting as the rain blustered around his face.

"Where are you? What you doing?" He growled.

Frightened, Sarah turned and quickly walked off down the path as Sunisa turned to face him.

"Who was that?"

"Oh, just some woman, selling some stuff." She replied, before quickly squeezing past him, heading in the direction of the hatch.

After standing there for a few seconds, looking down the path, trying to see who Sunisa had been talking to, but too late to really see anyone, he turned and headed back inside.

* * *

Inside, Sunisa had already taken off her coat and had locked herself in the toilet. She held the wet scrap of paper that Sarah had given to her, trying to make out what the numbers read, as the rain had caused some of them to merge. Hearing the hatch close and the trudge of Graham's heavy footsteps down the stairs, she stuffed the piece of paper into her pocket. She flushed the toilet, waited until Graham had passed and took a deep breath, before unlocking the door and stepping out into the hallway.

Entering the living room area she saw Graham open another bottle of beer, letting the bottle cap fall to the floor.

The sound from the television filled the room, which he then muted.

"So, what was she selling?" He asked, before taking a swig from his bottle.

Sunisa looked puzzled.

"The woman you spoke to outside."

Fear could now be seen on her face.

"You know, that woman." He said now thinking Sunisa's reaction looked a bit suspicious.

"Err, yes, yes, the woman." She replied, the fear of being caught the only thing she could think of.

"Well, what was she selling?" He repeated.

Sunisa quickly scanned the room and focused on the blanket that he'd brought out from the bedroom.

"Blankets!" She blurted out.

"Blankets?" He asked disbelievingly and furrowed browed. As it was raining; and where would this woman have them stored?

"Yes, It was a gypsy woman, selling blankets. She said winter was coming and would I be interested in buying a blanket. I said no."

"Hmmm, OK." He replied, before the images on the TV caught his eye. Turning the sound back on he listened to the weather report.

'**Eleven people were rescued from caravans in North**

Yorkshire as heavy rain threatened towns and villages across the county, while the Met Office issued a weather warning for south-east England and east Anglia.

'The Met Office said temperatures across Britain are expected to drop to as low as -4C over the next few days, and heavy rain is predicted in England and Scotland over the coming week, potentially hindering recovery efforts in flood-devastated areas of Cumbria.'

'North Yorkshire fire and rescue service said they were summoned to Knaresborough, four miles north east of Harrogate, at 2am this morning.'

'Eleven people in total were assisted from caravans by ourselves at a caravan park near the river Nidd in Knaresborough overnight," a spokeswoman said.'

'There is a risk of further severe weather conditions which threatens to affect parts of the UK later this week.'

'Showers are likely to be heavy and frequent at times across eastern parts of the UK'

\* \* \*

"I think we should go to Northampton to see my mother." He said as he lowered the sound on the television.

Sunisa didn't respond straight away, always wary when Graham spoke to her without raising his voice.

"What do you think? Do you want to meet my mother?" He continued.

Sunisa nodded slowly.

"OK that settled then, we'll go to see my mother on Friday. You have to take some warm clothes. OK?"

Sunisa joined him on the couch, as he picked up his mobile phone and dialled a number and seconds later was shouting into it.

"Hi, yes mum it's me. Yes, it's Graham, we're coming up to you. Yes me and the girl; By Barge. OK I've got to go now, but we'll be up in about five days. Bye"

Sunisa thought for a second, *warm clothes, by barge?*

He hung up and turned to Sunisa.

"We'll be taking the barge up, when we go to see my mother, it should be OK."

"What about the weather warnings?" She asked, now showing some concern.

"We'll be fine."

"But it just said that!" She just had time to say before he interrupted.

"I said we'll be fine!" He shouted, unable to contain himself.

She cowered, "OK, OK we'll be fine." She repeated back, before he returned to his relative calm.

"We'll be safe, you'll see," he said grinning broadly. Get me another beer."

She got up and headed for the galley and stooped; her

backside facing him, to pick up the top from his last bottle, which he'd left on the floor.

He made her jump up straight when he slapped her bottom, causing her to miss the bottle top. Turning to look at him as he smiled a smarmy smile.

"I've got something for you tonight," he said, raising his eyebrows and trying to give a sexy grin.

Turning back she stooped with a look of disgust on her face, this time grabbing the bottle top from the floor before he had the chance to touch her and then disappeared into the hallway.

\* \* \*

At 10pm, Sunisa and Graham sat in front of the television, Graham unconscious from a large meal and nine bottles of beer that he'd consumed and snored loudly.

For the past three hours, Sunisa worried about the trip he'd planned, and the suspicious way he'd been acting. She put her hand into her pocket, feeling for the phone number Sarah had given to her, somehow knowing that she had to use it, knowing that somehow her life depended on it. After finding it, she looked at it once before it returned back to her pocket.

"Graham, Graham!" She said, shaking him, trying to wake him.

He groaned and then belched.

"Graham, come on, time for bed."

After standing up, she pulled his right arm, willing him to stand up and when that didn't work, she knelt down in front of him and gently slapped his face.

"Graham, come on."

He belched again, this time into her face, which made her wince and then exhale. Now angered she slapped him harder.

"Graham, come on!"

He woke this time, "What is it? What?" He said before closing his eyes again, the red shape of Sunisa's hand beginning to appear on his face, where she'd slapped him.

"Graham!" She shouted and was about to slap him once more, when he woke.

"OK, OK."

"Time for bed!"

She stood up, helped to pull him to his feet, and as he swayed she supported him, leading him through the hallway in to the bedroom. Helping him into bed fully clothed, she switched the lights out and closed the bedroom door.

Sitting back down in the living area, she stared at his mobile phone, which he'd left on top of his book on the old coffee table.

## CHAPTER 28

Sarah, already in bed received a call on her mobile and as she picked up the call. *Don't recognise this number*, she thought.

"Hello."

At first there was no reply, only the faint sound of a television in the background could be heard.

"Hello," she repeated.

When no answer came back, she hung up, again thinking that she didn't recognise the number, but before she had the chance to put the phone down, it rang once more. *Same number?*

"Hello, hello." Again the faint noise coming from a television could be heard. *There's someone obviously there.*

"If you keep calling, I'm going to call the police." She said, now thinking it was a crank call.

Moments later.

"Hello," said a voice on the other end, which for a  moment filled Sarah with excitement; butterflies in her stomach, as the person on the other end sounded so much like Toi, but realising how ridiculous that thought was, she then recognised it to be Sunisa's voice.

"Hi, is it you?" I'm Sarah, I came to see you earlier, are you OK?"

"Yes, my name is Sunisa."

"Sunisa." Sarah repeated back. "Graham's wife? Are you

ok?" She asked once more.

"Yes, I'm Graham's wife." Sunisa whispered.

And now not knowing where to start, she whispered, "I'm scared."

"Why, is he beating you? Threatening you?"

Sunisa was silent.

"Come on Sunisa, you can talk to me."

"No; I mean yes, he does beat me, but," said Sunisa, now pausing for a second.

"Go on," urged Sarah, "I'll try to help, I promise."

On the other end, Sunisa wept.

"He's changed," she sniffed, "I mean, I know he's planning something, I don't know what, but." She paused once more. "I'm sorry," she sniffed, "I shouldn't have called."

"Yes, yes you should, I want to help. Please don't hang up."

"But he's been so good to me, I would have been sent back to Thailand if it wasn't for him."

"But he beats you and God knows what else. Whatever he's done for you is not worth your life, you do not owe him that. Just leave him."

Now, only Sunisa's whimper could be heard on the other end.

*Easier said than done,* thought Sarah, remembering her own situation. *OK change tact.*

"What do you think he's planning?" She asked

"I don't know." Sunisa sniffed.

"Well how has he changed?"

"I can't explain it." Sunisa replied, before silence once more.

*I'm not getting anywhere,* thought Sarah, now remembering the book.

"OK Sunisa, has Graham got a book; It's white, with a glossy cover and a picture of a man on the front of it?"

On The Duck, Sunisa silently stared at the book. *What is it about this book?* She asked herself.

"Yes. " She replied, still staring at it.

"Good, do you know where it is?"

"Yes, it's here."

"What, you've got it there with you, now?" Sarah asked not believing her luck.

"Yes."

"OK," said Sarah barely able to contain her excitement, "I want you to be safe, so only do this if you can, without getting into trouble, do you understand."

"Yes." Sunisa replied, now drying her face with her free hand. "It's OK, he's in bed, besides, he's drunk. But we have to make this quick, or this call will be on his bill."

"OK, look in the back of the book, is there writing in it?"

"Yes, there is, I know there is, I saw it the other day, but my

English is not good and I don't understand it."

"So there is writing in the back of it?"

"Yes," said Sunisa, clearly sounding a little impatient.

"Look I'm sorry, I just want to be sure: It's a shame that you can't read it: Look, I'll arrange something within the next couple of days; we've got to get you off that boat and away from Graham."

"Can you do that?" Sunisa asked surprised.

"Absolutely! And I will make sure of it. Just sit tight and I'll figure out what to do, OK?

"OK." Sunisa replied with a definite lift in her tone.

OK, I'll see you in a couple of days; bye for now."

The women hung up their respective phones, Sarah, concerned but excited by what she'd heard and Sunisa, frightened about what was to come. It was only when she went into the bedroom, taking Graham's phone into him that she realised that in her haste, she'd not told Sarah about the trip that Graham had planned.

\* \* \*

"Can I speak to DS Kirkland please?" Sarah asked as she stood trembling in the middle of her living room.

After a few seconds, an operator replied.

"DS Kirkland has gone home for the evening, can anyone else help."

"No thanks, can I just leave a message for him, can you tell him that Sarah Braithwaite called, and could he call me back as soon as he gets this message. Oh! Is he in tomorrow?" She asked, not wanting to leave it too long.

"Yes," the operator replied.

Sarah spent ten minutes pacing up and down the living room, wondering what she should do, *Clearly Sunisa was scared; but of what? Well Graham I suppose. And, how can I help?*

Doubting herself after what had happened with Toi and now giving Sunisa similar assurances, Sarah found it hard to concentrate on what really needed to happen, in the end opting to go to bed, deciding that it would be better to try to get something done within normal working hours.

* * *

She awoke the following morning to the sound of rain splashing against her bedroom window after failing to get a particularly good night sleep. Louise brought her in a cup of tea to rouse her from her slumber.

After a quick shower, she organised Carl and Louise, before dropping them off at her mother's house, as it was autumn half term break and she still had to work. Work for her started at 12pm today, which gave her enough *time to make some phone calls.*

After dialling the local police station and asking for the person who had taken over from DS Kirkland, she was kept waiting a couple of minutes.

"Hello," It was DS Shrives.

"Hi." Sarah replied.

"I believe you want to speak to the person who has taken over from DS Kirkland. That would be me; my name is Detective Sergeant Shrives. Can I help you?"

"Err, where do I start?" Sarah replied. Well..."

Sarah began to run through Toi's story and after a minute, DS Shrives interrupted.

"I'm familiar with this," she said abruptly. "Sorry, what did you say your name was?"

"Oh, I'm sorry, didn't I say, my name is Mrs Braithwaite, Sarah Braithwaite."

"Ahh, yes, Trevor told me about you."

"So, you know Mr, I mean, you know Trevor then?" Sarah asked, deliberately throwing DS Shrives a morsel; name-dropping, revelling in self-importance, revealing a kind of jealousy that showed she still had feelings for him.

"Yes, I worked with him before he left for Northamptonshire. But, as I said I'm familiar with what happened with, what was that man's name? Mm, Mor."

"Morton," Sarah replied, "Graham Morton."

"Ahh yes, yes, Graham Morton. I remember now. OK so what's the story now? The last time I spoke to Trevor, he said that you'd be keeping an eye on the woman he's now living with."

"His wife, yes that's right."

Sarah then went through what Karen had suggested, the subsequent visit she'd made to see Sunisa the previous evening, and the telephone call. DS Shrives was intrigued to say the least.

"I've seen the way he treats her and now it seems as though she is in fear for her life. OK Mrs Braithwaite, leave it with me. I'll get a couple of uniformed officers to pay them a visit today and perhaps I'll go to see her myself tomorrow. Don't worry, I'll get this sorted."

"What about the book?" Asked Sarah.

"Well doing something with that's going to be harder, but I think, after hearing what you've told me, you know, his arrogance; if we give him enough rope, he'll hang himself. We just have to gain access to the barge legally, well; we just have to play it smart. So, one thing at a time, let's get this woman safe first."

# CHAPTER 29

Under a bridge on the River Nene, The Duck fought the fast moving current, its engines whining under the strain, belching out black sooty smoke from its exhausts.

Wind and rain gusted and howled through the bridge arch, making it almost impossible to see or stand on deck. Only a tiny dim light of The Stag's Head pub half a mile away could be seen and in an eerily and almost ghostly way, The Duck stood in total darkness.

Out on deck, Sunisa struggled with a barge pole, trying to prevent the barge from colliding with the walls underneath the bridge. On the starboard side, she shuffled from bow to stern, while Graham watched from the wheelhouse, trembling with fear, but knowing that this night should make him fifty thousand pounds.

He waited for Sunisa to shuffle past and then shouted over to her.

"I'm going to switch the engine off, we might be able to drift back, just keep us off the walls."

From underneath her yellow hooded jacket she shouted back, "OK!"

After turning the engine off, Graham slipped out of the wheelhouse on the port side. Holding on tight to the guide rail he moved to the bow and hid, his black raincoat providing sufficient camouflage.

As he waited for Sunisa to pass, he felt a cold breeze wisped passed his left cheek, causing him to take a sharp intake of breath. Now looking to his left, he was startled by a small hooded figure that appeared out of the darkness. Someone that he thought he knew.

"What are you doing here, who are you," he asked, squinting to improve his vision and clearly surprised.

"Don't do this." A voice came back from underneath the hood.

Recognising the voice, he could not believe his ears and with his eyes now bulging and gripped with fear, said.

"It can't be you, I saw you: You're dead."

"Don't do this." The voice replied.

\* \* \*

Suddenly and with a start, Graham woke from his slumber, breathing heavily and sweating; he quickly rose looking around the room, ensuring that he was still in bed.

Relieved, he relaxed back on to his pillow, closing his eyes, *it was only a dream,* the same recurring dream that had haunted him ever since Toi's death.

He now enjoyed the usual smell of the full English breakfast Sunisa prepared for him. She'd been up for a couple of hours getting the barge straight; cleaning up and had also taken the opportunity to venture out on deck during a slight lull in the rainfall to put the rubbish out. Now she cooked

Graham's usual, ready for when he woke up.

He lay in bed, fully clothed, his mouth dry and head aching; both symptoms of dehydration following last night's drunken binge; but *breakfast would make it all better,* he thought.

As usual, he checked his mobile phone to see if there were any missed calls and expected the usual; none. He was surprised to see that his phone displayed a 'minutes left' message, as if the phone had been used. Puzzled by this, he flicked through the phone menu trying to view 'in coming' and 'outgoing' calls, to see what numbers showed up.

His club like thumbs messed up twice before they finally took him to the screen that he wanted. To his surprise a number appeared on the 'Last Number dialled' screen, which he studied; there was something familiar about it, but thought, *I don't know, I suppose it's just a telephone number.* He didn't know any off by heart so *how can this one be familiar,* he told himself.

After changing screens once more, the phone displayed that there had been a call made from the phone at 10pm last night, which lasted five minutes. *But how can that be, I had the phone on me. This has to be wrong..*

"Sunisa! Sunisa!" He shouted.

*What does he want now?*

Seconds later she popped her head around the bedroom door.

"Your eggs are just on you've got to make this quick.

Graham glared at her for a moment, before asking.

"Have you been using my phone?"

Sunisa paused just long enough to cause suspicion and said while shaking her head.

"No."

"Are you sure?" He growled. "If I find out that you have?" He threatened.

"No, I haven't."

"OK," he replied, "just checking; when will breakfast be ready? I think I'll have it in here."

"OK, I'll bring it in, should be a couple of minutes."

*She'd never use my phone. Best check with the phone company; don't want them over charging me.*

* * *

He sat up when Sunisa brought breakfast in on a large silver tray, Tea, toast, two eggs, three rashers, sausages, beans and hash browns.

"Thanks love." He said taking the tray and placing it on his lap.

He took a sip of tea before stuffing a piece of toast into his mouth and while fumbling around with a runny egg on the end of his fork mumbled.

"The phone company said that a call was made from my phone, last night, at ten o'clock."

Sunisa sat silently on her side of the bed watching as he ate the egg, dribbling some of the yolk on to his chin and then wiping it away with his right hand.

"Oh where's the sauce?" he asked, "You've forgotten the sauce.

Sunisa quickly left the room then returned seconds later with a bottle of brown sauce, which she handed to him before sitting down on the bed once more.

"Well," Said Graham as he squirted the sauce on to the plate. "Did you use my phone?" Thinking that Sunisa's earlier silence was a clear admission of guilt.

Shaking her head, she said. "No, I promise, I didn't use your phone. The phone company must have got it wrong."

On the end of his fork, Graham dipped a sausage in to the sauce on his plate and bit the end off.

"So you didn't use the phone then?" He mumbled, while chewing the meat.

"Yes, I mean, No." She blurted.

Now clearly suspicious, "Well what is it?" He said, now smiling, "did you, or didn't you."

"No, I didn't use your phone, you're confusing me, I didn't use the phone."

After putting the rest of the sausage into his mouth and washing it down with the rest of his tea, he held his cup out in her direction.

"I'll have a cup of coffee this time."

With Sunisa out of the room, he quickly put his hand into the slit in the mattress and rummaged around for moment, before pulling out the old mobile phone. Holding it up, he pressed the on button and waited for it's operating system to load and the signature tune to play.

Sunisa returned and almost stopped in her tracks when she saw that he had the old phone out of the mattress, but she kept her composure and carefully placed the cup onto his tray.

"You've seen this phone before, haven't you?"

"No," she replied, now knowing that somehow he knew that she'd been into his stash.

He smiled at her, however, didn't reply and continued to sip his coffee.

They both sat in silence for a couple of minutes while Graham finished his breakfast, the sound of the rain starting to fall heavier out on the deck above, the sound slowly beginning to engulf the room.

Sunisa stared into space, trying not to make eye contact, feeling uncomfortable, knowing that he suspected her and him still carrying on strangely: And Graham, suspecting that somehow she'd used his phone and was now lying to him.

Handing Sunisa the tray once he'd finished his coffee, he watched as she left the room, before holding up the old phone and punching a couple of its buttons. While looking at the screen on the old phone, he pressed a button on his phone and then compared the data on each, then nodded. He did recognise the number after all, the last numbers dialled were a match and on Toi's old phone, Sarah's name appeared against the number. In the hallway, the rattle of the cutlery as Sunisa rushed off from just outside the door, gave away that she'd been watching him through the crack. They now both knew that they had to act.

* * *

While Graham performed his morning ritual in the toilet and bathroom, Sunisa now determined that she must leave, started to pack a holdall; and as if a weight had been lifted from her mind, she found herself almost in a trance like state, as if outside of her body, observing herself as she packed. Surreally and showing her state of mind,  she took her time and slowly folded each item of clothing, even taking the time to pack some makeup.

Suddenly and with a jolt, Graham's shouting from behind the toilet door dragged her back to reality.

"Who's that?" he shouted, "Sunisa, get the door. Sunisa?"

From outside, someone banged on the hatch.

Quickly, she zipped up the holdall and placed it in the corner on her side of the bed, where she thought Graham wouldn't find it. Rushing out into the hallway and up the steps to the hatch, she took a couple of deep breaths just before reaching the top. As she reached the top, two more thumps on the hatch startled her, before Graham shouted out once more.

"I've got it." She shouted back.

As the hatch creaked open, she was filled with fear as two police officers stood out on deck. Seeing her alarm, they looked at each other before one of the officers tried to reassure her.

"There's no need to be alarmed, we're just in the area and calling on the local residence to make sure that everything's OK. There's been a spate of burglaries." He then sneezed, "Oh, I'm sorry," he continued, "yes there's been a spate of burglaries and we're just checking up on all the local residents."

Sunisa was silent and tried to avoid making eye contact, instead looking down at their feet, noticing that from the lower thigh downwards, both officers were soaked, their waterproof vortex jackets efficiently channelling rain off from their upper bodies, onto their trousers. For a moment, she felt sorry for them, thinking how uncomfortable they must have been feeling.

"Madam, are you OK," said the other officer, the rain dripping off the peak of his helmet.

"Who is it?" Graham shouted from inside.

"Is everything alright," asked the first officer, "are you OK?"

"Do you speak English?" The other officer asked when Sunisa didn't reply.

"Who the bloody hell is it?" Shouted Graham.

"It's the police," she replied.

Seconds later the toilet flushed.

"Madam," said the first officer now with some urgency, "we just want to know if everything is OK here."

Sunisa slowly shook her head; a shake that slowly turned into a nod as she sensed Graham's approach.

"Who did you say it was?" He asked as he pushed past Sunisa. "Oh, what can I do for you two?" He continued, on seeing the police officers.

The constables glanced at each other before the first one said.

"There's been a spate of burglaries and were just checking."

"Look, I've heard it all before." Graham interrupted. "And I want you off my barge. Please go."

"But Sir, all we're trying to do is." Said the first officer, before Graham interrupted once more.

"Can you please go," he repeated, "and you," now directing his attention at Sunisa, "go inside."

Graham addressed the constables once more.

"Please leave my property or I'm going to report you." He said before turning and closing the hatch.

The officers stood there for a second, before deciding that

no crime was or had being committed, and though Sunisa was fairly unresponsive, she looked and sounded OK. They had gathered the information they were sent out for.

Inside, Graham watched through the forward facing starboard porthole as the officers slowly walked up the canal path, passing the long boat in front and then the one after that, confirming what Graham had thought all along; their appearance having nothing to do with burglaries in the area.

He watched as the officers disappeared into the distance, and then sat down on the couch next to Sunisa, putting a hand on her knee before saying.

"We're going to see my mother tonight."

"But, I thought we were going tomorrow." She replied surprised.

"No, tonight, we're going tonight."

## CHAPTER 30

Graham and Sunisa, instinctively knowing that something horrible was going to take place whilst away on their trip, still had a chance to change the course of events, but they appeared powerless, or even unwilling to avert what surely was going to be a deadly experience.

Graham's hand had been forced; it was now time to put his plan into action, and throughout the day he watched with increasing interest, which didn't go unnoticed, the weather reports, which predicted severe weather.

Sunisa's holdall remained packed as time after time that day she tried to gather enough courage to leave the barge, even appearing out on deck at one point, while Graham had gone to the toilet, and then returning inside, tiptoeing back past the toilet, letting fear get the better of her.

\* \* \*

Deep in thought and cooking dinner, Sarah received a telephone call and after turning down the heat under the pans, leaving them to simmer, went through the living room, relaxing into her favourite armchair.

"OK, you ready for me now?" Kirkland asked sarcastically. "As I said, I'm just returning your call."

"How are you? I'm OK, how are the kids? Oh they're good." Sarah replied sarcastically, letting Kirkland know that he had not even bothered with the pleasantries.

"Oh, I'm sorry." He said. "We've just been so busy with the floods, you know getting people out of their houses. But, I suppose that's no excuse for being rude. Anyway how are you?"

"Oh I'm OK." Sarah replied, before bursting into laughter. "I see some things never change," referring to Kirkland not knowing when a joke was being played on him.

He listened as Sarah spent a few minutes running through what Karen thought about Toi's death, the conversation with DS Shrives, her trip down to the canal the previous night, and the call from Sunisa.

"So you guys have been busy then?" He said. "It sounds as though his wife: What did you say her name was, Sunisa: she's ready to leave him."

"Yes, she sounded really scared, and I suppose after what happened to Toi, I'm feeling scared for her. We've got to do something."

"Well, by the sounds of it Carol's got it in hand."

"Carol?"

"I mean. Shrives, err, DS Shrives." He replied now sounding a bit defensive. "I'll give her a call to find out what's happening."

"OK." Sarah slowly replied, trying to read Kirkland's emotions and starting to feel a bit jealous.

Suddenly

"Oh I've got to go, I'll call you later."

"What?" Said Kirkland surprised.

"I can smell dinner burning, I'll call you back." She said before hanging up.

* * *

"Sunisa!" Graham shouted from outside, "I need you."

Sunisa sat on the side of the bath in the locked bathroom, feeling sorry for herself, wishing that she'd taken the opportunity to leave when she had the chance.

They began their journey to Northampton at 6:30pm, in the pouring rain.

While Graham waited in the general warmth of the wheelhouse, Sunisa had been sent out in the pouring rain to make The Duck ready for the voyage, almost slipping off the bank and into the canal while untying the barge from its moorings.

Once they were underway, Sunisa took the opportunity to spend some time in the cabin, warming herself up, as well as taking the chance to get away from Graham if only for two hours; the time it would take to reach the first lock. She spent most of that time locked in the toilet worrying; trying to figure out a way of getting away from him.

Not long after they got underway, Graham dressed in a black two-piece, zip fronted coat like wet suit and green rubber boots shouted through the open hatch as the rain poured through it onto the steps.

"Sunisa! Where are you?"

Unlocking the bathroom door, she stepped out into the hallway still wearing her yellow hooded coat. Now looking up through the hatch, the cold rainwater fell through onto her face, making her squint.

"Get me a beer and then come out, I'm going to need some help with the lock." He ordered.

This was exactly what she dreaded, it was dark, wet, and she worried that no one would be around. *He could do anything to me and no one would know,* she thought.

After taking a beer from the fridge, she slowly made her way along the hallway, up the steps, and then pulled her hood up before opening the hatch. The excess rainwater that covered the top of the hatch splashed through onto her coat, hands and the inappropriate sandals that she wore, sending a shiver down her spine.

The rain had let up a bit since she was last out, but after nearly falling into the canal earlier she still moved slowly, holding on tightly to the guide rail, wanting to take no chances.

With only the light of a dim yellow lamp that Graham insisted on keeping in the wheelhouse, which defused in the spray that the rain caused, ensured it remained dark out on deck.

On reaching the wheelhouse, she smiled at Graham before handing him the beer. He smiled back an almost reassuring smile, before saying.

"Go inside for now, we'll reach the first lock in about an hour, I'll need some help with it, so I'll call you."

\* \* \*

While the wind whistled around outside, inside, Sunisa spent forty minutes pacing up and down the bedroom, trying to figure out how to get off the barge, without incurring Graham's wrath.

*Perhaps I can enlist some help,* she thought, remembering the mobile phone hidden in the mattress.

Kneeling on his side of the bed, she put her hand into the slit and pulled out, first the jewellery, the money, lastly the mobile phone. With everything placed on the bed, she sat down next to the items, her attention drawn to the roll of money, which seemed to be slightly larger than it had been before.

Leaning back across the bed to where she'd hidden her holdall, she rummaged around in one of the side pockets and pulled out the scrap of paper that contained Sarah's telephone number. After slowly dialling the number, she was surprised by the display, as Sarah's name appeared on it. *Why is this name in the phone?* She thought, comparing the phone display with what Sarah had written on the piece of paper.

"Toi!" Said Sarah when she answered. "Toi, is that you?" Knowing full well that it couldn't have been her.

Sunisa paused for a moment.

"Who is this?" Sarah asked.

"It's Sunisa."

"Oh! Sunisa," Said Sarah, surprised, a tinge of disappointment now clearly heard in her voice. "Where, where did you get this phone?"

"It's Graham's. Can you help me? You said you'd help me." She blurted.

"Slow down, what's going on? Are you OK?"

"Yes, I mean no: We're on our way to Northampton."

"Northampton!?" Said Sarah, now sounding alarmed.

*'Balance is low,'* said a telephone company service voice cutting into the conversation.

"What? On the barge?" Sarah asked voice raised.

"Yes, on the barge, why, are you asking?"

"Look, you've got to get off the barge as soon as possible." Said Sarah, deliberately ignoring Sunisa's question and not wanting to alarm her.

"I can't, I mean I don't want to make him angry." Sunisa replied, before another service message indicated again that the balance was low.

"Where are you now?" Sarah asked, now showing real concern.

"On the canal somewhere, but why are you so worried, you're making me nervous: And why is your telephone number in Graham's phone?"

Sarah thought for a moment.

"OK, look, I didn't want to worry you," she said before pausing and taking a deep breath.

"But Graham's last wife died on a trip to Northampton just over a year ago and I don't think it was an accident. I think he killed her; that's why I want you to get off the barge as soon as possible. And the reason my name is in that phone, is because it was her phone. She was my friend."

Sarah waited for a response, which did not come; the line was dead as Sunisa's phone credit had run out and now she had no idea how long she'd been talking to herself.

"Sunisa! Sunisa!" She shouted into her receiver before trying to call back.

'The telephone number is temporally unavailable, please try again later.' Said the service message.

She tried once more and got the same message.

*  *  *

On the barge, Sunisa hadn't heard any of Sarah's explanation and was startled when Graham opened the hatch, calling for her help as the first lock approached.

Quickly switching off the phone, she gathered up all of the items from the bed and stuffed them back into the mattress, taking a second to examine the bed, ensuring that it didn't look too ruffled. She then made her way up onto the deck, where the wind and rain beat down on her.

In front of them, the light from the lock keeper's house was more of a hindrance, and coupled with the weather the pair struggled to see the waterway in front.

Graham barked out his instructions then went back into the wheelhouse. Sunisa took one of the starboard mooring ties and stepped off the barge onto the canal path. As the barge slowly moved forward, she ran up some steps to the first paddle and twisted a crank. The paddle creaked into life, the noise echoing briefly against the moss fill walls of the lower pound, before being drowned out by the rain.

She continued to turn the crank until the paddle was fully open, allowing Graham to move the barge into the pound and then turned the crank the other way closing the paddle.

Spray from the rainwater, still like mist, filled the air, as Sunisa taking a welcomed respite from turning the crank stretched, relieving the pain in the small of her back induced by the activity she'd just undertaken.

She watched, positioned at the paddles of the upper pound as The Duck slowly rose, the water gushing through the upper pound paddles and slowly filling the pond below.

In the darkness, Graham climbed the steps out of the lower pound and crept along the canal path, his black raincoat providing the perfect camouflage.

On the opposite bank, in a dimly lit cottage, the lock keeper looked out of a window; spotting Sunisa's small frame covered by her yellow coat through the spray and the darkness, decided to see if she needed a hand and after sitting down grabbed a pair of heavy walking boots and began to pull them on.

Outside, Graham slowly crept up behind Sunisa, stepping into a large puddle, resulting in a slight squelching sound; he then stopped and stood motionless, hoping that she wouldn't turn around.

With her hood up, the sound of the water moving through the paddles, and the rain falling, muffled the sound of his steps. But, it was obvious that she'd heard something, so she looked to her left, then right, peering off into the blackness and on seeing nothing she continued to watch as the water gushed into the lower pound.

Suddenly she was forced to double take as she looked at The Duck, expecting to see Graham's large silhouette in the dim light of the wheelhouse, instead seeing nothing. As she leant forward to get a better view, Graham now only four feet behind her, held his breath and slowly raised a crowbar that he'd taken from the wheelhouse. He squinted as he brought the crowbar down, but pulled it away from Sunisa's crown when a blinding light from the cottage across the canal suddenly came on, illuminating them both and causing them to shield their eyes with their hands.

"Do you two need any help?" The lock keeper shouted across, lowering the elevation of the beam slightly, after seeing that he'd obscured their vision.

"No were alright." Graham shouted back from behind Sunisa, frightening her, causing her to turn and slip forward towards the canal.

He had to grab her left arm to stop her from falling in.

"Are you sure? The lock keeper asked.

"Yes, yes we're fine." Graham replied, pulling Sunisa to safety.

"OK, I'll leave the light on to help you see. Be careful," he said before waving at them and turning and  disappearing back into the cottage.

He now watched from a window, as outside in the light, Sunisa and Graham seemed to argue, Sunisa pointing to the crowbar and Graham seemingly ordering her back on to the barge. *What are they doing travelling on a night like this*? He thought.

After the lower pound filled, Graham opened the upper pound paddles and then manoeuvred The Duck through.

The ever helpful lock keeper reappeared and waved, indicating that he would close the upper pound paddles. From the wheelhouse, Graham acknowledged by waving back, continuing to steer The Duck out into the darkness.

* * *

After her conversation with Sarah, as promised, DS Shrives made her way up the canal path at Croxten.

She fought against the wind as the rain lashed down, her umbrella threatening to blow inside out several times, as her muddied court shoes not offering much grip, forced her to take small steps as she tried to stay on her feet. It didn't help that it was evening and dark.

Following the report that she'd received from the uniformed officers, she was more determined than ever to see that Sunisa was alright, no matter what Graham had to say.

Checking the names of the barges as she walked by, she reached the end of the moorings having not found The Duck and squinted, peering off into the darkness up the canal to see if any other barges were moored further on. But, it was too dark and she saw nothing as the bluster of the rain further obscured her vision.

*What the bloody hell am I doing out here?* She asked herself, now disappointed that The Duck was not here. She turned and started back, the wind forcing her to take larger steps than she would have liked, causing her to slip a couple of times. About half way along the moorings, she recognised a barge.

'The Pride of Croxten, it had been next to The Duck the last time she was here.

*Perhaps they'll know where the Mortons' are,* she thought, seeing that a light was on inside.

Stepping onboard, she stumbled forward, her hand leaning against a rope guide rail: *for God sake!* The rail was soaking wet, the cold water from which ran from her hand, through the cuff of her blouse, down her elbow and then armpit. She shook her arm, as if to force the water back out, already knowing the action would make the arm of her blouse and red fitted moleskin coat, which already felt damp, wet, but she did it anyway. Now fed up and ready for home, she knocked on the grey/blue Dutch oak hatch and waited. A few seconds later Mr Jenkins appeared.

"Oh hello," said DS Shrives, holding her warrant card up for an uncomfortably long time, ensuring that the squinting Mr Jenkins had a good look at it. "My name is DS Shrives, I'm enquiring about your neighbours."

"You mean the Morton's."

"Yes, do you know them?" She asked, putting her card back into her coat pocket.

"Yes, is there something wrong? There is something wrong isn't there? I knew there was something," he rambled. "She's so young and he's not very nice to her."

"What do you mean?"

"Well," he said after a short pause, leaning forward and shifting his eyes from left to right.

"I don't want to be a gossip, but I often hear him shouting at her and sometimes hear her crying." And now lowering his voice to almost a whisper said. "I think he hits her."

"Really!"

"OH!" he said, his voice returning to normal, "You didn't hear that from me."

"Of course not," DS Shrives whispered. "OK, but how do you know that he hits her."

"Well, I sometimes see what looks like bruises on her arms and wrists; she had a black eye back in the summer. And the way he orders her about, it's not right." He replied now noticing DS Shrives's good looks.

"Do you want to come in, out of the cold?" He asked, now looking her up and down and smiling.

Ignoring the question, she asked.

"Do you know where they've gone?"

"No, but they left a couple of hours ago. You sure you don't want to come in for a warm drink"

"No," she replied sternly, shaking her head, her face now wearing a worried expression.

"I've got to go, but I may call back if I need to."

A few minutes later, she was back in her car fumbling around with her seat belt when her mobile phone rang, *Bloody hell,* she thought, before quickly rummaging around in her coat pocket, then producing a phone.

# CHAPTER 31

In her car, DS Shrives had just finished speaking to DS Kirkland and now talked to DCI Thornton.

"Look. I know what you think, but I know something's going to happen to this woman."

"Kirkland's got you thinking the same way as him. He's got a bee in his bonnet about this man, and like a dog with a bone, won't let go." DCI Thornton replied.

"But I told you what the neighbour said; he beats her."

"Has he seen him beating her?"

DS Shrives paused and then said.

"No, but."

"That's what I mean." Thornton interrupted. "No evidence, of any kind: and I know that Kirkland was pretty screwed up about this one."

"But what about the woman who called Kirkland; she said that the wife sounded scared. Look, I know it's all hearsay, but if anything happens now, how stupid are we going to look?"

Thornton thought for a moment.

"OK," he sighed, "I'll ask the Chief Sper if he can spare a couple of uniformed, but I don't want to throw loads of resource at this. You don't even know where the barge is going do you? And we can't search the whole of the Grand Union."

"I'll find out; just arrange for the uniformed officers to

contact me."

"OK, just don't mess up."

"When do I ever?" She replied sarcastically.

\* \* \*

Graham moored the barge four miles from the lock at Cassiobury, in Bourne End, a small and quite inconspicuous town in Hertfordshire.

It had stopped raining about half an hour before, but it was still windy, and as Graham stepped on to the sodden canal path, the ground squelched underfoot.

Looking in through a rear portside porthole, he stared at Sunisa for a moment, on his mind, how he was going to justify sneaking up behind her at the lock. She caught a glimpse of him outside as he turned and continued fixing the barge to the bank.

Across a bridge he saw that The Three Horse Shoes pub was still open, and rather than face her, decided that he would go and conjure up some courage from the bottom of a beer glass, and after turning the wheelhouse lights off, he made his way across the bridge and into the pub.

Onboard Sunisa sat, now more annoyed than frightened that Graham had seemingly tried to hurt her, and though he said that he'd taken the crowbar just in case it was needed to free the crank that opened the lock paddles, she struggled to believe him.

Back at the lock she'd stood up to him, and for the first time saw fear in his eyes, a kind of fear that indicated to them both, that their relationship was somehow nearing its end, which now seemed to spur her on. But if she tried to get away now, he would surely find her, besides she had no idea of where she was.

*  *  *

On the road at Croxten moorings, lit by the yellow street lamps, wet leaves now leapt up from the sodden and well-manicured grass verge, and made mini typhoon like funnel shapes, as they danced around on the wind.

Only the occasional splash of droplets that had collected in the crevices of the large oaks that festooned the bank, sporadically blew down from their branches, hitting the car in which DS Shrives sat, sometimes giving the impression that it had begun to rain once more.

She'd already spoken to a uniformed police officer and had asked her and a colleague to speak to the lock keeper at Cassiobury lock, to see if he'd seen The Duck. Failing that, to head back down the canal path to Croxten, checking the identities of all barges moored between the two points.

DCI Thornton was right, they couldn't check the whole of the Grand Union, but given the time Mr Jenkins said that the 'Morton's' had left, realistically they couldn't have gone that far. However, it was getting on for 9pm and with only two officers at her disposal, if they didn't find The Duck between Croxten and Cassiobury, it would be a couple of days before they could mount any sort of proper search as the weekend was upon them.

\* \* \*

After her telephone conversation with Sunisa, Sarah first tried to contact DS Shrives at the police station, but was told that she'd already gone home for the evening. After leaving a message, she phoned DS Kirkland whose phone was first engaged and the next time didn't even ring, and frustratingly just asked her to leave a message; which she finally did.

From the kitchen, she rushed into the living room, splashing a bit of the hot cup of rooibos that she carried onto her hand. *Shit!* She thought, putting the cup down onto the coffee table, before answering the phone.

"Hello!" She said angrily.

"Hi, it's me, Kirkland, I thought you were going to call me back?"

"I was, but unlike you, I do have other dependents."

"OK, OK, calm down." Said Kirkland, sensing some tension in Sarah's voice.

"I am calm. I tried to call but it just went to answer phone."

"I know, I'm just returning your call: You OK?" He enquired now sensing her anger.

"Yes, I'm OK; I've just burnt my hand rushing to answer

the phone." She replied, now examining her hand.

"Burning your dinner, then your hand, always burning something." He quipped.

Sarah, not amused just got down to business.

"So where were we?" She asked, before answering her own question, updating Kirkland about the conversation she'd had with Sunisa.

"Now that sounds disturbing." He said once Sarah had finished. "I spoke to DS Shrives, she's arranging something your end, besides they can't have gone far."

"But what if he does something?"

"Look, don't worry; we are going to get this guy."

"Yeah, but that's what you said the last time." Sarah replied smugly.

"That's not fair." He replied angrily. "I thought you were trying to be positive."

"I am, but fair or not, we know what happened."

"There you go, trying to lay blame."

"I'm not, I just want something done, and I just feel so helpless: I just want to help."

"Look, it's a police matter and we'll deal with it." Said Kirkland, now sounding official. "We'll get him this time and before anything happens."

With that, Kirkland's phone bleeped, indicating that he was receiving an incoming call.

"Hang on," he said, looking at the caller display. *DS Shrives?*

"Look, I've just got to take this call, don't hang up."

"But!"

It was too late, Kirkland was gone, off taking the call, and while she waited, Sarah relaxed back into her armchair, pushed her slippers off and sipped her tea. The heat emanating from the cup reminded her that she'd burnt her hand, so she sat there for a minute examining it, occasionally gently blowing over the affected area

A minute later.

"Hello."

Kirkland was back.

"Hi, I've just been speaking to DS Shrives. There's been some further developments." He said, trepidation now clearly heard in his voice.

"What? What is it?"

"Well after you spoke to Carol, she sent a couple of officers out to look for the barge and they couldn't find it this side of Cassiobury."

After a short pause:

"What does that mean?" Asked Sarah

"Well, they could be anywhere. Well not anywhere, but, we don't know where they are."

Sarah stunned into silence said nothing.

"You still there?" He asked on hearing her silence.

"Yes, err yes. Well, what are we going to do?"

"Well, Carol is going to be looking for her tomorrow."

"Tomorrow!" She replied seemingly surprised.

"Look, They could be anywhere; have you seen it out there, it's dark and raining, and with no lights on the canal, you could walk straight past the barge and miss it."

"Yes, and she could be dead. Why aren't you, I mean, why aren't the police, launching a major operation to find this woman? It's like she has to die before anybody will do anything."

"I know what you're saying, but no crime has been committed and the woman."

"Sunisa." Sarah interjected, reminding Kirkland that 'The Woman,' had a name.

"Yes, Sunisa, she must have had a chance to leave him before now, and she's still with him?"

Sarah sighed heavily.

"Just like a bloody man, to come out with something like that."

"But I'm right. Aren't I?"

"You may be right, but you're definitely a man, lacking understanding. She's scared of him and has been since day one. You're just so typical."

"OK, OK point taken. But it doesn't change the fact that no

crime has been committed, or reported, so a full scale alert or search won't happen, I don't know what to say."

They were both silent for a moment before he continued.

"You said that you wanted to help, right?"

"Yes, yes you know I want to help." She replied angrily.

"Well, perhaps you could; you and your friends from the kitchen. Perhaps you could help with the search tomorrow. I know that Carol and a couple of officers will be searching from here to about Aylesbury, maybe slightly further."

"What, work with the police?" But I thought you said that this was a police matter."

"It is. But I want to keep you out of harm's way, I mean, if this guy is dangerous I don't want you anywhere near him. Besides, I don't think Carol would be very pleased if she found out that I asked you to help."

"OK, well how would this work then?" She sighed.

"Well we know there are a number of moorings and locks along the canal: do any of the other women drive?"

"Yes, if I get Jenny and Karen to help, we'll have three cars, but Karen's probably going to be busy..."

The pair planned what they were going to do the following morning, and where they were going to search. Sarah would contact the women directly after their call, print maps off from the internet, and would check all the moorings that they could find the following day; and call Kirkland if they found anything, who in turn would inform DS Shrives.

"Look, before you go." Said Sarah, "I just want to remind you how you felt when Toi died: The way we both felt."

"Don't remind me."

"Well, let's have a good outcome this time."

\* \* \*

At the lock keeper's cottage earlier.

"Yes, a couple went through the lock at about eight thirty," said the lock keeper as he talked to the uniformed officers, who had arrived two or three minutes earlier. "They went through alright, but there was something funny about them."

The lock keeper sat back in a high backed lime green cloth cover chair; something reminiscent of the 1950s. Indeed, the whole cottage had a 50s charm  about it; not only were the fixtures and fittings from that era, the clothes he wore, the high wasted trousers, green armless sweater, and striped collarless shirt with rolled up sleeves was in keeping with the surroundings. The officers spent some of their time pre-occupied, admiring some of the items that had actually come back into fashion.

"Funny how?" Asked  the female officer.

"Well more funny peculiar if you know what I mean, you know, odd. From what I can make out the man was middle aged and the woman was oriental and quite young. But, saying that, I really didn't get a good look at them. I found it odd that they were travelling on a night like this, given the weather warnings"

The second police officer recorded the lock keepers statement in a small leather covered notebook.

"Is there anything else you can tell us about them? He asked.

"Well, they seemed to be arguing. I don't know what about, but he did push her."

"Did he?"

"Yes; one other thing, come to think of it. He had a crowbar in his hand."

"A crowbar?"

"Yes, waving it about he was, I don't know what he would want that for, I maintain all the fixtures out on the lock. He should know that, he's used the lock often enough."

"I thought you said you didn't get a good look at them."

"Well, I didn't, but I know the barge; not long refurbished, looks quite nice. The Dick, no, The Duck I think it's called. But it's been through here loads of times."

The officer nodded.

"Well, thanks for your time Mr Moore," she said, "If there's anything more, we'll be in touch.

"My pleasure, glad I could be of help."

The officers left the cottage not relishing the search that they had to undertake, from the cottage to the moorings were a couple of miles and would take some time, given the weather and the time of night.

* * *

Graham returned to the barge at 11:30pm, the heavy shuffling of his footsteps on deck giving away that he was very drunk. He mumbled to himself as he fumbled around with the hatch lock, trying to get the key in, missing the keyhole a couple of times before pushing it in then turning.

As the hatch opened, he was startled by a spot light that came on from behind. The bright light hurt, and blinded his eyes as he turned and for the second time that evening, he put one hand in front of his face and squinted to see. From behind the light, a man's voice shouted over.

"Are you OK?"

"I would be if you'd turn that bloody light off." Graham replied.

"OK," the voice came back, "there's been some burglaries just recently. I just…"

"I know, I know," Graham interrupted, "Do I look like a burglar? Just turn that light off; I live here!"

"Oh, OK. I just heard some noises and came out to investigate."

In his stupor, Graham then realised that the man was the owner of the neighbouring barge.

"Just turn that bloody light off." He slurred, before turning and opening the hatch.

The man watched as Graham lumbered down the first couple of steps and disappeared behind the hatch door.

Inside, Graham made his way down the steps into the hallway; Sunisa already in bed, struggled to get to sleep after what had happened earlier, so was easily awakened as Graham stomped around outside the bedroom door.

"Sunisa, get out here." He shouted.

She lay there in the dark, not wanting to move, pretending to sleep.

"Sunisa, I want something to eat; come and make me something to eat."

It was no use, he would continue until she complied, so she got up and went into the living area, where he sat there looking at the television.

"Make me something to eat." He said, eyes still firmly fixed on the television.

"What do you want?"

"Oh, anything, surprise me."

She stared at him for a moment and wished that he were dead. From his periphery he caught sight that she was still in the room and looked up at her from the television and smiled. Disgusted by his whole demeanour, she turned and disappeared down the hallway into the galley.

Twenty minutes later, she returned with his meal to find

him fast asleep, snoring loudly. She put the sandwiches down on the table next to his book and returned to the kitchen to clear up.

Wiping up, she subconsciously left the large kitchen knife that she'd used to cut the sandwiches till last. Looking at the knife as she dried it, dredged up thoughts from the darkest corners of her mind. In a trance like state, she played his death over in her head.

*One stab, one twist. No one would know, No one would miss him, No one would care? I hate him and surely everyone would understand.*

Returning to reality, she found herself in the lounge, staring at him while he slept. Looking down to her left hand she held the tea towel and in the right the knife.

'*His mother would miss him.*' She thought.

# CHAPTER 32

By the canal the following morning, the sky painted in shades of grey threaten rain, as dark low clouds raced across the sky. The wind stripped the last deciduous leaves from the trees, and as the wet horse chestnut, oak and ash leaves fluttered about on the pavement they tried to gather lift, only to gather in the gutter, or stick to the sodden grass verge, with some ending up floating off in the fast moving waters of the Grand Union.

The air housed the beautiful and natural autumnal decay of animal and vegetable; the distinctive aroma of the canal.

Four women red faced from a sometimes-stinging north-easterly wind, peered in at DS Shrives through the steamed up windscreen of her car as she pulled up. It was Saturday, 9am, and they all looked tired.

Sarah had called them the night before and filled them in on what had been happening, and though it was short notice, they were all eager to help.

Unlike the women standing on the pavement, DS Shrives looked fresher, movie star like, wearing her red moleskin coat and matching bright red lipstick, *hardly the look of a police officer.*

"Morning." She said, as she walked past heading towards two police officers already standing on the canal path.

"Morning," said the women in unison, jealously gazing at

the blond hair and perfect makeup, against the stark red of her lipstick and coat.

"OK," Sarah whispered, "Obviously they're the police, and they'll be looking as well. But remember, DS Kirkland said, if asked, whatever you do, don't tell them what we're doing."

"Why?" Asked Jane.

"I don't know, he said that she wouldn't like it."

"Wouldn't like it?" said Debbie, "They're having a bloody laugh; after what happened to Toi, you would think they'd take all the help they could get."

"OK Debbie," said Sarah, "DS Kirkland's just trying to help."

"Really," Debbie replied, "So where is he then? I don't see him standing here, in the cold."

"Look, this is off his patch so he can't be here, but if they reach Northampton, or near Northampton, he'll take over."

"She doesn't even look like a police woman." Said Jenny jealously.

"Yeah, I know." Said Jane, "All tarted up like that."

Together, the women now looked over at the three police officers, which caught the eye of DS Shrives, who looked back and smiled.

"OK that's enough," Sarah whispered. "She's on our side. So let's get on with this."

"OK, so what have we got to do?" Asked Debbie

Sarah handed each of the women a map.

"Well, as we only have two cars we'll split into two," she said, "Debbie will come with me, and Jane goes with Jenny, OK?"

After a short pause to cater for any objections she continued.

"OK, on your map, it shows you where to search. It'll either be moorings, locks, bridges or something like that and there maybe: No, there will be a lot of walking involved. Is that OK with everyone?"

The women nodded, apart from Jane who seemed hesitant.

"You OK Jane?" Asked Sarah.

"Yes," she replied again rather hesitantly.

"What is it?" Asked Sarah, knowing that there was something up.

"We need to know; someone's life may depend on what we do now, so what is it?"

"No pressure then." Said Debbie sarcastically, to Sarah's annoyance, who glared at her momentarily, before turning to Jane waiting for an answer.

"Well I've never read a map." Said Jane.

"Is that it?" Sarah chuckled.

Come on let's go through it.

The other women took the opportunity to brush up on their map reading skills as Sarah ran through where they had to go, and what had to be done. She also explained that Karen would be joining them a bit later, and that they would, depending on what happened during the day; perhaps meet up later in The Horns pub in town.

So engrossed were they in their conversation that they didn't notice that the three police officers had got into their car and driven off. Eventually Sarah did notice and started the ball rolling.

"Remember what I said, we've got to be thorough, and we'll meet at The Horns at 5 o'clock."

As Jenny and Jane drove off to start their search, Sarah and Debbie started their search where they were, and hurriedly walked along the canal path to Croxten Moorings, just in case Graham had returned during the night.

\* \* \*

The noise as The Duck's engines spluttering woke Sunisa, who was surprised to find that Graham was already up, given his state the night before. This was very unusual, and looking to his side of the bed, saw that he must have slept in the living room. Even more unusual, he didn't wake her. Rolling back onto her right side, she felt something under the cover. Now all of the feelings from the previous night came flooding back as she slowly pulled out the knife from under the quilt.

In the cold light of day, she felt ashamed. *I can't believe it, I was going to do it, did he really try to hurt me*, she thought now doubting herself. *It was wet, cold and dark last night and I didn't want to come. Perhaps he was really trying to help me back at the lock.*

Feeling a bit confused, she now realised that she had to get away from him as soon as possible.

Putting the knife on top of the packed holdall she got up, and now looking through a porthole saw that the barge was moving quite quickly. She watched in the relative warmth, as from time to time the canal bank opened up to reveal quite beautiful green fields set before the rolling Chiltern hills, while in the foreground, craggy leafless oaks and sparsely wooded areas portrayed a melancholy mood, just as she felt.

An hour passed before she noticed that the barge began to slow down; they were at another lock: The first of the Marsworth locks, and now her mood changed. She worried about what she would do when she saw him.

Sitting down on the bed, she waited, expecting Graham to open the hatch, and to call for her to help. Looking over to her wardrobe, she tried; willed her legs to move so she could find something appropriate to wear. Even after hearing the heavy shuffle of Graham on deck, she still didn't move. A minute or two passed, and still Graham didn't call, then through the porthole she saw the walls of the lower pound starting to lower. *He must have got help from the lock keeper.*

Relieved, she lay back onto the bed for a moment before

crawling back under the covers onto the cold sheets. She pulled the edge of the cover round her front trying to prevent her bodily warmth from escaping.

Eyelids feeling heavy and almost asleep, she opened her eyes once more, and found herself looking at the knife perched on her holdall, which she stared at for a moment before pushing her hand through her warm cocoon, picking it up and pulling it underneath the cover.

* * *

In the wheelhouse, with the sound of the old crackly radio playing in the background, Graham, still breathing heavily from putting the barge through the first of the locks, was on autopilot.

'**Members of the public are advised to only travel when necessary as severe storms are expected throughout the night...**' Said a news reader.

But Graham heard nothing, as he played what he had to do over and over in his mind.

Before long the barge entered the upper pound of the third lock in the system and he stepped out once more.

# CHAPTER 33

"You're the second lot of people to ask after that couple." Said the lock keeper.

"Really?" Sarah replied.

"Yes, the police were here asking about them yesterday."

"Oh?"

"Yes," he replied, now being coy. "So, err, what's going on." He asked inquisitively, leaning forward in his armchair.

The women glanced at each other before Sarah unconvincingly replied.

"Nothing. Well nothing of any significance." She said looking down at the floor then glancing at Debbie once more.

Relaxing back into his chair the lock keeper smiled, knowing that he had no chance of gleaning any information from the women.

"Well, I'll tell you what I told them; the man was middle aged and the woman was oriental, they seemed to be arguing, and he was waving a crowbar around."

"What?" Said Sarah, "A crowbar? And you told the police that?

"Yeah, I mean it wasn't as bad as it sounds, I mean he wasn't hitting her with it or anything like that. Well," he thought holding his chin. "He wasn't really waving it around, but he had one in his hand."

"OK, we'd better go," said Sarah, now looking worried.

"Thank you for your time."

"That's OK," he said, getting up from his chair to see them out, "I hope I've helped and more importantly, I hope you find them."

Outside, the women rushed to the car.

"What's next?" Debbie asked.

"The Marina at Apsley. We'll check in with the others when we get there."

\* \* \*

The women were silent for most of their journey, cocooned in the warmth of the car as the promised rain began to fall. Their journey would take half an hour and induced by the soothing drone of the engine, Debbie soon fell asleep.

As the rain fell heavier, the Saturday morning traffic in and out of the town centre increased and soon they found themselves in heavy slow moving traffic, which frustrated Sarah. *Always happens when you're in a rush.* But now she had time to think, time to try to focus on something other than Sunisa, Graham and the situation that they found themselves in.

She looked at Debbie as she slept and smiled. *At least things are working out for you.* She thought, as Debbie looked so content.

\* \* \*

Just as Sarah had predicted, Debbie had been promoted to

kitchen manager when Karen left and was by all accounts doing a good job. With some positive help from her violent brother, she'd sorted out her private life; well, Michael, her wife-beating ex partner. Now with her job and an increase in salary, she was able to afford and live the normal family life that she'd always craved. She now displayed much more confidence in her abilities, her children were happy and getting on well at school, and though she retained some of her old traits, in essence she was a good and caring manager.

\* \* \*

"Debbie, Debbie," said Sarah, voice raised. "We're here."

Debbie woke from a deep sleep with a start, feeling heavy eyed.

"Sorry," She groaned. "We here already?" She asked, looking around.

"Yes I think we've got to go to the marina office." Said Sarah, pointing at a location through the rain soaked windscreen. "It's across the bridge; I think there's a row of shops over there."

Debbie yawned, "Sorry," she repeated. "I mean, for falling asleep like that," she said before stretching both elbows out to the side behind her back, pushing out her chest, arching her back and stretching.

"That's OK I know what it's like. Anyway, we'd better get going."

"I thought you were going to call the others?" Debbie enquired.

"Oh yes," Sarah replied, reaching for her phone, which rested in the unused front ashtray.

She thought for a second before deciding not to call.

"No, I'll call them when I get back from the office."

As the wind sprawled the rain about, which occasionally lashed against the car, Sarah buttoned up her coat and grabbed her umbrella.

"Look, you don't have to come; we both don't have to get wet." Said Sarah.

"You sure?"

"Yes, I'll be back in a minute."

Sarah opened her door, letting the wind and rain in for a second and now squinting got out, slamming the door, and quickly headed along the canal path to the bridge.

Inside the car, Debbie pulled her coat, which rested on her lap, over her body and up to her neck, ensuring that her elbows and arms were inside and then closed her eyes.

\* \* \*

Again, Debbie woke with a start in what seemed to her to be about thirty seconds later, when the car door flew open; Sarah had returned. As the rain dripped off her face, her expression told Debbie what she needed to know.

"No joy then?"

"No" Sarah replied, "The Duck wasn't here last night."

Debbie yawned once more, "What now?"

Sarah stared out of the windscreen for a moment before grabbing a hand full of McDonald's embossed tissues from her door compartment and while drying her face said.

"We'd better check in with the others, they may have had better luck."

* * *

At Bourne End Marina, Jane and Jenny stood on a bridge on the canal, overlooking the marina 50 metres away. They had been over to the marina offices which were closed and had already searched along the barges berthed on the moorings; The Duck wasn't there. Across on the other side, there were a few barges moored on the canal itself, so they decided to take a look at them.

"We're never going to find this boat." Said Jane, as they continued to make their way across the bridge.

"Barge." Jenny replied, correcting Jane's obvious mistake.

"What?"

"I said barge," Jenny repeated, "They're call barges."

"Barges, boats, ships, yachts, whatever they're bloody called, they're all the same to me. We're never going to find it are we?"

"Jane, we will find it. We have to. Anyway don't be so negative.

"I'm not. Well even you've got to admit, this is going to be like looking for a needle in a haystack."

"There you go again being negative. You of all people."

"Yeah, I know, but..."

The women continued over the bridge and so engrossed were they in their conversation, that they didn't notice DS Shrives and the two police officers coming the other way.

"Morning again." Said DS Shrives, as the women drew close.

"Morning," they replied in chorus as the officers passed.

"Oh my God." Whispered Jane, "I hope she didn't recognise."

"Don't worry." Jenny interrupted, not allowing Jane to finish her sentence, "we're just two women out for a walk."

"Yeah, but what if she recognised us."

"She did." Said Jenny, as she looked back at the officers, seeing them reach the end of the bridge and then disappear into the marina.

"Don't look, don't look," whispered Jane.

"It's OK, see they're gone."

Jane stopped and turned around,

"That was close." She said.

"Come on, it looks as though it's starting to rain again, let's check these boats before it starts bucketing down." Said Jenny.

"Barges, they're called barges." Jane replied sarcastically.

As the women reached the first of the barges, Jenny felt a vibration coming from her coat pocket, denoting that her mobile phone was ringing. Pulling the phone out, catching a bit of her 'Chariots of fire' ring tone.

"It's Sarah," she said before pushing the answer button and pressing the phone to her right ear.

"Hi, Sarah, no, no sign yet, were just checking a few other, barges!'" she said, while raising her eyebrows at Jane sarcastically, "on the opposite side of the marina. I take it you haven't found anything? She asked."

After a short pause, she said.

"OK, I'll see you soon," and then hung up.

"They're going to meet us here, get a cup of tea and then check further up at Berko and Tring."

"So they obviously didn't find anything down there then."

"No" Jenny replied shaking her head.

As the two women continued their search, Jane commented.

"Have you seen how slow they go, the barges I mean, they can't have gone far."

The women checked the few barges moored of that side of the canal and were about to leave when a man appeared from one of the cabins.

"Excuse me. Are you looking for them too?" He asked.

"For them too?" Said Jane, puzzled.

"Yes." Said Jenny, being canny. "Have you seen them?

"I thought you were." He replied, "Are you police too?"

The women didn't reply and just glanced at each other.

"Have you seen them then?" Jenny repeated.

"Like I told the other officers, they were here last night. He was very drunk and very rude."

"What, did the boat, I mean, the barge have a duck mascot on it?" Asked Jane.

"Yes, like I told your colleagues, it was called The Duck and yes it had a green duck mascot."

"What time did they leave?" Jane asked.

"It's strange, they left in the middle of the night,"

"The night?" Jane replied surprised.

"Yes, bloody woke me up with that rackety old engine. Yes he left about two thirty last night, in the pitch black and it can be quite dangerous, you know, if you don't know what you're doing. But I suppose I shouldn't be too surprised, given how much he must have had to drink."

*Nearly a seven hour head start, which means they could be anywhere.* Thought Jenny.

After thanking the man for his help, the women headed back across the bridge to the marina café.

Inside, Jenny called Sarah, informing her of what the man had said, but they still agreed to meet to plan their next move.

# CHAPTER 34

The four women sat in the Café at Bourne End Marina, taking a welcomed cup of tea, Jenny, Debbie and Jane all eating bacon sandwiches.

"So what's next then, they could be anywhere?" Said Debbie before taking a bite from her sandwich.

"We've just got to keep looking," Said Jane.

"I know that." Debbie mumbled, her mouth half full. "I just want to know whose going where and all that."

Sarah moved her mug before putting her hand into her coat pocket, pulling out her map, laying it in the space in front of her, folding it as to not encroach into any of the other women's space. In front of her, Jenny who'd already finished eating moved her plate to give more room for the map to be placed flat.

"Well," said Sarah, "we are here", pointing to a space on the map. "If they've had seven hours head start, then they still can't have got that far. If you think, a barge can only go something like, four miles an hour, or six at best. So they're only going to be about thirty five miles away, if that."

"See." Said Jane. Glaring at Jenny, who rolled her eyes.

"So they can be no further than Leighton Buzzard." Sarah continued, tapping the map. "We have to look in all the marinas between here and there. I mean they've got to stop sometime.

* * *

With similar thinking, the police offices headed to Marsworth Locks where there were moorings. They believed that the barge couldn't have gone any further and decided that they would work their way back from there.

It was lunchtime when they arrived at the lock, and rather than starting their search from the lock furthest north in the system, they started at lock 44, in the middle of the impressive 9 flight step, directly outside the lock keepers cottage.

The cottage, a turn of the century dwelling, stood on a bend, on the canal, with its bright whitewashed walls, brick red coloured tiled roof, white picket fence, and well manicured front garden, bore all the trappings of the English countryside.

As the rain began to fall once more, one of the officers knocked on the door of the quaint white cottage, however, got no answer.

Thinking that someone may have been home, DS Shrives walked through the well kept yet leaf covered front garden, around the side of the cottage and peered in through a window; there was no movement and clear to see that the lock keeper was out.

On the canal path, she looked up towards lock 45, but saw no one and then decided to head down to the start of the lock system. Hunger and the weather played an important part to that decision, as the 'old lock keepers cottage' at the start of the system, had been converted into a café some years earlier, and the lure of a warm drink and something to eat was too much of a temptation for her.

* * *

Unaware of the police presence, Graham traversed the final lock at Marsworth and was waved off by the lock keeper who had two barges further back, waiting to go through. It had taken an hour to pass through all nine locks and Graham feeling tired, was now ready for lunch.

Through the hatch, Sunisa now out of bed came out on deck wearing her yellow rain coat and carrying a tin foil covered plate: Graham's lunch.

The sound of the constant rushing water through the locks, twice induced her to go to the toilet, and after the second time, she couldn't get back to sleep and decided to get up.

While slowly getting dressed she tried to resolve some of the nagging issues that she'd had with Graham and now decided to find a way to leave him without arousing suspicion, so decided to behave normally, even if he did not; hence the preparation of his lunch.

Graham surprised to see her after their altercation, gladly welcomed the food, and after taking the plate asked her to "tie the barge up", when he stopped not far from the final lock. Those were the only words exchanged by them, as when she'd finished mooring the barge, she immediately returned to the cabin as the mere sight of him filled her with disgust, though did strengthen her resolve.

* * *

Over the next couple of hours, Sarah and the women walked the canal path, in addition to looking over bridges in the Berkhamstead area: The first on Little Heath Lane, where the excited Jane thought that she'd found The Duck, however, on closer inspection, she'd spotted a similar looking vessel. They then checked over the bridges on Bullbeggars Lane, Bank Mill Lane and Mill Street, *nothing*. They then moved on to Northchurh, Dudwell, before going on to Cow Roast Marina. *Still nothing*. On the canal path at Bulbourne still they found nothing, and by 3pm the women were starting to become disheartened.

"Look," said Debbie, "I've got to be getting back, I've got to get the kids and get dinner on."

"Me too." Said Jenny.

"Just half an hour more." Sarah pleaded.

Debbie and Jenny just looked down at the canal path, clearly not wanting to make eye contact, but resolute in their decision.

Sarah turned to Jane. "What are you going to do?" She asked.

Looking at the other women but directing a question to

Sarah, Jane asked, "What are you going to do?" before turning to face Sarah.

"I'm going a bit further up," Sarah replied, "as we're not going to The Horns now, and if you guys are going home, I might as well meet Karen later in Milton Keynes: I'll just take my time and have a good look up at Marsworth. I'll call Karen after this."

Jane thought for a moment. "OK, I'll stay with Sarah." She said, turning to face the other women.

Sarah smiled,

"Great."

\* \* \*

The women chatted for a few minutes and then said their goodbyes; Debbie and Jenny returning to where Jenny had parked her car, and then heading off home, while Sarah and Jane continued to walk along the canal path in search of the illusive barge.

In the squall and feet hurting, they slowly walked about five hundred metres then stopped: They decided to go back to the car and drive to Marsworth Lock as the moorings up there appeared on Sarah's map.

As they limped back, hikers, most of them fully clad in proper hooded waterproof jackets, walking boots, some even using hiking poles passed them.

They were surprised though, to be overtaken by DS Shrives

and the two police officers who had scoured the area up at Marsworth and were now on their way to Bulbourne.

"Afternoon," Said DS Shrives, recognising the women as they marched past. "Are you following us around?" She smiled, looking back at the women.

Jane laughed nervously.

"No. Just out for a walk." Sarah replied with a smile, but feeling stupid as the words left her lips, given the weather conditions.

The officers marched about fifteen metres before DS Shrives asked the constables to go on ahead and then stopped on the path. Standing on the grass verge at the side of the path, she waited for the women, looking at them and smiling as they approached.

"What are we going to do?" Jane whispered nervously.

"Don't worry." Sarah replied.

As the women drew close, DS Shrives asked.

"Excuse me, I know this is a strange question, but are one of you called Sarah?

The women stopped in the middle of the path and were silent.

"Sarah Braithwaite?" DS Shrives continued.

"Yes that's me." Sarah replied now feeling nervous.

"I thought so. After seeing you so many times today and looking at the way you're dressed, no one in their right mind would be just out for a walk in this."

As the words left her lips, a pair of middle-aged hikers, fully kitted up came up behind the women and waited to get past as the women blocked the path.

"Excuse me please." Said a silver haired hiker.

"Oh, sorry." Said Sarah, as the women moved on to the grass verge letting the hikers by.

They watched as the couple walked up the path a few metres.

"See." Said DS Shrives, illustrating how well dressed the hikers were.

The three women burst into laughter.

After a few moments.

"Yeah," said Sarah, "I'm Sarah and this is Jane. We're looking for The Duck."

"The Mortons, you mean?'" DS Shrives enquired and correcting Sarah.

"Yes, Graham and Sunisa." Replied Sarah attempting to go one better.

*Touché*

"Well I'm DS Shrives, I mean Carol Shrives, just call me Carol," the detective spluttered.

Yes we spoke the other day didn't we?" Sarah replied.

And after a short pause

"If I'd known you guys were looking for them this

morning, we could have pooled our resources and probably could have been more effective. But I suppose you weren't to know who we were."

For a moment, the looks on Sarah and Jane's faces portrayed one of guilt, which DS Shrives picked up on, and before she had a chance to continue, Sarah uncharacteristically when on the defensive.

"We, did know, but Trevor told us not to say anything if we saw you."

"Did he now? Just wait till I see him."

"Oh! Please don't say anything." Sarah pleaded knowing that she had put her foot in it.

"It's OK," the detective chuckled, "I won't."

After a momentary silence.

"Well we'd better compare notes." She continued.

The women talked for a few minutes about where they had been that day and realised that they could have searched as far as Leighton Buzzard if they had talked to each other earlier.

Jane noticed and became concerned by the tension that seemed to be building between Sarah and DS Shrives, as they talked over and interrupted each other.

When feeling that she should interject and about to do so, the two officers returned from their ten minute foray down the canal, abruptly ending the women's conversation, the expressions on the officer's faces giving away that they're search had not been fruitful.

So you're going to Milton Keynes then?" Asked DS Shrives.

"Yes," Sarah replied, "There are a few moorings on the way up there and we'll check around once we're there."

"Good, but unfortunately, we've got to call it a day."

"Why?" Jane asked, "As you said, the more pairs of eyes the better."

"Look, this isn't even an official search" DS Shrives replied rather sternly. "I mean we have no real reason to think that a crime has been committed and the resources that we're using here," she said turning to the officers, "have other duties; I was lucky to have these officers at my disposal for as long as I did, besides the light's going to be gone in an hour or so. So we won't be able to see anything out here soon."

*Excuses*. Thought Sarah, her body language giving away that she was annoyed with DS Shrives's comments.

"OK, were going to continue anyway." Sarah replied.

"OK, perhaps we can meet up tomorrow, if you haven't gone as far as Milton Keynes? I know it's out of my jurisdiction, but even after what I've just said, I'm still concerned; and, I'm on a day off tomorrow, so I can do what I like."

There was a momentary silence as Sarah thought; her body language and facial expressions depicting irritation.

"OK." She replied, "I'll call you, can I take your number?"

The women exchanged numbers, said their goodbyes, and went on about their business.

Sarah now saw that DS Shrives, like DS Kirkland last year, was torn between doing things by the book and her conscience: willing to give up her time to save a life. *Well why not, they are police offices, it's their job to look after the public after all.* She thought.

\* \* \*

As Sarah and Jane headed to the car, Sarah checked behind them and seeing that the officers were off in the distance, heading back to Marsworth thought it safe to talk.

"Rude, wasn't she." Said Sarah, staring into space, looking at the condensation of her breath is it left her mouth and nostrils.

"What do you mean?" Asked Jane.

*Shit* thought Sarah: She'd been thinking aloud and didn't really want to explain anything to Jane. Sounding judgemental was something she should have been practicing not to be and rather than resolving any issues she'd had with DS Shrives in her own head, she would now have to discuss them with Jane. Hesitating she made a meagre attempt to explain herself.

"Well, the way she spoke about the officers and in front of their faces. You know, calling them a resource; after all, they are human."

Looking confused, Jane shook her head and said.

"I don't know what you mean."

Then after a short pause said,

"But I did see some tension between you and that woman."

"Tension!" Said Sarah surprised, "what do you mean tension?"

"Well," said Jane, in a long drawn out way.

"Well?" Asked Sarah impatiently.

"Well, when you talked about that policeman, you know Kirkland, Trevor, or whatever his name is."

Sarah scoffed, "No, I think you're mistaken. You didn't see any tension from me."

"Yes I did," Jane replied sternly.

After a short pause she continued.

"Look, I don't know what's going on between you, that police woman and Kirkland; if you want to keep it private, that's fine, but you were the one that got me turned on to thinking positively, well, trying to be positive.

After a short pause and as if reading from a script, she continued.

"And being intuitive, recognising and responding positively to my feelings and now you're trying to lie to me."

Again, another momentary silence as Jane waited for a response, and when none came she continued on once more as Sarah's face began to flush.

"Look, you were the one who told me that when an opportunity came my way I should take it. Remember, when I got in trouble at the school."

"I know, I know." Sarah sighed.

\* \* \*

Six months after the *'lowered top incident'* involving Jane, Karen, JB and Mrs Mortimer, Jane left the kitchen to do an access course; one that, if successfully passed would gain her access to university.

She now attended The University of Hertfordshire, doing a teaching degree, and had also nurtured, to the dismay of his parents, a relationship with the now twenty one year old Kevin Mortimer; the boy who had almost cost her, her job.

Sarah's words had moved Jane to action and though she was still learning, *'The positive stuff'*, it had taken her to places, and opened doors that previously were only unattainable dreams. So now she believed in the power of thought and now couldn't understand why Sarah was now acting so strangely.

\* \* \*

"Well stop treating me like a child." Said Jane and after a short pause. "OK I know there was tension between you. Deny it if you want, but I know there was. "

"Yes there was. There is, I don't know." Sarah almost admitted. "I don't really want to talk about it." She said clearly flustered.

Jane glared at her, surprised.

"OK." She replied shrugging her shoulders.

The women walked back to the car in silence, Sarah wishing that she hadn't upset Jane, indeed, wishing that she could be more like Jane, also wishing that she hadn't opened her mouth.

As they drove the mile to Marsworth, Sarah began to critique herself: She'd taken this self-help and positive thinking to an extreme and now understood the space her ex-husband's mind occupied before she divorced him.

Although it was OK to be positive, there was now an air of self-righteousness about her, she acted as if she knew everything, or had all the answers and therefore subconsciously talked down to everyone.

*No wonder I upset Jane.* She had become like her Ex, conceited and almost intolerant and hated it.

Now knowing that she had drifted from the initial values that she'd once embraced, wanted to get back to them. Being judgemental was just one of the things that she recognised as polluting her psyche, and Jane's reaction to her negativity now reaped the wrong types of rewards.

As they pulled up at Marsworth, Sarah apologised.

"I didn't mean to upset you."

"You didn't; I just think you've been sounding a bit strange all day and it really came out when you spoke to that woman earlier."

Sarah nodded.

"Well," said Jane, with a smile "as Karen use to say we've got work to do."

In the fading light, the women got out of the car, the wind gusting through and forcing the car doors to slam shut; they then quickly made their way to the other end of the lock system.

# CHAPTER 35

Graham, having being in the wheelhouse for most of the day, apart from going in and using the toilet once, at lunchtime, was now very tired from the locks that he'd traversed, as it now approached 5pm.

They'd passed through the town of Leighton Buzzard and were a couple of miles passed The Grand Union pub at Three Locks; it was time to take a break. Inside Sunisa anxiously stared out of the starboard porthole, unsure of what to do, only knowing that she must get away from him.

After feeling the barge begin to slow, she made her way to the galley to prepare dinner. After peeling some potatoes and putting them on to cook, her eyes widened as she focused on a crate of beer that sat on the floor in the corner behind the galley door. She began to hatch a plan, *why didn't I think of this before,* she thought. With any luck, she would be able to sneak out after dinner.

She watched through a portside porthole as Graham moored the barge to the bank and step back on, before she hurried back into the galley.

Taking a packet of sausages out of the fridge, she placed them on the work surface, before stooping down to split the plastic covering on the twenty-four pack of beers; pulling out a bottle and then opening it. She listened while separating the sausages with a small knife, as Graham opened the hatch and climbed down the steps into the hallway.

Quickly laying the sausages into a hot lard filled frying pan, she waited for him to walk past the galley doorway.

"Oh you're in here. What have you been up to all day?" He asked.

"Nothing." She replied, handing him the bottle of beer. "Bangers and Mash for dinner." She continued. "Ready in about fifteen minutes."

Graham was silent; suspicious. *What is she up to?* He thought.

Before taking a sip, he stepped forward forcing Sunisa back, nearly on to the hob, where the lard and sausage filled pan fizzled. He looked at the pans over her shoulder, around the galley and then at Sunisa, who had both hands in her front apron pocket and defiantly staring at him then inadvertently glancing at the beer bottle that he held, which aroused his suspicions further.

"Here, you have some." He said, pushing the bottle under her nose.

"You know I don't like beer."

"Drink!" he growled.

Hesitantly she took the bottle and while staring up at him, sipped, smiled, then after a few seconds swallowed, and then moved to hand the bottle back.

"More! He said, pushing the bottle back, tipping it towards

her mouth, his eyes now bulging.

After quickly gulping a couple of mouthfuls, which caused her to cough as the bubbles filled her nostrils, he smiled, pulled the bottle back, *I don't want to waste this,* he thought, and with his head tilted back drank the whole thing in one go. Belching loudly, he handed Sunisa the bottle and motioned for her to give him another. Ripping the plastic packaging back a bit more, she pulled out two bottles and handed them to him.

"How long before dinner?"

"Fifteen minutes," She repeated, as he turned and headed to the lounge area.

Sighing with relief as he left the galley, she pulled the small knife she'd used to separate the sausages from her pocket, relieved that she didn't have to use it, throwing it into the washing up bowl that lined the sink.

Now reaching for a fish slice, she used it to flip the sausages that had begun to darken in the pan as a smile appeared on her face; her plan seemed to be working.

* * *

At 6:30pm, Graham sat in the lounge, exhausted, fast asleep and snoring loudly. He'd gorged himself on 8 sausages and a pound and a half of potatoes washed down with four bottles of beer; the bottles still lined up on the old coffee table. Knowing that he wouldn't be able to stay awake after consuming such a meal, Sunisa's plan had worked and now was her chance to get away.

Already in the hallway, she wore her yellow raincoat, carrying her holdall and trying not to breathe. Her face hot, beads of sweat now appeared on her brow, while Graham's snores grew louder and seemed to resonate off every wall.

With her heart pounding to the extent that she felt every beat in her breath as she slowly exhaled, she silently made her way up the stairs to the top of the hatch and took what was meant to be a last look down at the bottom of the hallway, before turning the handle.

But, there was a problem, it didn't turn, so she tried once more. *Nothing.* Now panicking, she tried harder, putting almost her whole body weight behind it, which caused her to slip forward and as she grabbed out at the rail to prevent her fall, she dropped her holdall, which made a loud thud as it hit the floor below.

In those few moments she felt that her heart would explode, as Graham's snoring suddenly stopped and now just a murmur came from the lounge. In a last ditched effort and prepared to leave her holdall, she frantically twisted the handle, but still nothing happened. It was locked, he hardly ever locked the hatch, but this time he had.

A few minutes later, Sunisa stood in the doorway of the lounge, staring at Graham, who was still snoring loudly, *he must have the key on him,* she thought.

Knowing that she must get the key from him, she put the holdall back into its hiding place, replaced the roll of money that she'd taken from the mattress, and now tiptoed across the lounge floor, having already searched his coat. It was only as she drew close that it began to dawn on her that she wasn't going to get the key without waking him, and as she stood there, he stopped breathing, which was something that he did often; and for sometimes up to about fifteen seconds. Knowing what was about to come next, she tried to leave the room quickly and quietly. But as she turned to go he let out a squeal like snore, as if trying to catch his breath, which woke him.

Wearily he opened his eyes and coughed, then seeing that Sunisa wore her coat and shoes asked.

"Where are you going?"

"Oh, I'm just going to put the rubbish out, but the hatch is locked." She replied hesitantly.

"No, No, I'll put it out later," he mumbled in his usual deep alcohol induced tone, still groggy from the beer that he'd consumed.

"I don't mind putting it out now."

"No, I'll do it," he said mustering a smile, "Wake me in an hour; we're going to get moving. We should get to Northampton by tomorrow. I'll put the rubbish out when I get up."

Shutting his eyes, moments later he was snoring loudly

once more.

Sunisa quietly returned to the hatch and tried it once more, but it was no use. *So much for my plan.*

\* \* \*

In Leighton Buzzard, Sarah and Jane spent an hour checking the barges moored around the well maintained canal path under the West Street Bridge, then moved on to the Old Linslade Road bridge as finally the light faded giving way to the night. After checking over both sides of the bridge and finding nothing, they stood on the north side, peering over its edge into the fluid darkness that ran beneath them.

"What now." Sighed Jane, tedium clearly heard in her voice.

"Do you want to call it a day?" Sarah asked.

"Well, it does seem pretty pointless carrying on now. I mean, it's too dark to see anything now.

After taking out her map, Sarah folded it, revealing the point at which they were and the canal ahead.

"I tell you what," she said, "let's go up to Three Locks, It's not that far. After we check the locks there, we can get something to drink if you want. What do you think?"

\* \* \*

A few miles past Three Locks, Sunisa woke Graham, who stood up, walked to the middle of the lounge, and stretched. She stood opposite him, hands behind her back still wearing her yellow coat, her face demure and almost emotionless.

"We'll be in Northampton tomorrow," he said smiling.

"I don't want to go." Sunisa replied, now staring at the floor.

"What?"

"I don't want to go, I want to leave. I don't want to be here anymore." She said looking up from the floor and shaking her head.

Stepping forward as he often did, he took up an intimidating stance, puffing out his chest, but was halted this time as Sunisa didn't back off.

Now enraged by her defiance, he reached out and tried to take hold of her upper arms, but buoyed by a newfound confidence she shrugged him off, flailing her arms around and for a split second bringing in to view a shiny object that she'd hidden behind her back.

"You ungrateful." He started, now filled with anger and raising his hand as if to give her a backhand. But, as it came down, he suddenly stopped, noticing that she did not cower or flinch and seemed unafraid; her eyes fill with hate and her face with rage.

Feeling something sharp pressing against his stomach, he slowly backed off, still looking into the rage stamped on Sunisa's face.

Now standing three feet away, he saw the shiny object that

had flashed before his eyes moments earlier. *No wonder she isn't scared,* he thought as the large kitchen knife came into view, its shiny tip glinting in the pale light and pointed in his direction, with Sunisa tightly holding the dark wooden handle with both hands. Shocked, he quickly patted around his stomach then examined his hands, checking for signs of blood.

"Why you!" he started, once more stepping forward, only to be halted in his tracks once more by Sunisa raising the knife and jabbing it in his direction.

"Don't come near me." She said, "I'll use this, I swear, I will."

"You ungrateful bitch!" Look at what I've done for you, if it wasn't for me, you'd be a whore. No, No, you'd probably be dead, your family would be dead and this is how you treat me. This is how you repay me?"

Staring at the floor, tears began to roll down Sunisa's cheeks, and she began to lower the knife.

"Come on love." He said stepping forward holding out a hand as if to take the knife and trying to take advantage of her emotional state.

"Stay back." She replied, taking a step back and resuming her pose, jabbing the knife in his direction once more, forcing him to retreat.

"Look, how long do you think you can stand there, the hatch is locked, how you gonna get out."

After a slight pause.

"Look, just give me the knife and let's talk about this." He continued.

"No, I just want to go."

But I paid for you; you can't go, unless." He thought for a moment. "Unless you give me back what I paid."

Angrily, Sunisa sniffed and dried her eyes with a cuff.

"What I've done for you in the past year is more than enough, I don't owe you anything."

There was a long pause as they both examined their options.

"Let me go." She whimpered, breaking the silence.

"Where will you go? I'm the only one that can take care of you."

"I don't know. Away from here, away from you."

"OK, I will." He sighed. "Just put the knife down and I'll let you go.

Sunisa, overwhelmed with emotion, wept.

"No, no you won't," She cried, "When I put it down, you'll change your mind, I know you will, you'll just keep me here.

"No, no, I won't." he replied, taking a step forward.

Sunisa responded by raising the knife and pointing it in his direction, but this time he held his ground.

"No, I won't love, if I'd known that you felt this way, I would have done something about it ages ago."

As the tears ran down her face, the tip of the knife began to fall; she moved it into her right hand, and then down by her side. Graham seeing his chance slowly took another step forward.

"Come on love, put it down." He said, taking a step closer.

Sunisa wanting to believe him was now completely off guard, tears streaming down her face and staring at the floor; time for him to pounce. Now less than a foot away, he suddenly grabbed out at her right wrist and then swung his right fist, punching her in the face, forcing her to fall. As she fell against the doorframe, he closed his eyes and swung once more, punching out and this time putting all of his weight behind it, this time missing her face and hitting her throat, forcing her to release the knife as she reached to hold the front of her neck. In her haze she looked up at him from where she'd fallen, before quickly scanning the floor for the knife. After locating it to her right, she slowly made a move for it, but with his full weight, he stepped on her hand and kicked out with his right foot, his shin catching her full square on the chin, forcing her head back against the doorframe.

Stooping, he picked the knife up and stood over her for a second, breathing heavily; she was out cold, blood slowly dripping from the corner of her mouth and left nostril. He now began to panic.

"I own you, I own you, why are you ungrateful? Why?

You're all the same," he mumbled to himself as he paced up and down the room, holding his head and occasionally pulling at his hair. After a few minutes, he stopped in front of her to ensure that she was still breathing, before rushing off down the hallway.

* * *

In the bar of the Parkside Hotel, Karen and Jane sat at a table.

"Long time no see." Said Karen.

Jane smiled, then relieved the strains the day had put on her back, by leaning back and sliding down into her comfortable Edwardian tub styled chair.

"You look so grown up now, and I hear that you've been busy." She continued.

"What with?" Jane asked, "Uni or the engagement?"

"Well both, Aren't you glad you ignored me?" She asked, referring to the conversation they'd had, in relation to Kevin Mortimer over fifteen months earlier.

"Here we go." Said Sarah, returning from the bar with a tray of drinks. "Get these down you." She continued, putting each drink onto the table before returning to the bar with the tray.

Looking around the bar as she returned to sit down, Sarah whispered.

"Everyone's staring."

The women briefly glanced around the brightly lit, light magnolia coloured room.

"Don't worry about it," Karen replied. "I get this all the time, it comes with the territory."

"So what's it like." Jane asked, "You know, being famous."

"It's OK, but tell me how are you all doing? How's Debbie and Jenny." Karen replied, taking a sip from her large glass of red wine.

"Everyone's fine," Said Sarah and then rushed through the pleasantries. "Of course you know about Jane: Debbie and Jenny are running the kitchen and doing a good job. I finally got the company to employ a couple more bods, so that Debbie and that, don't struggle too much now."

"That seems such a world away now," said Karen staring into space.

"Hmm, I can imagine," Said Jane.

Quickly interrupting, Sarah said, "Jenny's still going to therapy and getting better, or so she tells me and I'm fine."

"Good." Karen replied, now sensing the urgency in Sarah's voice. "Look, I'm sorry about today. I wanted to help, but it's been so hectic. But I do have a day off tomorrow though, so I'll be able to help."

Sarah nodded, "I'm just fearful for her, she sounded so scared."

"What did the police say?" Asked Karen.

"The usual."

"Yeah, you've got to be half dead before they'll do anything." Said Jane.

"What about your boyfriend, can't he do anything?" Karen asked, to Sarah's embarrassment.

"Boyfriend?" Jane asked surprised.

Sarah peered at Karen and if looks could kill...

"Oh, I'm sorry." Said Karen, "I thought everyone knew."

"Knew what?" Jane asked, "Knows what?"

"It's nothing." Said Sarah, still looking hard at Karen and now eyebrows raised.

"You may as well come clean," Said Karen, "She'll find out sometime."

There was a momentary silence.

"Well?" Jane asked.

Sarah sighed, "Kirkland, she's talking about Kirkland."

"What, the policeman Kirkland?" Then it clicked. "What, you and him. You're going out with him. Bloody hell! When did that happen then?"

Face red with embarrassment, Sarah butted in.

"Thanks," She said, looking at Karen. "Look, he's not my boyfriend anymore, it ended a while ago. 'Boyfriend, I hate that word, it sounds so, so."

"I don't believe it," Jane interrupted. "You and Kirkland," she said to Sarah's annoyance.

"Can you just get over it?"

"I don't believe it," Jane repeated, "just wait till the others hear this."

"Don't you dare!"

"OK you two, come on." Said Karen smiling.

After a slight pause.

"Well, let's get one thing straight," said Sarah, he is not my boyfriend and not a word to the others about this."

"OK." Replied, Karen and Jane in unison, before bursting into laughter, causing Sarah to smile then laugh along with them.

When they'd calmed down, Sarah answered Karen's initial question.

"I spoke to Trevor earlier; he said that he may be able to help tomorrow if we hadn't already caught up with the barge.

"Let's hope he does, because it looks like we're going to need all the help we can get." Said Karen.

"But I think there may be some jurisdiction issues though, well according to Carol." Said Sarah

"Carol?"

"Oh, sorry the police detective whose dealing with it from the Hertfordshire end.

"Ooh look at you," Karen mocked. "On first name terms with everyone, Carol and Trevor eh?"

"So tell me more about him then." Said Jane, changing the

subject.

The women caught up and for an hour talked about men, work and where they had searched that day, before Sarah remembered that she had to collect Carl and Louise from her mother's house, as it was already 8pm.

They agreed to meet up at the hotel at 10am the following morning to resume the search and as they got up to go, two women who had been staring over for the past half hour approached Karen and asked for her autograph. As she signed a couple of beer mats, Sarah mouthed and signalled that she had to go. Karen smiled and waved good-bye.

# CHAPTER 36

Sunisa regained consciousness at about 5:30am the following morning, still on the floor at the entrance of the lounge, face and head hurting.

Graham had switched the lights out leaving her in darkness, so it took a moment for her to regain her bearings. On hearing running water mixed in with the heavy rain that fell on the deck outside, she knew that Graham must be putting the barge through a lock and thought that if she could only get up, perhaps she could alert someone to her plight.

After propping herself up against the doorframe, she felt around her mouth, wincing when she accidentally touched her nose, which was badly bruised. Moving her tongue around inside her mouth, she felt that the inside of her lip was split and then ran her finger inside, checking the cut she'd already felt with her tongue.

Taking a deep breath, she tried to stand up, but even in the darkness, she immediately felt dizzy, tingling white spots appearing before her eyes, so had to sit down again.

After sitting still for a minute or two, she tried to stand up once more and when on both feet, clung to the doorframe, as she still felt a bit hazy.

Reaching out she switched the lights on, the brightness of which seem to glow off the magnolia painted walls; hurting her eyes in the process. This caused her to close them again and then open them slowly, squinting until she became accustomed.

After slowly looking around the room, she launched herself into the middle of it, pushing herself off the doorframe and awkwardly stumbling forward in the direction of the bow portside porthole.

*Made it:*

Peering out into the darkness, she could see from the slowly moving silhouettes of foliage on the bank, set against the dark dawn sky, that they were already on the move.

Disorientated, she listened for rushing lock water, which her eyes had already told her that she would not hear and only heard the sound of heavy rain above the hum of the engines.

Her eyes refocused on the light filled porthole, which gave her a hideous reflection, and on seeing for the first time the beating that she'd endured, she put her hand over her mouth and silently wept.

Blue and red swellings around her nose and mouth, and dry red to almost black encrusted blood on her nose and lip cracked, throbbed and stung as her face contorted, her salty tears running into the fresh wounds.

Turning away from what she saw and still feeling weak, she made her way along the hallway and climbed the stairs to the hatch, which was locked. After spending a few minutes trying to force the lock, she gave up, now feeling that she had now become a prisoner.

After spending half an hour in the bathroom slowly cleaning herself up, she returned to the bedroom, climbing into bed fully clothed, wishing that she'd never left Thailand, romantically and ironically only remembering the good things about her homeland.

Now with only the odd tear, it was as if she'd given up, resigning herself to her fate and drifted off to sleep as the dawn broke on a new day.

* * *

Sarah, Jane, Jenny and Debbie, met at 9am at the canal in Croxten.

The plan was to drive to Milton Keynes where Sarah, after a telephone conversation the night before, had agreed to meet DS Shrives and is where they would also meet Karen at 10am.

Jane waited in Sarah's car while Sarah under a large bright red umbrella explained to Jane and Debbie where they would be going as the rain tipped down. The weather reports predicted sporadic heavy rain and high wind; there were also flood warnings across large parts of the country, and members of the public were asked to travel only if absolutely necessary: Advice that had a familiar ring to it.

* * *

Both arriving at about 9:45am and being the only two customers in the lounge of the Parkside Hotel, Karen and DS

Shrives were shown to tables about eight or nine feet apart.

A waiter came out to serve them and on recognising Karen from the television, served her first.

The women sipped their tea in silence, DS Shrives trying not to make eye contact, but when she did, Karen smiled back at her.

"Hi," Said DS Shrives in an unmistakeable police officer's tone, "So what brings you here?" She asked.

"Oh, I'm meeting some friends." Karen replied, then taking a sip from her cup and turning to continue reading a magazine that she had laid out on the table.

"I've seen you on TV haven't I?" said DS Shrives, not letting on that she knew exactly where she had seen Karen before.

Karen smiled, "Yes, you probably did, at eight o'clock last night."

"It's not my thing." DS Shrives replied, shaking her head, referring to the television programme. "But I suppose it takes all sorts."

Karen paused for a moment, trying to figure out, if this woman was going out of her way to be rude, but giving her the benefit of the doubt said.

"So what brings you here?"

"Police business." DS Shrives replied, with an air of self-importance.

"Oh, you're with the police, you might be able to help." Said Karen before starting to go through the reason why she waited in the lounge. It wasn't long before DS Shrives interrupted, realising now that they were there to do the same job.

"So you know Sarah and the women from the school."

"Yes" Karen replied surprised, "I'm here to meet them."

DS Shrives gathered her things and moved to Karen's table.

"So how do you know them?"

"Well, I used to be in charge in the kitchen at the school a couple of years ago."

"Wow, big change then?"

Karen nodded, "Oh here they are now." She said, looking over to the entrance to the lounge.

Debbie and Jenny had arrived, water dripping off them, as the rain continued to pour outside. On seeing them Karen stood up and rushed over to greet them.

After hugging them both, she enquired after the others.

"Where's Sarah and Jane?"

"Oh, they're just parking up, they'll be in, in a minute. "Debbie replied. "Oh, I see the old bill are here," she whispered, nodding in the direction of DS Shrives, who was now standing, looking uncomfortable, hands in her jeans front pockets.

"Yeah," Karen replied. "Funny woman, anal."

* * *

"OK! Ladies," Said DS Shrives, I think it's time we got going."

The women had been sitting around drinking tea and chatting for about half an hour; the time now 10:35am. After introducing herself to the group, DS Shrives had been left out of the chitchat and apart from feeling a bit left out, now felt it was time that they resumed the search.

As if she was not there, the women carried on talking.

"Ladies!" DS Shrives repeated a little louder, now catching their attention.

"I think it's time we got going." She continued.

The women agreed.

"But first, we need to know where we're going to go and where we're going to search." Said Sarah turning to address the women.

"Well, I want to go with Karen today." Said Jane.

"Well I don't want to drive." Said Jenny.

The women bar DS Shrives and Karen began to talk over each other, as they all wanted their demands heard.

"Ladies, Ladies!" Said DS Shrives.

The women continued to bicker, before they were stopped in their tracks.

"Hey! We've got work to do!" That familiar voice; Karen butted in and there was an instant silence.

"Come on, were forgetting that a girl's life could depend on what we do now, so let's get this show on the road." She demanded.

"But all I was saying." Said Jane, before Karen interrupted once more.

"Jane, I don't want to hear it," she growled.

"But,"

Karen glared at her once more, which had the desired effect.

"Who's leading this?" Karen asked.

"I am," Said DS Shrives and Sarah in unison, glaring at each other momentarily before Sarah nodded, letting DS Shrives that she would not contest her being in charge.

"I am," repeated the detective. "Can I take your map," She said, holding her hand out in Sarah's direction.

The women listened while DS Shrives went through an action plan. She divided the women up into teams; Debbie and Jenny, Sarah and Karen, and to Jane's disappointment, she had been paired with DS Shrives.

The route would take them up the canal, through Milton Keynes in to the Northamptonshire countryside and ending at the entrance to the river Nene. They agreed to meet up at about 4pm, at The Walnut Tree Inn, to compare notes and to grab a bite to eat if they had not found the couple by then.

They left The Parkside Hotel feeling upbeat, confident that

they would find The Duck today.

* * *

Sunisa woke at around 11am and was quickly reminded of her situation, as when she moved to get out of bed she ached all over, especially around her mouth and throat.

In the bathroom, she took a couple of Ibuprofen to ease the pain, some of the water that she drank dribbling out from the corner of her swollen lips. Looking in the cabinet mirror, she believed that she looked worse than before, as while she slept, her facial and neck bruises had begun to ripen.

Feeling her stomach gurgle and then looking at her watch, she realised that she had not eaten in fifteen hours, but owing to the constant butterflies that she felt in the pit of her stomach, hunger wasn't an obvious feeling. Rather anxiety; anxious about Graham and what he intended to do with her.

She took a sharp intake of breath, alarmed when she felt the barge shudder as if blown by the wind. It was then that she realised that they were no longer on the move and on opening the bathroom curtains, through the steamed up porthole she saw that the barge was indeed moored.

She left the bathroom, quickly went back into the bedroom, where she slipped on her shoes and coat and then headed for the hatch, where she spent a minute or two pulling at the handle, which was still locked, before thumping the hatch and shouting for Graham to let her out; only the patter of the rain her answer.

After another few minutes of banging on the hatch and now crying she gave up, climbing back down to the hallway, taking off her coat and slowly making her way to the lounge. She sat looking through the bow, portside, porthole, waiting to catch anyone's attention, but given the amount of rain that now fell, *'no one would be out in this.'* She thought.

Just over a mile away at the Grey Hound Inn, just outside of Northampton, Graham, feeling quite tired, after travelling through the night, had just finished a mixed grill, which didn't help the way he felt. Leaning back into his chair, he sipped a pint of beer:

*Tonight, if all goes well, fifty thousand; easy money.* He thought smiling to himself.

## CHAPTER 37

Over the next five hours the women searched every lock and mooring on their maps and others that were not. At 4:15pm Debbie and Jenny were the last to arrive at The Wall Nut Tree as the light began to fade and were soaked as the weather began to worsen; hair stuck to their faces and looking bedraggled.

Looking across the bar area, Debbie spotted the others, and the pair made their way over.

"Bloody weather." Said Debbie as she drew close to the others.

"You girls want a drink?" Karen asked.

Debbie looked down at the table, seeing various drinks, tea coffee and a couple of the alcoholic kind.

"Tea for me." Said Jenny.

"Oh, err, I'll have a G and T." Debbie replied.

As Karen went off to the bar, Jenny sat down; taking off her wet coat, rolling it up and putting it under her chair; Debbie pealing hers off, as if it was stuck to her.

"No joy then?" Said DS Shrives.

Shaking her head Debbie sat down.

"No, nothing but bloody water."

"Same thing with us." Said Jane.

"But we've got to stay positive," said Sarah, "We'll find them."

"Yeah, but we're going to lose the light fairly soon." Said DS Shrives.

After a moments silence, Sarah turned to Jane and Debbie.

"Have you guys got to do stuff at home? You know, make dinner, or collect the children."

"Oh sorry, I should have said," Said Jenny. "Mine are with Steve."

"OK," Sarah a replied, turning to Debbie.

"Steve's my husband." Said Jenny, now turning to DS Shrives, who just nodded.

"Mine are at my mum's." Said Debbie.

"And I haven't got any, thank God." Said Jane, causing the women to burst into laughter.

"Good," said Sarah, "It means we can keep looking."

"Well, unless we've missed them out on the canal somewhere, I reckon they'll be in Northampton by now." Said DS Shrives.

"From what I can remember, when he took Toi to Northampton the last time, he'd done the trip in two days." Said Sarah

"Two days?" Said Jane in disbelief, "Have you seen how fast those things go? If he is even in Northampton now, that would be a miracle; he would have had to travel for two nights and two days, with no sleep."

"We'll see," said Sarah, as Karen returned with the drinks.

"I've got us a table in the restaurant and it's on me; and I'm not taking no for an answer." She said, putting the drinks onto the table.

"But," Said DS Shrives.

"No buts." Karen replied, "Let's get something down and get out again, we've got to find this woman."

After a moments silence.

"Come on," said Debbie, "I don't know about you, but I'm hungry."

* * *

After being on his feet for the best part of seventy-two hours, Graham was now exhausted.

Mooring the barge near Northampton Aquadrome, he now sat calmly in the darkness of the wheelhouse looking through its steamed up windows out onto the river, with his crackly old radio as company.

As the weather reports predicted, this was turning out to be the worst day so far and even he pondered the risk of damage to the barge in the activity that he'd planned.

Down below Sunisa also sat in darkness, still fearing the worst. She told herself that if he came near her again, she would give as good as she got, and though Graham had removed all of the sharp implements from the kitchen draws, she kept a heavy paperweight handy.

The pair of them in almost trance like states, listened to the sudden and noisy arrival of the rain as it beat down onto the deck.

It was time: Graham put his hood up and braved the squalor while untying The Duck from its moorings, having to jump back on board, knocking over a couple of beer bottles, as the barge bobbed about in the water and moved out two feet from the bank owing to the wind. *Bloody weather.*

He turned the engine over, which spluttered into life.

*'What is he up to?'* thought Sunisa, who got up and stepped on a plate containing a couple of slices of toast that she'd made and tried to consume earlier, but had trouble swallowing owing to her throat being swollen. She hopped half way across the room with a piece of buttered and jam covered bread clinging to her foot, the filling beginning to seep between her toes, before pulling it off and wiping her foot on a bath towel that had been left on the floor.

Now looking out through the bedroom porthole, all she saw was rainwater as it splashed against the steamed up glass.

\* \* \*

"I get off in about an hour," said Kirkland, "I'll meet you by the Hospital car par, the Cliftonville entrance."

"OK." Said Sarah.

"If you haven't found them by the time you get here, I'm not sure that you will, well not tonight anyway, have you seen the weather out there?"

"Yes, we've been out in it all day." She replied, looking at her map, "we're still in Blisworth, and it's going to take longer than an hour to do all the locks and moorings, between here and the hospital."

"OK what time then."

"Give us about three hours."

"Three hours!" He replied, seemingly surprised, then after a pause said, "OK." Looking at his watch. "About nine then."

"Yes, nine will be OK, I think."

"Look, I've got to go, I'll see you at nine," he said before hanging up.

Sarah returned her phone to her handbag and entered the restaurant, where the other women were finishing their dinners.

"What'd he say," asked Karen.

"He'll meet us at nine at the Hospital. Anyway, we'd better get going, it's dark already and it's going to be murder trying to see anything out there."

Five minutes later, the women were outside, having already decided where their teams were going to look. They said their goodbyes and were off again conducting their search.

* * *

Over the next few hours, the women frantically searched along the Grand Union.

The rain was constant and blew about in the wind, just off a roundabout in earshot of the M1 motorway, where Debbie and Jenny stood looking over a bridge.

They were well and truly soaked when an articulated lorry drove through a large puddle, which splashed dirty gritty gutter water onto them.

"Bastard!" Debbie screamed, as the lorry passed, water dripping off her face and having to spit to get the grit out of her mouth.

"I've had enough of this." She continued, putting two fingers up at the lorry, as it disappeared onto the motorway slip road. "We'll never find them now."

"We've got to stay positive." Jenny replied.

"You know who you bloody sound like?" Debbie replied sarcastically.

"I don't care; all I know is we've got to stay focused on trying to find that barge."

"It's too bloody dark now. I'm going to call Sarah, I think we should go home."

Jenny knew that Debbie was right, they could not see anything down on the water and it was definitely too dark for two women to be walking about on the path itself; and the weather made everything miserable.

\* \* \*

At 7:45pm on the Banbury Lane Bridge, DS Shrives and

Jane sat in the car, hazard lights flashing, making that rhythmical clicking sound inside, as the rain, so heavy that it fell; they had to wait for a break, before venturing outside.

"So they had a relationship." Asked DS Shrives, referring to Sarah and Kirkland.

"Yes, but it's all over now though."

*That makes sense and that's why she always seems a bit funny when we talk about him. Clearly a bit of feeling still there for him.* Thought DS Shrives.

"So what happened then, why'd they break up?"

"I don't know," Jane replied, now regretting that she'd started talking about Sarah at all. "Whatever you do, don't say anything to her about it. She gets a bit touchy, you know."

DS Shrives nodded.

"Look the rain's dying down a little," said Jane changing the subject, "Shall we have a look here?"

"Come on then." DS Shrives replied.

* * *

"OK, just meet us at the hospital." Said Sarah, before hanging up her phone.

"Debbie and Jenny have had enough." She said, turning to Karen. "They want to go home."

"You can't blame them." Karen replied.

"I suppose not and this weather isn't helping."

After a momentary silence, "I'm going to call Trevor," said

Sarah, "perhaps, he'll meet us earlier."

"Yes, we'll have to let the others know. I hope he's got some suggestions on how we can speed this up."

Sarah nodded before taking out her phone and dialling his number.

# CHAPTER 38

The women arrived at the hospital car park to see DS Kirkland braving the weather; standing under a large umbrella next to his car.

In the headlights of a long almost continuous line of cars that arrived with visitors, DS Shrives and Sarah got out to meet him, huddling under his umbrella and one that Sarah had taken from her car.

"Hi ladies, glad you could make it." He said sarcastically.

Not seeing the funny side, Sarah immediately looked at her watch, seeing that they had actually arrived five minutes earlier than they had agreed.

"So I see there's no need for introductions." He continued.

"No, we all know each other, don't we?" Said DS Shrives eyebrows raised..

There was a slight pause as Kirkland glared at Sarah.

"Err, yes." He said slowly, clearly embarrassed, given his relationship with Sarah. "It's a long story."

"Actually, not that long." Sarah replied, attempting to cut through the tension. "But we're not here to talk about how we know each other are we?"

"Yes, I mean no; of course not." Said DS Shrives, now thinking that she'd almost instigated an argument.

"Yes," agreed Kirkland, now blushing.

"OK," Said Sarah now taking the lead.

"We've looked at every lock and mooring from Croxten to here and found nothing, and under almost every bridge. It's like they've disappeared."

"Let me stop you there." Said Kirkland butting in. "Now, we're saying that Morton's done this before right? And got away with it? So what's to say he won't do the exact same thing, in the same place?

The was another momentary pause as the women waited for Kirkland to continue.

"Don't you see? The last time, Morton said that he got stuck under a bridge in Northampton. Now from where we are, there are only two bridges left, before we hit the River Nene proper. And one of those is where he got stuck the last time; so I'm betting that he's so arrogant that he'll try something under the same bridge or one very close to the spot."

"Hmm, I don't know." Said DS Shrives, "I can't see him doing that, I mean that would be total arrogance, foolish. I'm not sure."

"But what have we got to lose?" Sarah interrupted, "If they are the last two places left to search today, then I say let's do it."

Kirkland turned to DS Shrives,

"Look, you know how arrogant he was when you met him a few months ago?"

She nodded. "I suppose you could be right."

"OK. He said. "Carol you take two cars to the Hardwater Road Bridge: It's on the map; and I'll go with Sarah to the one after that, I think it's on some farmland. I'll call if I find anything. You do the same."

"OK." Said DS Shrives. "Let's go."

*  *  *

The bridges that crossed the Grand Union around the Hardwater Road area were in the middle of open country, dark, secluded and hardly used. They were low and renowned for trapping the inexperienced boat master when the water was high; and tonight the water was high, and the current fast moving.

As The Duck approached a bridge, with his heart pumping furiously and filled with anxiety, Graham slowly turned the noisy engines to full speed, something that he hardly ever did.

Because of this, below and still in the dark, Sunisa knew something was wrong and through the porthole, though still dark, she saw that the atmosphere seem to illuminate slightly, as unbeknown to her Graham had turned on his spotlight, and now she could just about make out the silhouettes of trees and bushes as they quickly moved by.

In the wheelhouse Graham watched as the bridge drew closer, so held on tight to the wheel and braced himself for impact.

Sunisa turned to make her way back to the bed and suddenly screamed as she was violently thrown to the floor when The Duck hit the bridge. The noise as the wheelhouse scraped against the underside of the bridge made a deafening sound; wood and metal against brick and concrete.

Panicking, she quickly picked herself up, switched on the lights and rushed back to the porthole, now only making out brickwork outside.

After slipping on her coat and then shoes, she made her way to the hatch, trying the handle once more. *Still locked.* On hearing more scraping outside and gripped by fear, she banged on the hatch shouting.

"Let me out. Help, please, somebody help."

She waited a second, before hearing the engine go off, then on hearing the unmistakable shuffle of Graham's feet as they grew louder as if heading towards the hatch, she quickly made her way back down the steps and into the bedroom, then scanned the bedroom floor for the paperweight that she'd planned to defend herself with.

Gripped by fear, she waited in silence as he unlocked the hatch and twisted the handle, opening it.

"Sunisa," He shouted. "Sunisa!"

Still gripped by fear, she said nothing.

"Sunisa love, I need your help."

She was still silent.

"Sunisa!" He shouted, once more. "We've had a crash and we might sink. I need your help. Please!"

Now thinking that he sounded serious, she slowly made her way out of the bedroom, through the hallway, and stood at the bottom of the steps.

"I'm sorry about what happened last night, but you gave me no choice."

Ignoring his words and just wanting to get out, she said.

"What do you want me to do?"

"Come out and I'll show you.

Slowly she climbed the steps, hiding the paperweight in her pocket, before stepping out into the wind, and having been locked up for the past couple of days, took a deep breath, closing her eyes and enjoying the smell of the fresh air.

It was dark as she looked around suspiciously, still refusing to trust him.

"This way." He said, pointing towards the stern.

"Look." He said pointing to the top of the wheelhouse that rubbed against the top of the bridge as the barge bobbed about in the water, grating and occasionally making that screeching chalk against blackboard sound.

Looking out onto the water, she saw that they'd not gone too far under the bridge and things didn't look that bad.

She would take the first chance to get away, thinking that as soon as they were free she would jump on to the path or into the water.

"We need to get it out of here."

"What do you want me to do?" She repeated.

"I'm going to slowly reverse the barge up; I need you to use the bargepole to keep the barge in the middle and off the walls. That could completely tear off the wheelhouse." He said pointing to the bridge arch.

"Here" he continued, picking up a thirteen-foot pole from the deck and offering it to her, knocking over a couple of his now water filled beer bottles, which rolled off and splashed into the river.

"I'll start the engine, just remember, keep us off the walls." He said now handing her the pole.

"Can't you turn the light on?" She asked, struggling to hold the pole.

"No, he replied hesitantly, "It's, it's broken."

She looked at him disbelievingly, as she'd seen the light earlier so knew he was lying, but now chose to say nothing through fear of angering him. Besides, she had her plan and would get away soon.

"Come on then!" He said voice raised, sparking her in to action.

\* \* \*

After talking to the other women, in convoy, they left the hospital car park.

With her windscreen wipers on full and the demister struggling to keep the windscreen clear, DS Shrives used her sleeve to clear enough of her windscreen to see to drive.

"So, something did happen between them." She said. "You know between Sarah and Trevor."

"Trevor?" Jane asked puzzled.

"Yes, Trevor Kirkland."

"Oh yes, well I did say that earlier." Jane replied, now remembering Kirkland's first name.

"Do you know why they split up?" DS Shrives asked once more.

"No, I don't really know much about what went on between them. All I know is that she's changed."

"Changed how?"

"Well, I don't know." Jane replied, now pensive. "She used to be so positive; you know, always thinking in a positive way. She helped me and come to think of it, she helped all the others too; you know, all of us that worked in the kitchen. Every one of us have had good things happen to us in the past year, but Sarah."

Jane paused.

"But Sarah?" DC Shrive asked inquisitively.

"Well I think ever since Toi died." Jane paused once more. "Look, I don't think I should talk about her."

After a momentary silence and seeing that Jane didn't

really want to talk.

"OK, suit yourself." Said DS Shrives.

"Look," said Jane pointing out in front.

Sarah's car, hazard warning lights came on, giving the drivers of the other vehicles in the convoy, DS Shrives and Debbie, the signal that they should turn off on to the Hardwater Road Bridge, which was only half a mile away, while Sarah, Kirkland and Karen would continue onto the farm bridge.

\* \* \*

The Duck's wheelhouse scraped along the bridges arch, juddering and making a horrendous noise. From Sunisa's point of view, the plan didn't seem to be working as the barge had moved three feet: Indeed, instead of reversing the barge had moved forward.

Out on deck the wind howled through the bridge arch carrying rain that lashed against her small frame while she struggled with a pole more than twice her height.

Inside the wheelhouse, Graham sat, trying to summon up some courage, but only trembled with fear.

Out across the fields, in the darkness, only the light from a few of the houses a mile away could be seen, as Sunisa felt her way along the length of the barge, using the barge pole against the walls of the bridge as her guide. As she reached the wheelhouse Graham shouted over.

"I'm going to turn the engines off to try and drift back. Go down the front and keep us off the portside." He said, pointing to the left side of the barge.

She nodded, before starting to make her way to the front, as he reduced the engine speed, letting the barge drift back, the top of the wheelhouse scraping along the arch, occasionally making a squealing noise.

* * *

At the Hardwater Road bridge, DS Shrives, Jane, Debbie and Jenny, stood under the cover of their umbrellas, peering over the sides; two of them on the side up stream and two on the south side. DS Shrives shone her torch down into the black fast moving water on the north side, then shouted over to the others,

"Can you see anything?"

"No," Debbie shouted back.

"I'm going down there." Said DS Shrives, before sighing heavily and shaking her head, knowing she was about to do something silly.

"You can't" Jane replied.

"I'm going down!" DS Shrives shouted over to the other women, who quickly crossed the road, joining her.

They all now wore worried expressions.

"Look, shouldn't you wait for Kirkland." Said Jenny.

"I'll be fine!" insisted DS Shrives; feeling a bit annoyed,

thinking that the women probably thought that she shouldn't go down because she is a woman.

After a momentary silence, DS Shrives responded, trying to alleviate some of their fears.

"OK, OK, I'll call him." She said shaking her head, "But only when I'm down there. "Come on give me one of your numbers just in case I can't get hold of him.

After tapping Jane's number into her mobile, she climbed the three foot wire fence that separated the road from the canal bank and then scrambled down the steep heavily mudded bank towards the path, clinging to bushes, small trees and shrubs to slow her descent.

Soaked when she reached the path, she took out her torch, flicked it on, having to hit it lightly a couple of times before it flickered into life. Pointing it downward to look at her shoes and trousers, she sighed heavily once more, as they were now covered in mud. *Bloody hell* she thought, shaking her head, before lifting the beam and shining it under the bridge.

Struggling to see, she wiped the rainwater from her face and shielded her eyes with her free hand. *Bingo!* There in front of her was a barge. *OK, time to get Kirkland over here,* she thought, turning the torch off and hiding by the side of the bridge.

* * *

At the farm bridge, Sarah, Karen and Kirkland stood on top

peering over the north side down into the water. In the light of Kirkland's torch, they caught sight of what looked like the stern of a boat.

"There!" Karen shouted, "There it is again."

"Yes I see it," said Kirkland. "It could be any barge, but I'm going to have to go down there to take a proper look."

"How are you going to do that?" Asked Sarah, clearly concerned. "How are you going to get down there? It's got to be 20 feet."

The bridge crossed the canal in the middle of an extremely muddy field, with barbed wire on either side, designed to keep cattle from getting close to the canal. The only way down was over the side of the bridge and they all knew it.

Kirkland looked down over the side once more, his body language giving away what he had in mind.

"Come on, you can't be serious." Said Sarah.

"Look, it's not that much of a drop."

Karen laughed. "Come on Mr," she said, "Be sensible, one slip and you'll be in the river."

"Or even worse," said Sarah, "You could hit your head or anything."

Kirkland thought for a second.

"Listen. This may be our only chance of saving this girl and I'm willing to take the risk."

The women were silent as deep down they knew he was

right.

"Come on, you know it makes sense." He continued.

After a short pause, Sarah said. "Just be careful." Before taking and squeezing his hand.

"OK." He said, handing her his torch. "Shine the torch onto the boat, I'll hang then drop down onto it. Then I want you to drop the torch down. I'll signal you, OK?"

"Yes." Sarah replied, "Please be careful.

Kirkland smiled. "Aren't I always?"

Though still windy, there was a lull in the rainfall and now was the best time to go. Kirkland thought about removing his jacket, but changed his mind, opting for warmth over agility. He then climbed onto the edge of the bridge and then slowly lowered himself down.

Sarah shone the torch light onto what could be seen of the boat and touched his hands.

"Be careful." She said once more.

"See you later." He replied, before letting go.

# CHAPTER 39

As the wind whistled loudly through the concrete bridge arches, Kirkland sat in the darkness on deck clutching his left elbow. Having landed awkwardly, he twisted an ankle on one of the empty beer bottles that now rolled about on the deck; which made him trip and hit his elbow. After about thirty seconds spent rubbing his arm and looking around, squinting into the darkness he just about made out the Duck mascot. *Found them.*

Looking up over the side, he squinted, as for a second the light from the torch blinded him. Shielding his eyes from its glare with his right hand, he held out his left and whispered loudly.

"Drop it now."

When nothing happened, it was clear that the women hadn't heard him, his voice obviously being lost in the wind and the scraping of the wheelhouse against the bridge arch. Not wanting to call any louder, he stuck his hand and arm out from under the bridge as far as it would go and then opened and closed his palm, hoping that Sarah would know that would be the signal to drop the torch.

"Drop it now." He whispered once more, just as his mobile began to ring.

*Shit!*

He quickly moved both hands to his pockets, before the

torch flashed passed and splashed into the canal. Looking over the edge he saw the torch light disappear into the dark water, before flickering and then going out. *Bloody hell,* he thought before quickly pulling out his phone and then rejecting the call, then scrolling through the menu and setting the phone to silent.

* * *

Under the Hardwater Road Bridge, DS Shrives stared at her phone, *Another bloody unreliable man. I'll have to go it alone,* she thought, after calling Kirkland and getting no answer.

Turning her torch on, she shone the beam up the river bank, checking behind and then turned it towards the barge moored under the bridge. *Surely it's dangerous to be moored in a place like this,* she thought, now feeling some apprehension and trying to justify going onboard.

Shining the torch down the path and seeing its light disappear off into the darkness, she took a deep breath and then slowly walked along, stopping only when she'd reach the barge, facing it with her back pressed against the cold concrete bridge wall.

There was no movement inside as she stepped onboard and now as the heavens opened up once more she stopped as fear took hold. Shining the beam up then down the path into the now mist filled atmosphere, she checked that she was still alone.

With the noise of rushing water in the background, breathing heavily, and heartbeat raised, she started from the wheelhouse and scanned along the length of the barge, looking for signs of foul play.

Every so often, on hearing a creek, she flashed the torch behind, checking that she was still alone and then quickly moved the torch back in front. *There!* Another creak; she moved the torch up in response, catching sight and being surprised by the barge's mascot. She stood there for a second looking at it before lowering the torch; suddenly she felt a strong hand on her shoulder which filled her with fear. She gasped and took a step back, almost feeling weak at the knees.

* * *

Kirkland thought that he would wait a few minutes, until his ankle eased before getting up and while sat there he noted that the engines where on; just about running, but the barge was going nowhere. *It's as if he wants the barge to stay under the bridge?* He thought.

As he began to stand, he heard the approach of footsteps, along with a tapping that seemed to phase off the bridge walls, so ducked down again, unaware that it was Sunisa using the barge pole, herself unaware that Graham carefully kept the barge under the bridge, steering too close to the wall, keeping her busy.

*It's time,* thought Graham.

"I'm going to move it forward and then steer it back." He shouted, "Just keep it off the walls."

Sunisa moved back towards the bow as Graham released the throttle and the barge juddered forward fifteen feet, debris from the top of the wheelhouse falling into the canal.

He then lowered the speed holding the barge in position. *OK time to do this,* he thought.

As he got up from his seat, he caught sight of a small blue light emanating from behind the wheelhouse, which slowly moved around to the starboard. *What the hell was that?*

Seconds before, DS Shrives had once more called Kirkland, who had taken the vibrating phone from his pocket and whispered into it.

"I've found them," He said, "call Sarah; and get a unit over here straight away." She didn't get a chance to speak before Kirkland ended the call.

From the corner of his eyes, Graham had caught a glimpse of the bluish light of Kirkland's mobile phone display a few minutes earlier, when DS Shrives called Kirkland the first time, but had thought nothing of it. But, this time he knew someone was out there.

Ducking down below the line of the glass on the wheelhouse door, Graham trembled; now feeling his heart beat with every breath, as he tried to breathe quietly. As Kirkland passed just outside, peering in above Grahams head into the blackness of the wheelhouse, Graham waited, trying not to hold his breath for too long and listening for anything that signalled that the intruder had shuffled past.

There was a screech, as the top of the wheelhouse bobbed onto the arch of the bridge, causing Graham to lose his footing and fall onto the floor with a thud. Both men paused, on opposite sides of the wheelhouse door, almost holding their breath in fear of being caught. In the darkness, Graham reached for the crowbar that leant in the corner.

\* \* \*

The storm now reached Sarah and Karen, who were still standing on top of the bridge, the wind gusting at over 60 miles per hour, causing Karen's umbrella to blow inside out for the umpteenth time.

Sarah reached for her mobile phone when it rang and seeing who it was on the caller display spoke as soon as she answered.

"Carol, did you find anything." Shouted Sarah above the wind.

"NO, Yes, I mean No, It wasn't the right barge; I mean just listen," DS Shrives blurted out.

"A unit's coming out to you." She continued, before the reception started to break up.

"What, I didn't hear that, say it again." Sarah replied.

What came back was a garbled metallic, echoing type voice.

As Sarah looked up at Karen, "I can't hear a word she's saying." She said, before pressing the phone against her ear once more.

"I can't hear you!"

"I'll be there in..." Was all Sarah heard, before the call disconnected.

"What did she say?" Asked Karen.

"She said something about a unit coming over. I think."

"A unit?" Karen replied, puzzled.

\* \* \*

The noise from the wind, rain, and the top of the wheelhouse against the bridge arch obscured almost everything.

Graham, genuinely frightened, stood up and peered over the window line, holding up the crowbar ready for action. He saw no one in the darkness, so tentatively opened the wheelhouse door, letting himself out onto the deck.

Hanging on to the guide rail and keeping himself as low as possible, in the darkness he sensed that someone was not to far up ahead.

Through the noise, he heard the phased tapping of the barge pole as Sunisa headed towards the bow, but on the portside. As he moved forward, just in front of him he heard one of the beer bottles rattle and then roll over the edge of the barge splashing into the canal.

"Shit!" Whispered Kirkland, cursing as the bottle splashed in.

Graham, now seeing his chance quickly moved forward.

"Who's that?" he said, waving the crowbar in the air.

The startled Kirkland who started in a crouching position quickly stood and turned, and now frightened by Kirkland's movement, Graham instinctively brought the crowbar down, hitting Kirkland's temple. He caught a glimpse of Kirkland's face before he fell to the deck, and now panicking Graham raised the crowbar once more, this time bringing it down with greater force, only stopping when it registered who it was that laid before him.

Kneeling down to the unconscious Kirkland, he whispered into his ear.

"What are you doing here?"

Kirkland groaned, took another breath, exhaled, and then nothing. *He's not breathing!*

Panicking, Graham grabbed the lapels of Kirkland's jacket and through clenched teeth, shook him violently.

"What are you doing here?" He whispered knowing that he would get no answer.

Then after a few seconds, *I'll deal with you later,* he thought, releasing Kirkland, letting his limp torso and head fall heavily to the deck.

The sound of the wheelhouse buffeting the bridge arch, as

the barge slowly moved back in the current, reminded Graham what he had to do, and now he listened for the tapping of the barge pole. Still clenching the crowbar, he followed the sound to a gap between the hatch and roof of the cabin. Hiding there, his mind wondered, and he thought of the money, the fifty thousand pounds and how he would spend it.

\* \* \*

Sarah and Karen rushed over as two police cars arrived, pulling up quickly, red and blue lights flashing. A police sergeant and four police officers got out all at once it seemed.

"Who's DS Shrives?" Asked the police sergeant.

"She's not here.' Said Karen

"She said she would be here soon, that was a few minutes ago." Said Sarah

"So who are you?"

"We're members of the public." Karen replied.

The sergeant now recognising Karen's voice, then her face as the red and blue lights lit up the road, introduced herself.

"I'm Sergeant Lucy Travers. We've had a call to say that an officer was in trouble, do you know anything about that."

"What do you mean trouble?" Asked Sarah, clearly worried.

"Calm down," said Karen, before addressing Sergeant Travers. "It's a long story, but your man is on a barge under the bridge."

There was a look of puzzlement on the Sergeant's face as she looked over the side of the bridge, then to the left and right.

"How'd he get down there?" She said bemused, then shaking her head, almost knowing what was to come.

"He jumped," whispered Sarah, before clearing her throat.

"What? He jumped?" Travers repeated back.

The women nodded.

"OK" said, Travers, still shaking her head and then turning to a young fresh faced officer.

"Get Trumpton down here and tell them were going to need climbing equipment."

"Trumpton?" The young officer repeated back, puzzled.

"The Fire Service!" Travers shouted, "Get the Fire Brigade!"

"Yes Sarge." Said the officer, before turning around and speaking into his airwave radio.

"Do you know who the officer is?" She asked the women.

"Kirkland, Trevor Kirkland." Sarah answered.

By the look on the sergeant's face it was clear that she knew him.

"Bloody cowboy, always trying to buck the system." She muttered under her breath, before calling two other officers, asking them to go to see the farmer, to get a tractor to drive across the field to the canal path.

DS Shrives and the other women arrived a minute later.

"Stay here." Said DS Shrives to Jane as she jumped out of the car and headed toward Travers and the flashing red and blue lights.

The two women seem to argue for a moment, before DS Shrives hurried over to Jenny's car, had a quick word, and then got back in to her car joining Jane, now seeming a bit flustered.

"Everything alright?" Asked Jane.

"Yes, everything's fine. We've got to move the cars off the track, to let the emergency services through."

"No, I mean with the others. Where's Kirkland? And why are there so many police here?"

"Knowing Kirkland, taking matters into his own hands." DS Shrives muttered under her breath before starting her car.

\* \* \*

Kirkland gasped, as he fully filled his lungs for the first time after regaining consciousness. His groan was muffled by the screech on the wheelhouse as blood trickled from a large gash on his forehead, first feeling warm, almost comfortable as it came out, then quickly cooling in the wind and feeling less so. He lifted his head which throbbed and stung at the same time as he opened his eyes, trying to focus in the darkness.

Sunisa now tired, arms and lower back aching, looked towards the wheelhouse, but couldn't see anything clearly: Though there was a red and sometimes blue tinge to the darkness which wasn't there earlier. One thing she was sure of was that the barge was still well covered by the bridge.

*This isn't working,* she thought, as she strained to push the barge back off the bridge wall once more, before deciding to speak to Graham, to see if anything else could be done to move the barge back. Heading back towards the wheelhouse she approached the hatch, where Graham waited.

He smiled as he thought about the money and now readied himself now hearing her approach. Still feeling the beat of his pounding heart as he breathed, for a split second he remembered how Toi had died, thinking how upset he'd been when the deed was done: And now, feeling nothing, he realised that he had no real feelings for this woman.

Sunisa shuffled passed, moving gingerly into the gap between the hatch and the cabin as Graham raised the crowbar ready to strike and now biting his top lip, took his first swing, bringing the crowbar down with force. It was then, just like in his reoccurring dream that he felt a cold, almost freezing wisp of air on his left cheek. Turning slightly to his left, he gasped, as there in the darkness he glimpsed an outline of a figure.

Sunisa dropped the barge pole as she screamed, before crumpling into a heap on the deck. The crowbar had missed its mark, but had hit her left shoulder with brutal and bone crunching efficiency, chipping her shoulder blade. Now on all fours, she cried with the pain that shot through her back, as

Graham momentarily distracted by the dark figure to his left moved forward to strike once more.

"Don't do it." Came a voice from out of the darkness.

In his mind his nightmare had become a reality.

"It can't be you." He said, as he spun round to face the figure, now backing off. "You're dead! You're dead!" He shrieked.

Raising the crowbar once more, he took a step to the side allowing him to take a full swing at the figure, in doing so stepping on to one of his empty beer bottles. His right leg flew forward, putting him off balance, causing him to stumble backwards, colliding with Sunisa who was still on all fours on the deck. Dropping the crowbar, he instinctively grabbed out at the guide rail, instead finding thin air, and tripping over Sunisa's curved spine in an almost comical fashion. He called for his mother as his head hit the bridge wall on his way down into the canal.

* * *

"Help me!" Graham shouted, as he coughed the freezing canal water out of his lungs.

"Sunisa, please help me." He called, terror clearly heard in his voice, as he was now trapped between the bridge wall and the barge's hull.

The wheelhouse screeched along the top of the arch, more debris falling into the canal, as the barge, engines still set low and in reverse bobbed in the water, and was now finally moving back under its own steam. He screamed once more for her help as the barge juddered its way back.

From the starboard side, the figure that had frightened Graham appeared. It was DS Kirkland clinging to the guide rail, groggy and still hurting. Using the light from his mobile phone display, he answered Graham's call.

"Where are you?" He shouted.

"I'm here." Sunisa mistakenly groaned, now sitting, both legs stretched out on the deck, using the hatch as support, and clutching her shoulder.

"Are you alright?

Squinting into the light, she made the mistake of nodding, and then winced as the pain shot through her shoulder.

"Yes." She replied.

"Help, I'm down here." Graham shouted. "Get me out! Please help!"

The Barge juddered back moving closer to the bridge wall.

"Leave him!" Sunisa shouted, ensuring that Graham heard. "Leave the Bastard." She whispered, before bursting into tears.

"Please help," Graham continued.

Kirkland paused for a moment, deep down wanting to leave Graham, but swung the beam from his phone around the deck in front of him looking for something with which to pull Graham up. Then his phone beeped, indicating that the battery was low.

"Please," said Graham, and now losing himself in rage. "Don't listen to that bitch, she's the one that hit you; she's the one that pushed me in, just wait till I get out, I'll show you. Get me out, just get me out." He ranted.

Kirkland shone the beam back onto Sunisa's face just as the wheelhouse broke free from the arch, the barge floating back towards the portside. On seeing the dried blood and bruising Graham had inflicted on her, he shouted back to Graham.

"Just wait! I'm trying to see what you've got up here that will help pull you out." *'You Bastard.'* He thought.

His phone bleeped once more as he continued to shine the display light around, frantically looking for anything that he could use; the only things coming into view before the battery died; beer bottles, which rolled about the deck.

It was too late and Kirkland's demeanour showed it; it was as if he'd given up, shoulders slumped and head lowered, and now waiting for the inevitable.

"Help! Sunisa! Help!" Graham desperately shouted once more as the hull slowly moved towards him; seconds later slamming him against the bridge wall.

He screamed for his mother once more before a cracking sound; his skull crushing under the weight of the hull was heard. Now brain matter, bodily fluid, along with his broken body drifted off with the current as the barge slowly began to move starboard.

His terrified cry had sent shivers down the spines of Sunisa and Kirkland both, and they were silent in the darkness for a few moments; only the sound of rain and the silky movement of rushing river water audible.

Kirkland sighed as the barge cleared the bridge; he then took off his jacket, carefully covering Sunisa's shoulders, and then sat down next to her, both of them leaning against the hatch for support.

A deluge of water greeted them, as there was no let up in the rain: they were also greeted by bright blinding and almost warm spotlights, which had been erected by the emergency services, which pointed down from the top of the bridge.

Amidst the ensuing hive of activity on the bridge, Sarah shouted down to them.

"Are you alright?"

To which Kirkland gave her the thumbs up.

## CHAPTER 40

The rain had stopped, giving everyone a welcomed respite, but the wind still gusted, sometimes hindering police frogmen, who searched along the riverbank.

On the bridge, the illuminating red and blue lights of the emergency services lit the immediate area, while their bright spotlights scanned the canal for Graham's body.

Officially he was missing, well, until a body had been found, but there were rumours circulating that he was dead; not being able to survive being crushed by a 26 tonne vessel. Everyone on the bridge had heard his terrified screams, so did not hold out much hope of finding him alive.

The women stood back and watched as Sunisa in a gurney blew about in the wind as the emergency services winched her up from the bank, and on top an ambulance waiting to whisk her off to Northampton General.

Once on top of the bridge, Sarah moved to greet her and was shocked by the extent of the bruising to her face. Exhausted and tearful, Sunisa reached out and held on tightly to Sarah's hand.

"Thank you." She croaked, as the paramedics first raised the gurney onto its wheels, giving Sarah a chance to kiss Sunisa's forehead, then lowering it again, realising that the track was too rough to push the gurney and decided to carry it the short distance to the ambulance.

"You'll be fine now," said Sarah, as she let Sunisa's hand slip from hers.

Debbie, who had been hankering to go home, complaining that she'd not seen her kids all day, quickly volunteered herself in a nosey sort of way, to sit in the ambulance with Sunisa and could be heard saying.

"I'm Debbie, everything'll be OK now," as a paramedic closed the ambulance doors.

"We'll go to the hospital to see her later." Said Sarah

Karen nodded, knowing that Sarah was more concerned about Kirkland's wellbeing, who was winched up next, and asked for his gurneys wheels to be folded out, allowing him to sit up when he reached the top.

"Look, you may have concussion, we need to get you to the hospital." Said the attending paramedic.

"OK mate, I'll just be a minute." Kirkland replied as he held a blood stained antiseptic wipe to his temple.

Turning to face the women, he said smugly,

"Well, we got him."

The women nodded, before Sarah, not being able to contain herself, fell on him, giving him a long hug, and kissing him on the cheek.

Kirkland coughed, "I never knew you cared." He said sarcastically. "Come on you're squeezing the life out of me.

"Well I do, I do care." Sarah whispered as she pulled away

now red faced and feeling a bit stupid.

"What happened down there?" Karen asked.

"Well I let my guard down, that's for sure." He replied as he smiled and then slowly lay back, closing his eyes.

"Are you OK?" Karen asked.

"Yes, well, I just feel a bit sick."

"That's it!" Said the paramedic, waving for his partner. "You're concussed, we'd better get you looked at."

"You'll hear no complaints from me." Said Kirkland, as Sergeant Travers appeared.

"Oh no," Kirkland continued, "I'm in for it now."

"Too right!" Said Travers, "The governor's going to have your balls for this…"

As the paramedics carried Kirkland to another waiting ambulance, Travers continued to give him a dressing down.

Karen looked at Sarah.

"Well." She said.

"Well what?"

"Well, I can see that you want to go with him. You know, in the ambulance."

"No, I'm OK, we can go in a minute."

"Look, I'll take your car." Said Karen, "Go before it's too late.

"You sure."

"Yes, go."

Sarah rushed over to the waiting ambulance just as the doors were being closed; she climbed in, sat down, and took Kirkland's hand.

* * *

An hour later, the other women were greeted by Sarah and Debbie as they arrived in the Accident and Emergency foyer.

"Sorry we're late," said Karen shaking her head, "we had to get something to eat."

"Where's ours?" Asked Debbie.

Karen sighed. "Sorry, I didn't think soggy Mc D's would have gone down that well."

"I'm only joking, Debbie replied. "We had something here."

"How are they," Jane asked changing the subject. .

"They're OK." Sarah replied, with a smile, "They're both being kept in for observation tonight. So did they find him?" She said referring to Graham.

"No," Jane replied shaking her head.

"It's like he's disappeared." Said Karen, "But I think they'll get him. I mean, where can he go?"

"So did you ever find out what happened? Asked Karen. "I mean how did Kirkland get lumped."

"Well," said Debbie, who was to her annoyance quickly interrupted by Sarah.

"He said that, he's not sure who hit him as it was too dark

to really see anything, but he kind of remembers Graham talking to him, but he can't be sure. He says that there was definitely someone else on the barge."

"Really?" Jenny asked.

"Yeah. He said that he was knocked unconscious, totally out of it, and then he woke up with a start. He described it as, you know when you've been sleeping for a few minutes and then you wake with a jump. That sort of thing."

Karen nodded.

"Well," Sarah continued, "as I said, he woke up and felt cold; uncanny he said, like really cold as if in the middle of winter.

'It is winter," Jenny quipped. "You seen the weather out there?"

"I know, but colder." Sarah replied, now a bit annoyed about being interrupted. "He said when he stood up he thought that there was someone else onboard, someone other than Graham.

I mean, at the time, he thought it must have been Sunisa, but thinking about it later he realised that it couldn't have been because of where he found her and how badly she was injured. Anyway, he said that the person said 'Don't, or don't do it', or something like that, a couple of times, then he heard Graham, shouting and screaming. He said he used the light from his mobile phone and as he put it on, he was sure that he saw someone in a yellow coat. But after taking that bash on the head he can't really be sure."

Karen sighed.

"How creepy," said Jane. "Perhaps the ghost of Toi has come back to take her revenge."

"Don't even go there." Said Sarah, her gaze now taken up by the ramshackle figure that was DS Shrives; her trousers, shoes and parts of her cheeks covered in mud and hair dishevelled, coming in through to the foyer. Seeing Sarah's gaze the other women too, turned to face her.

"Well, I think that we've had a result." She said, pulling a small opaque plastic bag from her coat pocket, inside, something that all the women recognised.

A self-help book, Graham's self-help book.

The women waited while DS Shrives fished out a couple of rubber gloves from her other pocket and started to put them on, holding the bag under her right arm.

"Finger prints." She said as she snapped the rubber rib of her left hand glove to her wrist.

Taking the book from the plastic sleeve, she then turned to the last few pages and said while looking at Karen.

"You were right. Here, he's fully documented why, when and where he was going to kill Toi, and dispose of the body and this." She said turning to the last page, "is what he intended to do to Sunisa. This is meticulous, premeditated, totally incriminating, and it's all about money."

The women looked on silently.

"How the hell do you read a book like this," she continued flipping the book around to the front cover and then back again, "and use it to plan to kill people?" Looking at the front cover once more.

"The Art of Positive Thinking & Creative Visualisation." She read, shaking her head.

"I think I've seen it all now. And why the bloody hell do people read this dross anyway"

The women still silent all looked a bit sheepish, which made DS Shrives suspicious.

"Is everything alright?" She asked, "You guys are a bit quiet, what's up? Is Sunisa and Kirkland OK?"

"Oh, they're going to be fine," Sarah replied. "They're staying in for observation.

"Well, someone will be in to take their statements soon, I'm just going to pop in to see them, anyone else coming?" Asked the detective.

"No, said Debbie looking at her watch. "I've got to be getting home"

"Me too." Said Jenny.

"Yeah, I think we've had enough for one day." Said Sarah. "We'll probably come back tomorrow." To which there was general agreement.

"Well, I think the police are going to want some sort of statement. Said DS Shrives, so please make yourselves available to them at some point."

One by one, the women shook DS Shrives by the hand and hugged before she turned and spoke to an attendant, flashed her warrant card and was taken out the back to see Kirkland and Sunisa.

* * *

In the car park, the women said their goodbyes and headed for home, Sarah taking Karen back to Milton Keynes.

"Well, what a day." Said Karen.

"Strange few days." Sarah replied. "And what Kirkland said about seeing someone else on the barge, that was just spooky."

"Yeah but in all seriousness." Sarah interrupted.

"Yeah I know what you mean."

"Stupid though; Toi back from the dead and all that. I just wish we'd help her like we've helped Sunisa."

"Don't beat yourself up about it." Karen chuckled. "There was nothing we could have done. How were we to know what that bastard was planning?"

Sarah turned to look at Karen, puzzled by her laughter.

"What's so funny?"

"No, nothing."

There was a short pause before Karen continued.

"DS Shrives just reminded me of a conversation we'd had, you know that one, about how planning and executing a murder could be a positive act. Well, depending on which side of the fence you're standing."

"Yeah and it's good that you did, or we wouldn't have caught him."

"Yes, but, that weren't it." Said Karen, "I mean Carol's reaction, you know, calling it dross."

"I know, what she doesn't understand is that it's not the book or the information in it that's bad, people are; or on the other hand, how they used the information."

It was like the old days as they talked about what was next on the horizon for them both and before long, they arrived at Karen's hotel.

"Looks as though it's clearing now," said Karen looking out of the front windscreen and up at the sky, as the moon started to appear from behind the dark clouds.

"Yeah, well I think we've had the worst of the weather."

"Well, I'll see you soon." Said Karen, leaning across and hugging Sarah.

"I'll see you first." Sarah replied, then pausing for a second.

"On TV tomorrow."

They smiled at each other before Karen got out and as she closed the door asked.

"The voice, you know the one Kirkland said he heard, did

he say whether it was male or female?"

Sarah thought for a second before saying, "He said it was a woman's voice."

* * *

Graham's battered body was found a week later, under a bridge snagged against a heavy roll of barbed wire that had been dumped into the river.

FIN

# EPILOGUE

After that first meeting, the woman, well, as you will have guessed by now; Sarah and I met at her house for the next few weeks; eight weeks in fact.

These meetings in a way became therapy for the pair of us, but more so for her, as it became apparent that she somehow needed to bare her soul and in the short time that we had known each other, it was kind of strange that she chose me as her confessor.

Like old friends, we talked about many things, but always came back to this story, as I became more and more intrigued as it came out, over a five-week period. At times I felt her discomfort and knew that something was wrong, as I had to tease her thoughts and feelings out.

She kept in contact and met up with Karen and the other women once or twice a year, even with Sunisa and Abhasra: And among other things they reminisced about was how if it were not for Toi, they probably wouldn't have ended up as lifelong friends. And how sadly it had taken the last few weeks of a beautiful woman's life and her subsequent death to really bring them together. But, no matter how many times they met and talked, Sarah always came away feeling incomplete, unsatisfied, and as we now know, unhappy.

I tried to get her to focus on her feelings and on how she felt about what happened, which surprisingly didn't come easy for her. I say surprisingly, because I know she'd read some of the same literature as myself, and I knew she understood the merits of exploring one's thoughts and feelings. But I suppose, books are there only as a guide and as we saw with Graham; what we do with information after we have assimilated it, is always open to interpretation.

Anyway, we eventually focused on, and explored her feelings about what had happened and found that she was racked by guilt, which was the main reason she devoted so much to charity. Her real angst being that she was the one that initially told Toi that everything would be all right and a few days later, Toi was dead, which wasn't meant to happen.

So, for years she felt that Toi's death was her fault and slowly, outwardly turned her back on the whole positive thing. Actually, that is not entirely true; she stopped being so preachy about it, and in the end became a bit more inward looking, which came out as the story unfolded, and I suppose, from the earlier parts of it, this may not have been such a bad thing.

We also found that there were peripheral reasons for her unhappiness, which were that, Graham never stood trial for what he'd done, and though he had died horribly, even if alcohol abuse and a strange relationship with his mother may have had something to do with his state of mind, in her words, "He got off easy."

In addition, she'd not attended Toi's funeral, failing to say a real goodbye, and to make things worse had missed a ten-year memorial service that had been arranged by the families of those that had perished in the flood. "No one was there for Toi, ether in life, or in death."

In the fifth week that we met and after the final instalment of the story, Sarah got a little upset and cried, which was something that she'd not done over the period that she'd told the story.

And after taking some time, allowing her to compose herself, I tried to make her see that, though Toi's death was tragic, she couldn't have prevented it from happening.

You see Toi had seen herself drowning so many times that in the end, that became her reality. At first this was hard for Sarah to take, however, she knew there was some truth behind a self-perpetuating dream or vision; after all, was she not living proof that creative visualisation worked?

By the time I left for home in that fifth week, though she wasn't entirely happy, she began to see this as being a truth, which served to alleviate some of the guilt that she'd been feeling.

On my way home that evening, I couldn't help thinking about the women involved, wondering what Toi was like, and how profound an effect she'd had on the whole group. I found myself questioning: What sort of person was she? Who were her family? What were the real circumstances surrounding her death and I suppose the real question how many other women, had, suffered the same fate.

By the time I arrived home, I was determined to educate myself: To find out what was happening in Thailand in relation to the whole Thai bride thing and possibly mount some sort of campaign, well not a campaign; but do something to stop what many of us would see as a major exploitation of women.

Of course, I knew that men the world over went to Thailand on sex holidays, where they played out their fantasies with young girls and boys; the younger the better in many cases. However, what I found out was; what I thought I knew was very far from reality. The story, unbelievably, alluded to high numbers of girls, women and even boys, just disappearing; being taken for this sex industry, but I found that the numbers surprisingly, were significantly higher than was stated in her story.

My research took me into a seedy world, where the exploitation of women and the trafficking in human cargo is big business, linked to the infamous cliché: sex drugs and violence. A business run by organised international criminal gangs, as well as seemingly respectable civil servants and officials.

It also took me to places where I found that Thai workers,

men, women and children alike, entered countries illegally and were exploited by the indigenous populations. In many cases they were forced to work and live in squalid conditions; conditions that were no better than where they had escaped. Many of them forced to live in cattle pens, metal underground tanks, even animal dens; and this was just the tip of the iceberg.

Trafficking and exploitation is happening the world over and though outwardly condemned by most governments, not enough, or very little in the grand scheme of things is being done to stop it.

That being said, I can say, that in recent years the Thai authorities have taken major steps to curb the exploitation of its nationals. However, to get round the fact that Thai women were now less likely to end up working in the sex industry, thousands of other women were still being trafficked from neighbouring countries, such as Burma, Cambodia and Vietnam.

I know I make it sound as if the exploitation is, or was unwanted and in ninety nine percent of cases, it is.

But, I found that some women took pride in returning home wealthier than they were when they had left and were able to buy land and amenities for their families: Their lives in prostitution overlooked; dirty little secrets that their families choose to ignore.

Unfortunately, seeing this only serves to encourage other women, who then become willing participants in the trade, or families willing to sell their daughters and wives into prostitution, or as wives to wealthy foreigners.

So, here we have one big circle that we in the west outwardly despise and on the other hand support by our demand.

And what of the battery, the mistreatment: It got me questioning, was this abuse, a man thing? Well, in the main men are the main contributors to the plight of these people aren't they? However, I began to see that though men were at fault, women in many cases were contributors to some of the most shocking treatments. I began to see that this whole thing as well as being about money, was more about power and control. The thing that as human beings, we continually, both consciously and subconsciously crave, seek out, and at some level somehow enjoy.

A more shocking discovery for me is the fact that worldwide, an estimated 1.2 million children, at the time of this publication, were being trafficked each year, many of them girls. That would be almost one quarter of the population of a city the size of London, taken into bondage each year.

It was kind of funny, well not funny, but strange, finding these things out, as like most of us, deep down, I already knew what was going on; like the exploitation of Africans in the gold and diamond mines, the Chinese and Indians in sweat shops, or the eastern Europeans used to prop up western economies. But, as none of this was on my doorstep, I chose to ignore it. But now that it was laid out before me, I couldn't just stand by and do nothing.

Sarah had devoted a lot of her wealth to the needy, as penance for Toi's death, and in those last few weeks that we met, I convinced her to divert some of her kindness to other charities. Charities that had been set up to help educate the young women of South East Asia to the perils that they may face if they chose prostitution, or tried to find rich foreign men to marry. It didn't really take much convincing, as to Sarah, this was life saving work.

What about my contribution? Well, my contribution would be this: I would tell Toi's story, and somehow get it out there into the public domain; to as many people as were prepared to, or cared to listen. It showed that the infectious Toi, and her story; the story of a real life and death struggle had got to me.

At our final meeting, Sarah seemed much happier than at any time during the time we had spent together. I quipped that not having to see me anymore after that meeting had put her into such a good mood, which she quickly and rather seriously rebuffed. Saying that I had played an important part in this chapter of her life.

When leaving a bit later, I hugged her, gave her a peck on the cheek and promised to keep in touch, before heading for my car. As I started the engine, an immaculate looking late seventies Triumph Stag rolled up, and a tall, well groomed, silver haired middle aged man got out.

Sarah, who had been standing by her front door, waved to me, indicating that she wanted me to wait, before greeting the man, who gave her a short, but telling kiss on the cheek.

I rolled down my window as they walked over to my car. Sarah introduced her husband, which came as a big surprise, as for some reason I thought that she'd remained unmarried, and had not once mentioned him in the weeks that we had spent talking. Well actually, she had. With a broad smile, she introduced "Trevor," before winking at me.

Printed in Great Britain
by Amazon.co.uk, Ltd.,
Marston Gate.